A Shot at
AARON

A Shot at AARON

The Trials of Iliana

Douglas E. Templin

authorHOUSE®

AuthorHouse™ LLC
1663 Liberty Drive
Bloomington, IN 47403
www.authorhouse.com
Phone: 1-800-839-8640

This book is a work of fiction. People, places, events and situations are the products of the author. Any resemblance to actual persons, living or dead, or historical events, is purely coincidental.

Published by AuthorHouse   09/30/2014

ISBN: 978-1-4969-3958-6 (sc)
ISBN: 978-1-4969-3975-3 (e)

Library of Congress Control Number: 2014916362

Any people depicted in stock imagery provided by Thinkstock are models, and such images are being used for illustrative purposes only. Certain stock imagery © Thinkstock.

This book is printed on acid-free paper.

To Jacqueline

CHAPTER 1

PUGET SOUND, WASHINGTON

Aaron Concord shuddered from the ear-busting blast outside. Clearly, it came from the down-slope side of the house, near the pebbly, oyster-strewn beach that skirted the east border of their property. A moment later, the front picture window disintegrated into a thousand tiny cutlasses—too close to where he sat dozing in the pale loom of an old floor lamp—a barely begun novel in his lap.

The covey of # 4 BBs that followed, sliced a path through the half-closed, blue muslin curtains with such force that it could have been a grenade, he thought, before he realized the concussion was that of a large bore shotgun.

Aaron sensed the absence of an aftershock—flying metallic shrapnel—having accommodated to the hazard when serving in Vietnam. Instead, an opaque cloud of crystalline slivers flew everywhere from the shattered 1/4" plate window he and his wife, Peggy, painstakingly emplaced during their last remodel effort.

Mid-January and blustery, a typically misty night on Olympic Peninsula's western-most waterway of Puget Sound, a rush of 42 degree outside air bellowed around him. Aaron shivered uncontrollably from the implosion of cold. His nostrils burned but flared with the combined infusion of natural perfumes from cedar, fir, and pine trees that blanketed most of their land around the house, garage, and his helicopter hangar, upslope, near the west property line.

First dumbfounded, though nearly paralyzed with raging fear, he sat motionless—no idea what to do. The startling invasion then strangely engendered more anger than fright. Amateur builders, Peggy and Aaron worked for days when they cut through the outside wall, built the frame, secured the 4" x 8" header to support the lengthy span, and installed the pane.

He admitted afterward that the new opening turned the remote cabin into a fish bowl from the front. The dramatic change in the erstwhile windowless façade, however, offered any onlooker one of the finest possible 180-degree vistas of the lusty, green-bearded, pewter surface that typified sixty-mile-long Hood Canal. While proud of that, all too suddenly the tableau turned to a shooting gallery, with Aaron as the moving target.

Instinctively, he closed what remained of the drapes from his seated position. He tugged at the looped cord next to his chair with short jerks, and considered it damned fortunate that his wife of thirty-three years was away. Peggy stayed a short time near Seattle with his aging mother, going on ninety, to assist the elder in recovery from a stubborn bout of pneumonia.

He finally reacted to the blazing shock that triggered old military tactics as though it were yesterday, and dove for the bottom of the artillery shell crater he envisioned a few feet away, in that fleeting instant. His body curled, fetus-like; he buried his head in the muck, clamped hands behind his neck, and remembered what he learned in basic and advanced exercises, at Fort Benning, Georgia, an idealistic, twenty-two year old enlistee.

Reactions like that also arose by rote, from months of specialized Ranger training in 1965, and later, while on seemingly endless search and destroy patrols in the open flats, jungles, and rice paddies within a half hour's flight radius of Long Binh Army Base. Sent to Vietnam as a greenhorn sergeant in the second Battalion, 16th Infantry Regiment, in 1966, the heat was on in Southeast Asia and he fell into the midst of it.

This is freaky ... so damned cold. What the hell is going down? I've got to get out of here. The forced air furnace ground at full tilt. Ribbons of ripped curtains fluttered into his space: drying dishtowels on a windy day. Aaron wanted to get up, move from the room, when the vibrating tangle of frightening sounds returned. Another deafening discharge stopped him and found its mark in the same area.

Again, it shattered the silence of the woodsy environs that encircled the house. The first took out the expansive plate glass; this one tore straight in, and with sledgehammer force, splayed a four-foot diameter, orbital pattern of small holes in the white plaster wall.

The impact centered just above the newly varnished mahogany wainscot. Aaron trimmed the front room with the four-foot high bead board paneling before Christmas, to give the well-used space a more traditional appeal. Two framed oils, painted by their thirty-two year old daughter, Beth, dropped to the floor in secondary crashes.

Well beyond petrified; Aaron wondered how long he could be pinned down before Cobra gunships with their vicious firepower, would drop in to take out the hostile troops. They had to be close by. Where were the ground hugging, patrolling Loaches; Hughes 500s—comparatively smaller helicopters—low level spotters for the heavily armed aircraft? He lauded the radio call for immediate air support whispered by his nearest companion, PFC-2 Broadman, who also hugged the ground close to where he lay.

Stout of frame, Aaron Concord stood just north of 5'10" and turned sixty-eight in April. Otherwise in good health, he remained as attractive to Peggy as ever: sinuous, slender, and strong for his size. He carried a healthy tan from lots of summer sunning at their Laguna Beach, California seaside home in Crescent Bay. Always an active mind, he read and learned everything possible about any new passion: flying, weather phenomena, instrument navigation among the latest. About to give in to the loss of an almost life-long, and ostensibly arrogant, chest-out, belly-in physical stature, his long-time regimen of vigorous exercise fell victim to a left knee injury, not the same after a ladder fall, when he waterproofed the cabin chimney during post-purchase restructuring.

Aaron pitched forward, still shunted pain from intermittent irritation when he walked or stood too long at parties. He sat much more, too, as he rehabilitated. While doing so, Aaron took particular pleasure working on the beginnings of his, "Great Western Novel," the fifty-odd page manuscript on which he dabbled for too many months, and often deleted pages from his computer more quickly than new text could be laboriously entered.

"Someday ... someday," he often proclaimed to those who did not hear the notion before, "I'll be recognized as someone beside the flat-foot investigator I've been all my work life. I've written medical-legal reports *ad nauseam*, for decades; exposed, if not covered for the human foibles and honest mistakes of physicians, podiatrists, chiropractors, hospitals and nurses," he would express in good humor. "Now it's my turn to spin yarns … my own passions … not simply report the antics of some young buck, impatient surgical resident who screwed up." Infatuated with western fiction for relaxation, Aaron always had one or more novels in the read.

Close friends laughed off his spirited if not feigned lamentations; yet down under, he harbored a definitive, deep-seated, sometimes driving, and irreconcilable resentment. Even rancorous at times, though fully retired from all of it, he remained bothered by the stark disdain he still held, for the way some lawyers could stretch facts or cover them, just enough to mitigate a serious claim or exonerate an otherwise liable client from punitive action.

As a valued independent representative of medical malpractice insurers and defense law firms, he occasionally, while rarely, was induced by defense counsel, "duty bound," as he would put it, to gloss over a client's negligent or willful errors, if not life-threatening, careless professional mistakes.

Clean-shaven, mostly because Peggy liked him that way, since they bought the cabin when he retired; she encouraged him to allow his lightly grayed, blond mane to grow much longer than he kept it during his work career. Those were dress-to-the-nine days: three piece suits, short hair, buffed nails, and well-shined, slip-on Italian shoes, completing the image of success and confident style.

Nearly to the shoulders, more rough around the edges—he kept his hair neatly combed straight back. It only draped about his forehead when he worked on the house or in the garden, or didn't wear his ever-present, navy blue baseball cap. Aaron's face, seen by most as slender, showed cheeks a bit hollowed, from eating less beef, he contended. Except when he flew, when corrective lenses were required, he used no eyewear.

Furry brows—rarely trimmed—still light brown; boxed deeply set, penetrating brown eyes, which Peggy loved when they sparkled and sent a compelling message of devotion. Empathy, too, exuded in his routine and natural expressions. Usually more a listener than a talker, that quality helped extract candid replies to his persistent yet disarming queries when interviewing recalcitrant witnesses.

Experienced trial lawyers for whom he worked, often took a back seat during tenuous fact-finding inquiries with medical professionals, and simply listened while Aaron cleverly painted finely detailed chronologies of events that led to an alleged error or omission. He took no shame when he second-guessed the most prominent of egocentric, teaching hospital attending physicians, and clinical professors. Concord dug for the truth in the first meeting, with the acuity of his inquiries, his broad, practical medical knowledge; and innate humility. Aaron's smile, sculpted to a consistent wide grin, never a smirk, revealed a healthy set of teeth. "His own," Peggy proudly reminded anyone bold enough to pass forth a compliment.

Soft of voice, Aaron cussed with the best of them, usually out of Peg's earshot, and he could talk anyone mute, given a spate of silence to fill. He fit well in cosmopolitan Southern California. Born, raised, and educated there, it became his workplace for close to forty years.

Yet his inherent softness and natural care for the other person, allowed him to blend quickly with, and befriend the quieter, earthy folks of the Pacific Northwest where he often traveled while handling cases. Peggy went along with his passion to live there in retirement, after she accompanied him on many business trips. She house shopped while he worked. They also turned increased interest to the region during visits with his aging parents, who built a home in the outskirts of Seattle, in 1994, to foster a lower-key lifestyle.

Peggy was first to broach the idea of bringing fancy to fact and actually relocating north—somewhere. Together, they discovered and became infatuated with the isolation and quietude of Hood Canal's western reaches, bespeaking their ideal picture of uncomplicated, slow-paced, rural living.

He thought hastily about his likeable qualities, as he lay prone, face glued to the deep blue, cut pile carpet, and wondered, while quizzing himself. *What provoked these obvious attempts to scare hell out of, if not kill me? What have I done, besides treating people right? Those were two damned close-range, well-placed shotgun blasts. Who did I anger enough for this, for God's sake? When, where … did my best to get along with people. Sure, I've had the usual hassles over the years, but, none would induce a try like this, for murder.*

He bled badly from one spot near his right elbow. Smaller, less severe glass lacerations punctuated both forearms. His forehead bled, too; he dug it deeply into a mass of splinters when he leapt for the floor. The injuries did not cause concern, once he realized none was serious. Aaron worried more about what his wife would think of the gunshots, bloodstained carpeting, and the mess. He grimaced, too, from dog hairs impacted in his mouth when he hugged the floor.

Yet another shot shook the stillness, and ripped at the exterior wall, this time below the window frame. Loudest report so far; the load smacked brittle exterior cedar shingles with chilling force. The shooter moved much closer. By then the acrid smell of gunpowder wafted through the gaping window, with the easterly breeze, to spawn added fear and curiosity.

The sonofabitch knows I'm on the floor and he's lowered his sights to take me out down here. Christ! What happens if he approaches the house? I left the front door unlocked and Duke is with Peg. Why did I say I wouldn't miss the old pooch? His determined bark would scare anyone away. Aaron's wife took their big male black Lab to help cheer up his mother, whose large rear yard, with a year-round pond, at the edge of winter, usually over-ran with migrating ducks and Canada Geese the retriever loved to harass.

Aaron's thoughts raced silently but he went on the defensive, when he realized the intruder's determination. All alone, a mile from the closest neighbors—an elderly couple to whom he had to yell to be even slightly understood—they could not help. *Probably wouldn't even answer the phone at this hour,* he muttered silently.

He belly-crawled through saw grass that cut through his knees, thighs and elbows, across a thorn-ridden rice paddy dike; stung from the bites of leeches that found uncovered skin in the musky water; smelled the sickening, rotten odor of the swampy 'Nam lowlands, and then lay dead still for a few moments. Face married to the mud, he listened intently for any Viet Cong movement and for their often-unchecked quaky chatter after a fiery offensive.

Sent on a find and kill operation, his squad dug in just across a small river from Bien Hoa Air Base, scattered personnel bunkers on which took a fierce siege of mortar fire earlier that night. They dispersed to locate and blow up nests in which the enemy likely took refuge. Charlie brazenly worked nights in that area, and hid in tunnels or thickets in the local hills during the daytime, to avoid detection by intense low-level army helicopter surveillance traffic from dawn to dusk.

No noises but the forlorn bray of a disgruntled water buffalo, probably a click or two from their position; so he crawled again, close enough, stomach-sliding side to side, to the wall where he remembered—when he snapped suddenly from the unexpected combat recall—the floor lamp cord was plugged. He grasped the wire, gave it a swift yank; the light flickered once, and went out. A few moments of quiet and he returned to reality in near darkness.

Grim as pitch outside, only a faint glow shone over the roadside border of the front yard, cast by a flood lamp loosely mounted on the branch of a red cedar tree. Aaron placed it there to illuminate the rural mailbox and driveway apron. Swinging in arcs in the midnight on-shore breeze, the light threw diffuse dancing shadows on the one lane road below.

Another report came from the same direction as the others, while this one did not ring so loudly. The lamp in the tree went out. Its large reflector sailed through the mist and landed in the shoreline muck with a tinny splash. Surrounded by the forest black, and with no moonlight, at least he would be invisible. The stakes were more even—no more sitting duck, lighted bull's eye—Aaron thought.

Unlike him, for he was a non-violent man with the patience of Job and rarely a perceptible grudge or chip on his shoulder, Aaron came to his senses; enraged and ready to retaliate. He slid across the broken glass-showered carpet toward the hall. Beyond the south living room wall, it opened to the kitchen on his left; the staircase, straight ahead; and to the den at his right. A small gun rack he built with six-point deer antlers—just above the Cordovan leather den couch—held his Model 98 Mauser .308 hunting rifle. Below it lay an old Remington hex-barrel, pump action .22, gifted by his grandfather when he turned fourteen.

Both guns he kept unloaded for safety's sake during rare grandchildren visits but he harbored an ample supply of shells in the top left drawer of a huge oak roll-top desk his grandfather constructed in the early 1900s. Otherwise, he used the imposing antique only to store receipts and pay bills. Peggy kept her recipes inside, and sat there to prepare shopping lists before they ventured to town.

Aaron arose, then well out of view from the front elevation, fumbled about the drawer in the lightless room, grabbed a box of rifle ammo, and shuffled in stocking feet toward the stairs, weapon in hand. Two dormer windows punctured the master bedroom, in the same perimeter wall as that which absorbed the blasts in the living room. He would be safer there; he considered. All lights were out upstairs. If he crept quietly and didn't step on the tread—second from the top—which groaned like a bullfrog as body weight bore down on it—his positional change might go undetected.

Carefully, he peered toward the water through a slit of space below the nearly closed window shade. He captured a faint figure; someone moved toward the mailbox. Beyond, he glimpsed at what appeared to be an older Ford van, stopped some fifty feet away on the northbound road shoulder.

The diminutive shooter, darkly dressed, crouched in an abnormal posture, he thought; crept slowly, with an apparent limp, ever closer toward the house, gun in ready-to-fire position.

Likely, the yellow cedar in the center of the front yard would be the shooter's next stopping place, he surmised. Two feet in diameter at shoulder height, it offered adequate hiding in the otherwise clear area. Hands trembled, arms sticky and bloodied from myriad glass cuts, Aaron quietly slid one cartridge in the chamber, slowly closed the bolt, opened the safety, then snapped in place, the magazine he filled with five shells, without so much as a click. This Mauser's action, he would argue with anyone, was the picture of smooth, noiseless perfection.

An eighth inch at a time, he carefully raised the lower panel of the double hung window, just enough to allow the gun's muzzle to extend to the screen. Accuracy, on the brink of marginal; the scope was of no use in the dark. Best he could do, he sighted along the barrel and let go a quick hail of three shots, as fast as he could withdraw the bolt, eject, and close it. He aimed generally at the base of the tree, to disable but not kill the intruder. Bark splinters flew everywhere. Resting warblers near the tops of several bare alders cackled, fluttered above their roosts, and settled back. He hoped to hit a leg or foot but his retaliatory action brought another blast from behind the cedar; that one, he could tell by the sound, struck the living room wall again.

"What the hell?" he audibly whispered, "if I can't hit you, I'll tear up your goddamned van." His hands and arms still shook with excitement. The back end of the Ford took two loud claps from Aaron's converted Spanish made WWII rifle and that left one cartridge in the chamber when the bolt slid closed after the second volley. The clash of lead to back windows and the van's heavy rear doors must have panicked the shooter's driver.

The starter motor stuttered, ground with a stubborn, then singing whine; the engine finally roared, exhaust smoke and mist blew behind, and headlights went on. Aaron heard the muffled call of a male from inside, "Forget it! You cannot hesitate. Hurry," the gravely, nasal voice resounded, with a distinct foreign accent. "Get the hell in here; we must go before we get killed." The van backed up, stopped, lunged forward a foot, then halted again with a brief tire squeak. He heard the transmission grapple when the clutch withdrew. A stick shift; that he vowed to remember.

Aaron just discerned through obscuring trees and fuzzy shadows below that the shooter loped away, likely a woman, he concluded, definitely in a right-leg-affected, stumbling gait, toward the passenger side, and out of sight. He fired his last shot, tried to hit the left rear tire, but heard the slug ricochet off the pavement and slam into metal, as tires screeched, smoked burning rubber, and spewed it backward in tumbling white clouds.

Clear of Aaron's line of sight, the shooter snagged the cuff of her black denim jacket on the doorframe, yanked it sharply, and barely boarded the van before it left. She flashed an ominous smile, opened her door a crack and tossed out a matchbook hastily snatched from her purse.

It appeared to be red when its lights went on; the van sped out of sight to the north. Tires squealed and slid at every twist in the pretzel-like, narrow road. Aaron thought it lucky he installed easy-to-raise aluminum frame windows throughout the house during the remodel or he would never have moved its former, sticky, double-hung wood counterpart, to fire back as he did.

What the hell to do now? He wondered, and shuddered involuntarily from the expected overdose of adrenalin. *Should I call police, vacuum the carpet, board up the window with plywood, clean and dress the glass cuts, or just plain get the devil out of here for the night? What if they regroup and return, more determined to find me?*

He considered firing up the helicopter; but by the time he would complete the needed pre-flight check, roll the aircraft to the pad and get airborne, finding the van in the dark would be futile. So much tree-covered terrain, and no moonlight; he would violate visual flight rules in the Federal Air Regulations. Common sense dictated the very real hazard of disorientation from vertigo on such a black night with hardly any ground reference lights for miles. That thought was clearly one to abandon.

"Damnit! I cannot believe, in the peaceful haven we've created, something like this could happen," he exclaimed, as though Peggy were there, "unless someone has a bone to pick with old man Bryson." The former owner's name still appeared on the mailbox. The Concords left "The Bryson Place," between their names and the street address, to make it easier for local delivery people and tradesmen to recognize. All the business folks in the area tangled with aging Ted at one time or another and knew his house well, without the five-digit address.

Though neighbors to the north described Bryson as a bit "rusty upstairs," even "nutty" by others, he built the place and lived there close to thirty years until moved east by his children. No longer could he care for himself in such an inaccessible area, they feared.

Peggy and Aaron stumbled on the house three years before, by accident, while they drove north on Highway 101 from Olympia to Port Townsend. She saw the sign posted at the Frontage Road cut-off, several miles north of Eldon, close to the south end of Jefferson County:

MUST SELL
WATERFRONT VIEW PROPERTY—FOR SALE BY OWNER

They continued northward a few minutes before Peggy, more adventurous of the two at times, shrieked, "Honey, stop! Let's take a break … go back … peek at that house, for what it's worth." Seemingly uninterested, Aaron kept his gaze on the road ahead, and adjusted the stereo volume. "Aaron—Sweetie, please," she pleaded. "Besides, the smaller sign on the post said, 'Blackberries for sale,' and I'm starved." She beamed with excitement when her husband made the U-turn without argument or comment. Peggy reached around his neck and pulled him toward her for a gratuitous but heartfelt peck on the cheek.

He loved her when she acted childish like that, beamed with her impish smile—prominent dimples aglow, even deeper than they were when the two first met. They were teenagers at the beach then, and the attraction was more about her sleek legs, he fast recalled.

Eyes of hazel, always alive and beckoning, her auburn hair turned gray, though she had it colored regularly. He thought the youthful hue cast a natural enough look, and swore, while she was three years his junior, it helped her appear ten years younger.

Olive skin, more wrinkled than many women her age, from so many years of California beach living, Peggy's was still supple and healthy; cheeks ever rosy. Always careful to compliment her, Aaron said her textured expression—whenever she spoke curiously of cosmetic surgery— was emblematic of fine character, not the aging process.

Any change from who she was in the flesh worried Aaron; he loved her without induced beauty. She maintained a decent figure by cooking mostly vegetable dishes in recent years, and still worked out or jogged every day, rain or shine. Peggy looked younger, too, by wearing a wide variety of over-sized, dangling turquoise and silver earrings, whether or not she was around home.

After a quick inspection and a chance meeting that afternoon with the owner's daughter, they walked the property for an hour, fell in love with the cabin and robust Canal view, and tendered a ridiculously low offer for the rare ten-acre parcel. Complete with six hundred feet of coveted waterfront, it offered unusual elements of privacy in an area sparsely scattered with high-priced seasonal vacation homes.

Quickly accepted, with little negotiation, escrow closed in two weeks and they had a spot—remote as could be dreamed about—the perfect retreat for retirement when they were ready.

Close by sparkled some of the Peninsula's best fishing streams, fed by year-round Olympic Mountain snowfields to the west. Equivalently alluring, he looked toward kayaking from their private beach, trolling for salmon in the sound, oyster harvesting at low tide, deer and bird hunting to his heart's content; and, last but not least; flying over some of the most beautiful wooded countryside anywhere.

"But, what about this shooting business?" he said soberly. Aaron often talked aloud when alone, a vestige he hoped stemmed from years of dictating lengthy investigative reports to his recorder—for hours on end, throughout his working life—rather than an emergent measure of encroaching senility.

"I can't tell Peg; she'll want to sell, move out … go back south without the slightest hesitation. I have to get this disaster area cleaned up, get a glazier to reset the window, fix and stain outside shingles, patch the plaster wall, replace curtains with the extra set in the attic, and then clam up. I can't call the law or they'll be all over us when Peggy returns.

I'll get to the bottom of what the shooting was all about, who the hell did it and, more importantly, for whom it was intended; me or maybe someone else." His former career as an investigator instantly bloomed with prospective areas of inquiry. "This can't happen again. I will figure this out or I'll be the first to offer a move home.

"What about my helicopter and the insulated hangar up the hill. Cost me thirty grand to keep it out of the wet weather, another ten to level and pave the landing pad in front, and top the downhill trees." During his final two years on the job, Aaron backed off working full time and took intensive helicopter flight instruction at Orange County's John Wayne Airport.

Flying almost daily, he acquired his private and commercial certificates, instrument and certified fight instructor ratings, and purchased his pride and joy, November 156 Yankee Tango. The new, bright-red Robinson R44, Raven II™, four-seat, fuel-injected helicopter, served him perfectly for low altitude, fair weather pleasure flying in the Northwest. A short run as the crow flew, to the dealer at Bremerton Airport; inspections and needed mechanical work were conveniently available.

His well-thought plans sounded shaky at that moment, though, still poised by the upstairs dormer window, elbows at rest on the padded settee cushion below it, rifle at the ready. He scanned the vista toward the Hood Canal while he conversed with himself for a half hour or more, when he took note of movement over the berm, on the beach side of the road.

He saw the flash; then heard the deafening report, followed by a scattering of shot that ripped at the window where he knelt.

Aaron cried out, flew backward, all his one hundred eighty five pounds dropped to the wooden floor in a loud thump, a hard enough landing to be easily heard from outside.

CHAPTER 2

She piled in the van after the last shot. The shooter saw a sign of movement at the upstairs window, took quick aim, and hastily pulled the trigger on the old Winchester 12 gauge pump shotgun. As before, the recoil nearly knocked her slender body down. The blast echoed across the mile and half-wide canal like a broken record. She fired at a shadow, saw a dust cloud puff away from the intended impact point, heard his shriek and what sounded like a body fall, as might a cement sack when dropped to a wooden floor.

Iliana Ona Gosnov was not happy to leave without knowing positively, her long sought target's fate; while her driver and partner, insisted he would take off without her if she persisted.

"We are most lucky not to have been killed by shots he took." His nasal manner of speaking irritated her; she withheld comment. "I told you this was stupid thing to consider. I tried to discourage it, but, 'No,' you insisted, 'this guy is mine and I'll get him if it's the last thing I do,'" the driver, Boris Kovansk Oligoff, scolded. He chose to go by Kovansk. Shooting was only to be a scare tactic, as far as he knew. "That was no scare ... murder in cold blood; it was ... terrible thing. You gave me no idea." Oligoff went on, angrier with each word.

A deeply furrowed frown on his otherwise young, smooth, and almost boyish face contorted it in a frightening way; gave him a terribly menacing look, not just one of aggravation or annoyance, Iliana thought. Nicknamed Kovi after his Russian born father, he harbored a dark side that Iliana did not understand. The sudden change in countenance involuntarily displayed itself whenever he raged or yelled at her.

Only days before while Kovansk impatiently awaited arrival of a prospective tenant for their Beverly Hills condominium, he displayed the same look ... rarely seen before Iliana began to plan the assault. Oligoff lost his temper that day while he spoke on his cell phone with the realtor, who tried in vain to explain her prospect's tardiness.

Absent apparent provocation, the otherwise even-tempered man slammed his right fist through the gypsum board drywall, and broke into the bedroom on the other side of the partition where they sat, in the dining alcove that overlooked busy San Vicente Boulevard. His forehead wrinkled frighteningly just before the outburst.

Iliana, proportioned like a fashion model, filled all Kovansk's desires; stood 5'8", narrow of face and hips. Small busted, she had finely carved eyebrows, full lips, and a pouty though unusually sensual expression. A passionate pulchritude, her coal-black eyes—large and alluring—spoke "I want you," without effort. Born in Los Angeles to a St. Petersburg, Russian-born physician father and Ukraine mother who modeled in France in her younger years and later on New York runways, Iliana conversed casually with a slight Russian accent. Her father spoke the mother tongue at home much of the time while she grew up with him.

A wedge in her dreams of modeling, she fought hard, to no avail, against the insurmountable barrier: an under-developed, spastic right leg, the skeletal and muscular structures in which—owing to a foreshortened tibia, fibula and femur, and a deformed foot—would never permit her to walk with a normal gait. In fact, she limped openly, quite incongruent with her otherwise exceptional beauty and grace. Too often, openly angry because of it, the debility enraged her almost daily, usually more when arising, especially after she learned of the cause.

"I'll get even with the SOB who did this to me," became a morning mantra, spoken rhetorically to anyone who might have caused or contributed. Memories of her father entered her mind at such times, filled her delusions of ineptness with hate and conflicting love. Iliana never learned that a simple choice could allow her to coexist with such a deformity, as so many learned to do with ambulatory problems much worse than hers. Much as she loved him, Iliana became strikingly inconsolable if Kovansk ever ventured into the forbidden territory of cause or, God forbid, as a fine surgeon himself, to explore prospects of correction. Iliana took any such commentary as a stabbing insult rather than support, as he would have it.

An unbending, if not threatening determination to hurt someone, anyone in the way, in response to it, drove the woman even further toward the unusual fixation with her right lower extremity. Oligoff became increasingly concerned when conversation about it instantly altered her personality, her outlook, and how it could bring on a projected contempt with the medical profession to which both dedicated their lives. What was the force that gripped her pathway to nursing in the first place? He often wondered if her curious need for revenge somehow pushed her into the profession in lieu of the more conventional philanthropic or humanitarian reasons.

Extremely intelligent, otherwise approachable and ostensibly sensitive—appealing as they come—she was born with unusual recall and a photographic memory. Iliana well used these attributes to attract and maintain Kovansk's affections since they met. Her insatiable appetite for sex, too, made it even easier for him to stay committed since they spent their first night together after their first coffee date in Westwood, a few blocks from UCLA Medical Center Hospital. When not in nursing attire, she wore tight-fitting designer jeans in lieu of a skirt or shorts. Much less revealing of her problem leg, she filled them beautifully, from Kovansk's viewpoint.

Rather than leave a trail to a car rental agency, with latex surgical-gloved hands, they broke into and absconded with the maroon, 70s vintage Ford van, earlier on the day of the shooting. After arrival at Sea-Tac Airport from Orange County on Alaska Airlines Flight 517, just before 11:00 AM, Kovi and Iliana crossed the pedestrian bridge from the terminal, went straight to the massive parking structure, and with a surprisingly short search effort, stumbled upon their transportation for the day.

Cautiously, they checked its tires and felt the radiator from beneath the hood. Both were cool. Coupled with oil drippings on the concrete surface below the engine, indications were clear: it was parked there for some time; they both agreed ... a safe bet that an immediate missing report would be unlikely in the few hours they would do the job and return it. The entry ticket stub, clearly visible in the open ashtray, assured an uncomplicated exit from the parking lot.

A hard push by Oligoff on the driver's side wind wing; the frail locking lever gave way, and they had their wheels.

Iliana sported a long blond wig that masked her natural ebony pixie cut and dyed bangs. She wore sunglasses and, though she walked awkwardly in them, 3" heels, to look unidentifiably different than she would without the accoutrements, for the return flight. Heavy cotton batting stuffed beneath her clothes, expanded her slender profile, illusory of thirty-five or more pounds of added body weight.

"I will be only too glad to get rid of this red wig, beard, and moustache. These—how you say—elevated boots, are killing me," Oligoff complained, when they boarded the van, after they decided it would be their transportation. He checked the parking lot ticket, date stamped three days before. Kovansk removed a $100 bill from his silver money clip to pay at the gate and fired up the engine by an easy hot-wire of the ignition from below the dash. They picked the older van for that reason.

"You did well with camouflage," he had to admit. "Not a soul on our flight could have come close to recognizing us with props," he continued. "You used masterful imagination at Hollywood thrift shop." Oligoff occasionally omitted articles when he spoke. Unlike English, Russian did not make similar use of them, he often argued in his defense. "Isn't there alternative ... a more reasonable method of frightening this man beside elaborate effort you planned?" He asked for the tenth time.

Scare? Hell, I'm going to blow his goddamned head off. She could hardly contain her anticipatory excitement, and simply returned his comment with silence and a cold stare, followed by her uniquely devious smile. Such expressions from Iliana, he knew, meant, "No more queries."

Next day's plans called for a flight—not back to Orange County, but for further obfuscation—to LAX. Taking that route home, surveillance cameras in the terminal and ticket sales records would be of no correlative help if police investigated. They discarded clothing worn for the trip north, in a Tacoma truck stop trash bin. Iliana acquired forged IDs earlier—something entirely new to them as medical professionals. For the flight to Washington, papers labeled them as Igor and Anna Massov— Roberto and Isabel Huerta for the return trip to LA. The sheaf of phony documents included forged California drivers' licenses, credit cards, and other complementary papers to add apparent legitimacy. She flatly refused to discuss with Oligoff, just how she assembled the paraphernalia. His vociferous outcries of curiosity ranted untiringly in the ensuing weeks.

Arrival at LAX, plans called for them to walk from the usual passenger pick-up zone, quickly beyond view of surveillance cameras, a quarter-mile or so east on Century Boulevard, then to hail a taxi, and exit several blocks from their condominium. They planned to walk the remainder of the way.

"We have done everything to the point of overkill to obscure our movements," Iliana had to assure Oligoff beyond doubt, before he reluctantly agreed to participate. It required interminable convincing, as Kovansk, a cautious professional, was, up to that point, the picture of propriety, certainly unwilling to do anything that might affect his hard-fought medical career.

"For God's sake, I'm a healer, a Doctor of Medicine, a good one, too, and you: a top-class educator, and neurosurgical nurse-assistant. We have suddenly become common criminals—how you say—cold blood killers. I stupidly joined effort, because of my love for you?" Oligoff snarled the query.

They sped south on Highway 101 after the shooting, past Eldon, a small village on the Hood Canal waterfront, closed tight at that hour—toward the end of the sixty-mile-long, blunt-ended waterway. A musty, foul smell that came from damp carpet in the back of the old van did not help Kovansk's attitude. Used to the sleek look and new-leather scent of his 2009 Porsche 911 Carrera—packed with 385 horsepower, and designed to own roads like the one they traveled—the van they took seemed an even more onerous ride.

"This is invitation to disaster, and we bought two tickets in front row," Oligoff said.

"Love?" Iliana finally responded to his first outburst with a delay brought by her desire to choose words carefully—but there was clear sarcasm in her tone. "Love, you say? Don't you think the half million borrowed against Papa's unsettled estate, even though discounted by the greedy lender, to set up your private practice, was a little more than barely motivating?" Let's be truthful for a moment, Kovi. Don't hand me this honor business; no guilt trips at this stage of the game; not now. She growled deeply inside, and silently foisted upon him, some of the wrath she tightly held for men, which she usually kept covertly capped and undetected.

"How could you know the fellow took a lethal blow," she snapped, "yelling for me to get in the car, before I was sure? So much planning— months and months of it—so many details, the chances we took; yet to be uncertain of the outcome before taking off, panicked though you became, was sheer lunacy."

"Lethal blow! You kid me! You said you wished to throw fear of God into the man, not take his fucking life." Kovansk fiddled with the road map again, checked their progress, and tossed it behind the seat. "What in the name of Vladimir Putin's mother do you say? Our lives, too, were on line. We were damned targets ... bullets struck the van, maybe us with next shots. We can verify by phone, can't we?" He inhaled deeply, took a few more breaths to calm himself, and said, with less panic in his voice. "We have home number and cell, too. We shall call from booth ... downtown Tacoma and Seattle—just before gun drop-off—not from airport where cops might think an assailant would go, to leave town. No answer ... no Concord ... correct?"

A dramatic discount to his suggestion, Iliana jerked her head close to the passenger door and away from him, sneered disagreeably, then stared out the window at the endless, near-black tree line that sped by in a blur. She saw only a whirling kaleidoscope: a viscous blend of unabated fright, the heavy beat of her pulse, dense woods, worry, mist on the window, dripping perspiration, the moving line of headlight yellow that traced the road's edge, and her rapid, shallow breathing. Sickened by all of it, she closed her eyes for a full disconnect.

"How can we be sure?" she finally turned to him and asked, eyelids raised to a fiery glare. "I want that man dead." Her jaw tightened; fists clenched. She involuntarily flashed to the memory of having related the same thing to her closest friend when stood up by Roger Banning, her twenty-one year old fiancé, practically at the altar, and with no forewarning. The memory, while painful and never welcome, arose from the depths too often for her taste, usually when she felt threatened by or was angry at a male, any male within reach.

Iliana, nineteen, and a naive college freshman, fell for him hopelessly in her first semester. Dating in high school, rare, unsatisfying, and perfunctory; never resulted in a lasting partner on whom she could depend.

They wanted sex; nothing seemed more important to them at the time, and she learned to offer it freely to keep them in tow.

She dated Banning for a year before she got pregnant; thought him a well-positioned young man, a mature college senior, who would be a good provider when he finished school with a degree in finance. Only son of two loving, very successful aerospace engineer parents, with lucrative careers, her regular at UCLA, much to Iliana's well-concealed envy, very well liked, and a fraternity man with an abundance of friends, skated on a full academic scholarship.

That legacy engendered frequent bouts of self-doubt and insecurity on Iliana's part, if not periods of despondency as she—a solo child, from a single parent home—felt insular, isolated from that lifestyle. Despite the disparity, she was urged by intrinsic forces, compelled to feel, what she thought was enduring love. Marred far too often, though, by her outbursts of violently expressed jealously and contempt, she must have irrevocably frightened the young man. She sensed his withdrawal whenever she lost control, and cast hurtful epithets, which flowed all too easily.

When Iliana confessed she bore his child, a product of their prolific and carefree amorous practices, it sparked, to her surprise, yet elation, an immediate proposal; a commitment from him to be her life-long partner, and a modest engagement ring she soon adored. A hasty wedding, planned by his parents, not her father—who wished nothing to do with the young imposter—would, she tried in vain to dream, bring them closer together. The Las Vegas marriage date, but a week hence, brought forth a terrible and unbearable shock when Iliana found her fiancé disappeared, apparently bound for the east coast—maybe Europe, his upset parents claimed— never to be heard from again. Strongly persuaded by her father, depressed Iliana underwent an abortion, immediately returned to school, though with a deep emotional scar and an underlying bender to get even, that never resolved itself. Only to worsen as the years passed; she lashed out toward any man in her way, at the slightest provocation, and with a curried vengeance she could not seem to grasp or comprehend.

Many years later, with no softening of her position, musings continued to turn attentions toward memories of her first love. Angrily, she visualized chocking him until his eyes bulged, with a garrote so tight he could not speak or call for help. Hopelessly, he struggled to free his hands from the bonds she affixed while he slept; his body finally went limp, and turned eggplant purple while he relinquished to asphyxiation. Strangely, such wanderings gave her solace, allowed her to cope, in a macabre way, with daily frustrations, and the right leg that persisted as an ever-present and embarrassing anathema.

Kovansk, sobered and frightened, by Iliana's sudden hostility, drove too fast on the winding road to respond. Nervously, he shifted glances behind, in the rearview mirror, and then quickly forward. The rear wheels slid on an outside curve. Iliana shrieked and continued, "If he finally answers one of our calls? What then?"

CHAPTER 3

Kovansk slowed and gathered back his senses with a lurch that snapped her head forward. He knew he risked a speeding ticket, even at that hour on the near-deserted road, southbound to Olympia, to pick up northbound Interstate 5 toward Seattle. Travel brochures he reviewed before the trip, warned, in spite of the area's remoteness; hungry cops abounded, on the loose for fast drivers.

Radar-equipped, aided by the confusing variety of speed limits, Mason County Sheriff's Deputies enjoyed a steady flow of tourist citations when they patrolled Highway 101 from Lilliwaup to the county seat in Shelton. He trembled with apprehension the more he thought about it. Kovansk's ideations centered upon worry ... a probable murder, bullet damage to the van that could link the vehicle to shots taken by Concord, and the innate curiosity of lawmen, if nothing else.

Police would soon find Aaron dead, his piece beside him, Kovansk thought, and expended cartridges. They would easily add up things. He grew more afraid of a stop for some minor infraction—discovery with a stolen vehicle, a shotgun smelling of recent firing, their false identifications, and disguises. *How would we explain the purpose of this trip in a routine stop?* He wondered, absent any plausible explanations.

"Simply being on record, driving through the state on date of murder, would place us in, how you say, 'Persons of interest,' category," Kovansk argued when Iliana asked that he stop for a snack and coffee.

"No! No more footprints will we leave around here … too damned much at stake as it is."

Iliana muffled her recant, afraid to confront the man under the tense circumstances. That ominous frown appeared again. She would get her time, she promised to herself. She clearly viewed the imagined terror on her first love's face as she tightened the belt around his neck until the buckle latched at the last hole. A devilish grin broke through at the illusory recall.

They passed the Highway 106 crossing, south of the southerly dogleg turn in the deep fjord, dubbed Hood Canal by Royal Navy Commander George Vancouver when he ventured there, under sail, in 1792.

"I did hear one hell of a fall from up there by window, and thereafter, no more retaliation … pretty sure sign," Oligoff acknowledged after a long, resigned sigh. "That was direct strike from my vantage by the street when you whispered that the window shade was moving. My only concern is longer distance that made shot less deadly by the foot."

"Let's consider him gone," Iliana said, only half believed. "Alone, he'll bleed to death up there, if he were not completely taken out by the blast. Two dozen or so metal balls should remove a face at that range. I remember, with a shiver, the damage # 4 buckshot did to the plywood behind our practice targets in the desert."

Russian born, an unusually attractive, talented and superbly trained ER physician of athletic build, he towered just over six feet, and looked younger than his thirty-eight years. Oligoff sported a neatly trimmed, very small, triangular, jet-black goatee in the midst of his chin, and a thin moustache, he shaved clean for the escapade. An enviable figure, he captured though easily ignored, continuous female stares he perceived whenever he and Iliana went out; so strongly did he feel for the woman.

After he spent close to half his life expectancy immersed in school and medical training, he dreamed of someone like Iliana, with whom he could spend quality time, marry, and have children, when he completed it. She was that rare person who could understand the self-driven strife for perfection in his work and elsewhere. Never, was he not meticulously dressed, down to his odd habit of wearing cufflinks, even on causal custom shirts he had tailored.

The unexpected intrusion, though, with recent underpinnings that spelled so much potential trouble, caused serious concern that his life fell far short of the path he thought it should have followed by then. This caper, though, would end their turmoil, he finally convinced himself, though he swam in complete denial of its obvious repercussive potential.

After studies to the doctorate level in microorganism physiology at the M.V. Lomonosov Moscow State University, the dark-eyed doctor emigrated from his homeland, entered the U.S., and completed medical school at Harvard University, Class of 2001. He became the lucky part of an exchange program for scientifically gifted bilinguals that followed the fall of Soviet Russia. Kovansk ardently pursued English throughout his education and in graduate school had the benefit of two advisors who trained in the U.K. He spoke the King's English well, but, still self-conscious about it; knew he sounded awkward at times, while mediated by an appealing British twang.

An honor student at Harvard, second in his class, he elected to make the USA his home, and, with his high academic standing, quickly accepted an internship and residency in emergency medicine and trauma surgery, offered by L. A. County USC Medical Center, in the heart of the big city. Finishing that five-year stint, and deeply in debt, he secured a fairly well endowed two-year neurosurgical fellowship at UCLA Medical Center.

There he met Iliana, twenty-seven at the time. She taught for two years on the neurosurgery rotation at the university's School of Nursing and snared him initially with her penetrating eyes that showed deep passionate interest, barely visible above the margin of her surgical mask.

The bespectacled, dedicated physician, beset with deeper crow's feet at eye corners, Iliana thought, than most males his age; gentle as a lamb for the most part, nevertheless had his weaknesses. Money was one of them, coupled with a history of larcenous behavior as a young boy in his homeland, where he endured life in Moscow, a city riddled with crime and deception—one's cunning, toughness, and bravado the God-given keys to survival. Poor then, cash broke and mortgaged to the hilt, he burdened himself further with an over-priced Beverly Hills condominium he couldn't sell when the economy down-turned. He bought a new home in the desert and his car—credit extended up to his neck—when he joined the Joshua Trauma Center staff two years before, and obligated himself even deeper, as a buy-in partner.

Nothing like the huge multi-disciplinary hospitals where he trained, the clean, 175 bed, near-new primary care facility, in California's stark though rapidly populating Mojave Desert, filled his every need by comparison. The usual nighttime array of grueling stabbings and gunshot wounds at the large inner city facilities ... almost unheard of there. The steady stream of indigents, with every discrete malady in the book, pleasantly absent from the picture, also made his work easier.

However, gone, also, were the rare opportunities he savored as a new medical school graduate, to learn myriad diagnostic techniques a small center could not justify to explore; and the finely trained senior attending staff members, always eager to impart what they knew. Despite that, he quickly accommodated to the flow of car and motorcycle accident victims, rattlesnake, scorpion, and spider bites, and the usual variety of off-roaders' spinal and head injury cases he felt confident and capable to treat, with his added neurosurgical training.

Single storied, shadowed by the San Gabriel Mountains in late afternoons, 100 miles northeast of his Beverly Hills condominium, the isolated hospital offered fresh air and a new start.

Oligoff moved his head slightly to his right, turned on the dome lamp, and flashed a smile to assure he was still capable of the gregarious persona he enjoyed expressing, that is until Iliana's venture into the unexpected began. He swept back his curly, medium-length dark hair, and again forced a feigned grin. The past two years or so, money finally coming in to create a modicum of positive flow, he kept the mane shorter, had it groomed weekly, just long enough to cover his ears, and down to the collar of the blue scrub shirt he wore while at the hospital.

Lifting his glasses to rub tired eyes, Oligoff glanced repeatedly into the rearview mirror and more critically studied his countenance while Iliana dozed—hand on his thigh, head tentatively balanced against his shoulder. She still smelled of the perfume he always suggested she wear, when she begged his preference before going out for the evening. *Was it the* Rancé Joséphine *I bought her in Paris? She would not remember, anyway.* He didn't really care at that moment, but it reminded him of Iliana's clean, spicy smell after she showered, at least on the few occasions she felt romantic of late. Iliana found herself irrepressibly stressed and all but completely unaffectionate since they embarked on this mission, and so soon, too, after her father's passing.

Kovansk felt rough, tired, and frightened and shifted his attention from the mirror, back to the roadway ahead. *What the hell have I done? Who is she? Do I ... will I ever know what other lies, if any, might exist behind all of this? What in God's grace possessed her—how I say—to take on job to kill a man, to end life of a human being, someone with whom she simply had a grudge? We did not even know him. Yes, we have years to pay debts at very severe cash flow sacrifice and I am closing on forty, but I stupidly became accessory. I cannot rationalize this as I did when committing misdemeanors with friends as struggling teenager.* Kovansk further frightened himself with other mounting concerns. He watched enough crime programs on TV to know he would be just as exposed as she would, if they didn't pull it off successfully. *I am not some stupid killer. I educated myself for eighteen years … earn large six-figure salary … profit sharing. But my fingers are as deep in the borscht as are hers.*

For a moment, the deep red Ukraine borne soup brought back memories of the old country. Made with beets, beef shank and miscellaneous vegetables—whatever was on sale and cheap at the time, in the central market—he and his roommates made it a staple while starving students at the State University. Life near the campus in their cramped flat in the Lenin Hills put them just outside the deep Moscow hustle.

As his mind drifted thousands of miles to the east, he silently reflected on his father. *He was a genuinely mean, terrible man by repute, a crook, cheater at heart, and just as bad in way he treated me. Thank God, though, he cared enough to inquire at Josephina Tratinov Primary School, how I had been doing at level six, and found to his surprise I displayed unusual attributes, far above my peers.* The ensuing transfer to Lennskiiy Intermediate School of Natural Sciences took young Oligoff away from home, doubtless, the best thing that could have happened.

At least he managed to leave the small collective farm, and receive an education paid for by the State, unlike his older brother who still labored there, and cared for his aging father. The old man no longer operated heavy equipment owing to a mild stroke suffered when Oligoff entered graduate school and began research into the mystical field of viruses. His father spoke awkwardly, due to facial nerve parasthesias. He became a most hateful person with the paralysis-induced drooling and slurred speech he found so humiliating.

Entry into the right lane of Interstate 5 was easy at that hour. Oligoff dutifully turned attentions back to the task of driving, used his left turn flasher to merge into the center lane, and once situated, leaned back to stretch for the long ride ahead.

His blood suddenly ran cold, though; skin goose-pimpled and his legs shuddered involuntarily. A quick glance in the rear view mirror, then beside himself, he caught an alarming sight: two sets of red and blue flashing lights no more than three hundred yards behind, and closing.

"Damned Troopers! They're gaining, one in my lane and one to left. Here we are: sitting Red Square pigeons, freshly fired shotgun, shells we intended to throw off the Highway 90 Bridge across Lake Washington … good solid evidence of a gunfight." More than panic-stricken, Kovansk turned helplessly toward sleeping Iliana for ideas, and sharply nudged her awake with his elbow as the patrol cars pulled closer behind and slowed, lights still ablaze.

CHAPTER 4

REDMOND, WASHINGTON

Peggy Concord felt her mother-in-law's forehead. Considerably cooler, no longer febrile, as she was intermittently, recent as three days before, she succeeded in her well-fought and nearly won battle with pneumonia. The aged woman, hospital-confined for ten days, beat the odds, and once again deterred the disabling lung infection.

Mother Grace—Peggy affectionately called her that for decades—became incessantly impatient for discharge home. The end of her fourth day there, Peggy would see her through the transition and determine, for the last time, whether the independent, almost virile woman could care for herself without twenty four/seven assistance. Grace lay supine, relaxed in her king size bed, beneath a faded rose, down comforter, head propped upon two overstuffed pale green pillows.

The room, too dark for her to read, had but one lamp on a tripod table close to the door. Peggy sat quietly, looked at the brood of plastic bottles stacked on one nightstand—prescriptions to continue until they ran out—and the ten or more framed family photos neatly arranged on the other.

She's over the tough part, but a fall ... pneumonia relapse, living here all by herself, pose big risks, if we are just two or so hours away. Missing her friends from the bridge club ... absences from Friday night bingo games at church could kill her, too, and maybe faster, with nothing more than bed confinement on the menu. Contrastingly important reasons to live, they awakened her will to heal, which we cannot forget to consider.

Peggy almost spoke audibly as worrisome thoughts plowed forth. Did they make the right decision? Would she and Aaron relinquish to the pleasant woman's insistence to shed the idea of extended institutional care, so harshly against their wishes?

Grace opened her eyes, made contact with Peggy's. She grinned in the same fashion, as did Aaron—convincingly, engendering spirited confidence—though all too feebly held up her left hand for Peggy to clasp and rub, while voicing gratitude for her daughter-in-law's indulgence. "Sweetheart, you can't appreciate what your being here has done for me ... gave me the courage not to cave in, to accept no substitutes but to rid myself of this raspy, danged respiratory congestion. I'm feeling so much better ... stronger by the hour it seems.

"I got this fight-back strength from Senior, my good doctor husband, bless his resting soul, and together we imbued to Aaron, the strengths he showed all his life: never-give-up attitude, unblemished integrity, likeability, and expertise to create the financial successes he achieved in business." Aaron's mother allowed lazy lids to slip down, cover her eyes, then opened them after a brief reprieve, with renewed vigor, to expose clear azure irises, healthy as those of a thirty-ear old might appear. She never wore glasses and cataract surgery was not yet a talking point, unlike most of her peers, many of whom who were ten to fifteen years younger and half-blind from one degenerative ocular condition or another.

"Land sakes, your husband managed to save much more money than Doctor Aaron Concord ever did," Grace said proudly, knowing just the same, her deceased mate left her well enough heeled to have no financial woes as long as she lived. Since Aaron Senior's demise a year before, she referred to him as, "Doctor C or Dr. Concord," as she did while she worked the front desk in his office for twenty years.

"No matter now, that Aaron Junior didn't go to medical school when he finished college," she continued. "At least he got a good taste of it working in surgery at the hospital through high school, and most of his available university days. Judging by his financial triumphs, Little Aaron took to heart all he learned as a business major at Cal State Long Beach, and mixed it well with the intimate working knowledge of surgery he gained with so much orderly and scrub-tech experience. He sure spoke the language of the physician if he weren't one. How his father loved to chat about the profession with him.

"We begged him to apply to Ivy League schools. However, he did well at State and enjoyed living part time at the beach with us, as a luxury he'd not have had in a musty, old, East Coast dorm in the midst of a large city. We had fun, Aaron and his friends around the place a mite longer than would otherwise have been the case.

"I must be honest, we were both disappointed in a way," Grace jabbered on, "Junior could have become a fine ophthalmologist like his dad, with the top grades he got in the sciences. When he made eyes for you, Darling, his pictured future, and ours, too, came to a screeching stop. Dad and I both agreed when we met you, however, that our Aaron made the right decision. When Beth and Robert came along in due course, two of the world's best grandchildren, we knew Aaron did right; that his life and yours would be good. I've been so enamored by our son's integrity and business acumen—yours as well, and how well received by the medical community he became, once his business was established. He even had lawyers for friends, not just as clients, if you can imagine."

Honesty, yes, for the most part, Peggy mused. *Aaron did have that affair ten years ago with Casey, the young hussy in his office. That certainly was not honesty and he came close to paying dearly for it. He'd have emerged from the short tryst with no family support, all alone, and tormented with the guilt that consumed him when he finally admitted to it and came clean.*

Grace and the doctor never knew of Aaron's temporary philandering. They kept it to themselves once Aaron agreed to, and completed a long series of therapy sessions to set his mind straight.

Peggy squeezed Grace's hand, smiled easily, and then spilled a few discrete tears with the mother-in-law's assertions. It was the first time she felt acknowledged to that degree and not viewed—as she always secretly thought herself, despite regular assurances to the contrary—an interruption in Aaron's parentally induced, pre-destiny to become an eye surgeon on his father's heels.

"I'm glad we decided to follow you to Washington," Peggy replied. When Dad retired, you two shot up here from Orange County like rockets. We truly thought you wished to get away from us. That is, until we got a taste of Pacific Northwest living ourselves. We fast realized we no longer needed the crowded beach and the continual skin cancer diagnoses our dermatologist began to bestow upon us as we got older. I do miss sounds of the waves crashing on the rocks below the house. Unarguably, though, our new digs became the best we've ever had. Do you still feel that way, now that we're up here with you?"

The aging woman breathed deeply. Her chest finally cleared of the alarmingly audible rales and ronchi—wheezing and rattling breath sounds—that typified fluid build up in the lungs, characteristic of pneumonia. She fell lightly asleep with Peggy's responsive chatter, but stirred again with partially opened eyes when Peggy spoke: "You go on; get your rest, Dear; try to sleep. Let me brush your hair a bit and lull you into a good night's nap," Peggy said, while she stroked the old woman's long, silky-white tress with patient deliberation.

"I must call my hubby before he's off to bed. Haven't talked with him for two days; we've been so busy with your recuperation. I will give him a good report, that you've been the ideal patient: walked well, up lots, helped me make soup today; that we sat in the den, watched a late movie; even took a stroll, and, amazingly, no adverse results but mild fatigue.

"You keep this up and he won't be screaming that you need convalescent hospital care the rest of your life. Above everything, I agree; you should stay away from those pockets of disease, greasy food, and germs of every description—helpful as they are when absolutely needed—until your health leaves virtually no alternative."

Stiffly arising from the uncomfortable dining chair she placed next to the bed, Peggy tightened the ties on her light green wool robe, shivered from the cool hall draft and quietly left Grace, who slipped back to sleep again, somewhere before she finished speaking. Tiptoed across the room, she turned off the lamp and swung the door mostly closed. A thin spear of yellow from the den across the hall sliced into the old lady's space, enough to peek in on her before Peggy, too, crashed for the night. Another long day and, to her surprise, nearly 1:00 AM—too late to call Aaron, she considered.

Dead tired, Peggy checked door locks, flipped light switches one by one, meandered through the large home to the guest bedroom, and fast slipped into an almost paralytic, pre-sleep relaxed state. She wondered if her children would show the same care Aaron and she did for his mother. If an accident, fall, stroke, or cancer debilitated one of them at a much earlier age than Grace's stray from her long-term picture of health; would they be able to spend as many years as they hoped, in the nest they made in the midst of nowhere; so far from their kids and grandchildren in Southern California?

Might it not have been more sensible to find a spot in Redmond? She wondered ... just east of Lake Washington ... closer to hospitals, the airport, and civilization as they knew it all their lives?

Peggy arose suddenly. She alerted to a soft call from Grace, not one of distress but a last minute by-the-way plea. Slippers and robe on again, in a flash, worried something went wrong, Peggy rushed to the chair beside Grace's bed, sat down gently, and listened to a somewhat mumbling monologue.

"Probably should have said something before, Dear, but it just occurred to me to mention that an old military buddy of Aaron's stopped by, looked for him not so long ago. You two went to California for that wedding, remember?"

Peggy shook her head side to side, and frowned. "Army buddy? Wha ... what Army buddy? Aaron hasn't heard from anyone in his old group for years and years. That is odd all right, but likely one of those who didn't make out very well after discharge ... needed to borrow money. That way for ten years or so after he left the service, such contacts were not unusual. Those less fortunate, without educations beforehand, or after, had a hard time of it in many cases: drinking, drugs, broken families, and other troubles—even homelessness. Aaron helped a few of his men get a foothold in life. Who was this; do you recall?"

"He freely gave his name, don't remember it now, a foreign sounding one, maybe Czech, Russian or even Polish; I don't know. Quite a charming man, he was ... bushy red hair and beard, the darkest eyebrows for that hair ... noticed that right away; and there was a lovely lady with him, blonde, looked like a model, but with a bad limp. Both simply asked for Aaron. They thought he lived here for some reason ... driving a slick little sports coupe ... silver one; looked new." Grace had Peggy's full attention. It sounded all too unusual.

"Well, what did you tell them?" Peggy was more than passively concerned.

"Oh, I just gave them your number, Aaron's cell, and directions—best I could—to your place out on Hood Canal. I said that was your home since you leased the Laguna Beach house, that you flew south, and would be there for a week or so." The gentleman said he would call Aaron, catch up with him on their next trip from San Francisco."

"San Francisco?"

"Yes, they were driving from there to Vancouver, B.C., for a vacation ... 'passing through,' they said."

"Mother Grace," Peggy retorted, and reluctantly shook her finger, "why didn't you say something about this earlier? I asked you before to not be so free, handing our address to just anyone. We're all alone out there, and at times I'm still a bit nervous, even with Duke around, whenever Aaron is away." Peggy reached down and patted the doting dog. He sat between them and looked up as if part of the discussion.

"Well, they seemed so pleasant." Grace rolled away from Peggy, toward the window, and sighed.

"Good night and sleep well," Peggy said, "I must get to bed, to arise with the chickens as you always do, no matter what time you retire." She felt betrayed at the disclosure the elderly woman made to someone she did not know.

Peggy lay awake for a few minutes and wondered about that unusual encounter. *What prompted the couple to stop at Grace's house like that? We don't know anyone fitting such a description from the Bay Area. Red beard?*

Must ask Aaron in the morning. Her head filled with a million stars and she dropped out for the remainder of the night.

CHAPTER 5

OLYMPIC PENINSULA, WASHINGTON

Oligoff slowed gradually and steered toward the right shoulder, frozen in fear. What would come next? His mind raced with possibilities. "Good evening … driver's license, insurance certificate, and registration, please," would probably be the first request, he worried. Then, "What's a feller with a fresh California driver's license doing with an old junker Washington-registered vehicle?" Finally, "You have some ID, Ma'am?" the officer might then inquire of Iliana.

Stupefied with his inability to concoct innocent sounding responses to such mundane yet expected questions, Kovansk nearly lost consciousness. Broken rear door glass, and evident bullet holes on the driver's side, could easily spark cautious curiosity.

"We're fucked." He said nothing more and turned toward his misted door window when the State Trooper motioned him to roll it down. Should he reach behind the seat for the shotgun? A momentary look in the outside rearview mirror; he saw the man's partner still in the second patrol car, mike in hand, likely calling in to check the plate against that day's hot list. Could the owner have reported it stolen? He wondered.

"'Evenin' folks." The officer bent forward slightly from just behind Kovansk's door and looked quickly at each of them, right hand on his holstered pistol butt. Before either could do anything but flash limpid smiles, the horn honked in the patrol car. "We're on a call … accident up the hill … must go. I just wanted you to know; your left rear tire is awfully low. It's not safe. Better get it filled. There's a truck stop up the way." The horn behind honked a second time. The Trooper's partner again motioned him back to the patrol car. Kovansk shook as if he contracted well advanced Parkinson's disease, he surmised.

"You folks drive safely; g'night, now, and get that tire checked ... other ones, too."

At the last minute, Oligoff mustered the strength to lean his head out the window, turn toward the rear, and, as the Trooper walked away, to respond with a feeble, "Thank you; and good night to you, officer.

"Jesus Christ! I have never in my life been so in shock by a police stop." Kovansk grabbed the wheel with both hands and leaned forward, rested his head on his forearms, until rapid breathing and throbbing pulse regained normalcy. Iliana's urge to cry, merged quickly into full-blown hysteria—the first time he recently saw her express emotion so openly, aside from the frequent but short-lived episodes of contempt when she started most of her days.

Kovansk felt unsure of his own ability to retain composure for the rest of the drive to the airport, exuded sticky perspiration, until sopping wet from the sobering encounter. Close to 3:00 AM; they did not stop to eat, and would barely arrive to make Alaska Airlines Flight 454 at six o'clock. They had little leeway to dispose of the gun and remaining shells in Lake Washington, from the Highway 90 bridge, according to plan. Certainly, they had insufficient time to get a room near the airport, freshen up, and arrange new disguises. That had to happen in the van, however awkward.

All movement halted in the Concord cabin. The owl in the tall fir by the road returned to its lofty perch, hooted softly after the gunfire disturbance; northeasterly breezes abated, and forest stillness reigned once more.

The bedside telephone's persistent ring invaded the quiet. It stopped when voice mail responded. Aaron's cell phone, knocked to the floor from his flannel shirt pocket, murmured its special ring tone; a clapping Vietnam-era Huey helicopter rotor blade and the background whine of its turbine. He paid $20.00 for the unique attention-getter, and always let it run to the last second possible, before responding. Five minutes passed; the same sequence repeated itself. There were no responses to the attempted connections.

Engine idling roughly, the van's musty exhaust belched blue smoke that hovered low to the pavement like a London fog. They stopped in an all night service station parking lot next to the off ramp for downtown Tacoma. Oligoff stood by an open pay phone booth, shivered from the dank, icy air that swirled around him each time a truck passed. He liked the name Kovi, even Kovansk, but hated his given name, Boris. As a boy in Moscow, that handle taunted like Gayle, Marion, Lynn or Tucker might for a male in the States—too often the subject of teasing by young peers.

"Boris K. Oligoff, get in this van, now; let's try again later. I won't sit out here and freeze another minute." Iliana rubbed her shoulders impatiently, shook her head side to side and slammed the passenger door. It took little for her to churn anger when irritated. Much to her chagrin, it was hardly unusual for her to throw kitchen utensils, smash glassware on the floor, and to sling forth vile insults when touched off with the slightest provocation, by a man.

No idea, consciously, from whence these latent episodes of rage were born, Oligoff usually wore the target. Then she remembered her first fiancé and the sadistic illusions her mind created, in which he twitched and trembled, succumbed to his crushed larynx, a leather belt taught around it. She heard the cartilage fracture—listened to him gargle for air, watched his movements cease, ever so slowly—and smiled grotesquely as he withered to complete immobility and terminal silence.

The doctor flushed red with anger at the insulting command and Iliana's intentional use of his given name, Boris, to focus attention. His face tightened; his forehead wrinkled involuntarily, the way that frightened her. He slammed the receiver down and sent his female companion a non-verbal message not to tempt him or she might be damned sorry.

Iliana grew anxious at his persistence with the pay phone, and the endless cacophony of clanking quarters after each dial attempt. They went out of the way to find change in a nearby mini-market when the service station cashier refused to part with the few coins he retained for the remainder of his shift.

Kovansk opened Iliana's door, tightened his fist on her shoulder as if he were lifting a barbell, until she grimaced. He cursed a streak of expletives in urban Russian, and froze her speechless with the heightened tone and unusual physical contact. She cowered sullenly. He went back to the phone, and dialed as before: the house, then Aaron's cell—again to the house—and brought about no answers to either.

He is dead ... poor bastard, he thought. "I'll try once more," he turned to Iliana, wreaked with guilt, face gray, and taciturn, "then we give up for while."

At times like this, Iliana thought, she would be on her cell phone, venting with her closest friend, Svetiia Kronoff. She and Kovansk, however, agreed to maintain complete insulation from any connection with Washington State during their two days there, and left their phones in Southern California as they did on their earlier motor trip. They encouraged friends to use the cells as much as possible, thus linking them to the L.A. area, while they were actually in Seattle, should investigative inquiries ever focus on the geographics of their cell use after the assault. She was glad they took the precaution but missed the many chats she and Svetiia could have exchanged as they did at home during idle or non-working hours.

Svetiia and Iliana studied together as undergrads at UCLA, and for three of their four years there, shared an apartment in a low rent area south of Santa Monica's main business district, near the west end of the I-10 Freeway. Much to her regret, Svetiia unwittingly involved herself in an irreconcilable financial bind when her mother filed bankruptcy in the midst of her first semester of post-graduate nursing studies.

She had no choice but to borrow money and banks were no help. Her desperate inquiries led to a source, through a "friend of a friend." She had no idea. The lender turned out to be a second level boss, one notch down from West L.A.'s most prominent *pakan*. The Russian Mafia, prolific in the area, operated with those top bosses as controllers of four crime cells, each led by a *brigadier* or local community sub-boss.

Iliana learned from her friend that the lenders, into every sort of illicit activity, including loan sharking, adhered to the strict code of conduct of the *Vory v Zakone,* "Keep your agreements or else." Unable to make promised progress payments on time, Svetiia left school, and was inducted against her will, into the *brigadier's* escort service. The alternative needed no elaboration, though still naively so, she understood the power and long tentacles of the organization's well-managed sub-cultural endeavors. Chernya Bostovitch—the *pakan's* strongest *brigadier,* a former KGB covert investigator in Moscow; tough and heartless, with few scruples—claimed ownership of Iliana's friend thereafter.

How could she have taken on the life of a hooker ... such a smart girl, and dear friend? God, how I wish I could somehow have intercepted her downhill plunge. Iliana could not resist thinking of her close friend and former schoolmate, enslaved for an uncertain future by a business as antithetical as possible to nursing. She could only imagine Svetiia's exploits, many too gruesome for Svetiia to relate, even to her; while she pictured, as her entire body shook with disgust, many of those her friend was willing to speak about on rare occasions.

Needing consolation, Iliana instinctively reached for her purse to phone Svetiia, but withdrew her hand with increased resignation. She called from the open door window—this time more respectfully—for Kovi to give up on the phone attempts.

The driver's door snapped open; Kovansk sat behind the wheel, and shook his head in disgust. "I think you did the man a lethal blow, Iliana. You must have killed him. More than ten times, I ring both lines ... nothing in response. We have to follow through, get on freeway, head for Highway 90 bridge, toss weapon, and then rush to airport to clear security, or we never make our plane. We have three hours to get this—how you say—crate, back to terminal. I called airport; plane is on time. We will leave as scheduled. I did my best for you and that is it. I am on duty in desert starting tomorrow at midnight. You are due at UCLA for three all-day teaching sessions the day after."

A searing twenty-four hours of excitement, uncertainty, and then, in conclusion, they would be homeward bound. Their senses of professional responsibility returned all too quickly. While Kovansk drove, he said little, ever vigilant to avoid a repeat performance of the earlier police stop. Next time, he pondered, they could not possibly be so fortunate. He filled all four tires, gassed up at the truck stop, checked operability of running lights, and assured himself that, if driving with traffic, they would not attract attention as happened earlier.

Iliana fell into a deep sleep once they entered the freeway. Her dreams nurtured, though with some tumult, until Kovansk paused on the bridge across the lake, assured no traffic approached from either direction, and tossed the gun and ammunition box over the side. Exhausted, she went out again until the van came to a bumpy stop at the airport parking lot gate, about to ascend the dizzying circular driveway to the upper level where they originally found the van.

As often occurred, sleepy wanderings took her to the shocking discovery she made after her father's demise, when she learned the truth about her malformed leg and how she came by it. The deeply ingrained anger, with which she often began her days, finally prompted incipient conversation with Oligoff about it. Somewhat relieved with the expected expository release, she whispered to Kovansk, and felt infinitely vulnerable. "I think I can muster the courage to tell you the story of my leg, this anatomical disaster, now that I have completed the mission of getting even."

Unaffected by her remarks, Kovansk spotted and swerved into a vacant space not far from where they found the old Ford. Clearly disinterested in any revelations at that point, he shut down the engine, and looked at his watch.

"That's fine, my *popka*," he replied—a word of affectionate Russian for little butt. "However," he twice more glanced at the time, "we must get on with our disguises for the trip south, and run like hell for departure counter, if we make our flight."

Iliana's sudden and unexpected will to consider opening up with her secret, swirled into oblivion as quickly as the idea was born. She reached behind the seat, opened the red duffel bag, and with one of her scowls, tossed their new adornments onto the center console between them. The two dismissed Aaron Concord and the need to call for him again.

CHAPTER 6

Seats 10-D and F on the Alaska Airlines Boeing 737-700, for Flight 454 that morning, were adjacent to the right side, mid-cabin exit, absent the usual third seat, exactly as the two occupants wished. Such placement eliminated possibilities of the usual nosey business traveler who would invade their space with questions, incite conversation, or look too closely at the subterfuges they employed.

The female, seated closest to the window, short black hair with bright red-dyed bangs, wore a cluster of yellow gold loops, twisted into ovals below each ear. She kept on her full-length white knit coat, tied at the waist like a robe, that showed only the top of a black turtleneck sweater beneath. Black designer jeans, sunglasses, tennis shoes, and an over-sized, old gold wedding band completed her simple ensemble.

Next to the aisle sat an attractive, tall man with wide-framed glasses and unkempt straight, rather bushy, light brown hair that dropped across his forehead and over his lenses—an oversized Elton John in the midst of a sweaty summer concert. His hands were delicate—long fingers, neatly manicured, and easily described like those of a surgeon, if not a violin player.

A padded, protuberant belly gave the impression he was disproportionally out of shape, that he weighed close to two-twenty or more. Unshaven for two days, he had a small black goatee a half inch below his lower lip; smooth, youthful facial skin—yet a most wrinkled forehead.

Oligoff, still in a sorry state, remained in emotional turmoil over the harrowing ride from Hood Canal. *We nearly missed carefully planned seat assignments. Stand-bys jumped up, disappointed, and many grumbled loudly when we arrived at the check-in counter, heaving and perspiring, to claim our seats.*

Iliana disposed of the blond wig with her other guises, while Kovansk wore the brown hairpiece to mask his curly, dark hair. It fit him to a T she thought; quietly she laughed inside at her lover's altered appearance. *A proud Russian,* she almost giggled aloud: *strong nose, prominent cheekbones, and wide jaw, with such a silly, incongruent hairdo!*

Embarrassed at the level to which they stretched to be covert, they still worried. Would someone they knew recognize them? They wrapped themselves in blankets, like cigar store Indians and were well asleep, head-to head, before take-off—dead to the world from the busy night. Both were oblivious to the two attendants who served drinks in their section.

"This is the Captain Speaking."

The blaring announcement startled Iliana from her rest. Nothing more than notice that, to their left, on the opposite side of the cabin, Mt. St. Helens, the recently active volcano, still emitted steamy smoke, and would soon be visible through a break in the cloud cover. Many of those on their side of the plane crowded toward the small window in the exit door across the aisle. Iliana felt intimidated by the closeness, frustrated with the grins and excitement, and rolled back against unconscious and exhausted Kovansk, to resume her nap.

Instead of sleeping, though, Iliana's aimless drifting turned to a phone call she received from her excited mother—at age thirteen—a long time before, but one she never forgot. It was something of a fulcrum on which her life thereafter teetered in a different direction.

Iliana's impersonal mother, to whom she referred for years as Ivana, her given name, called to say she found the "perfect new man." Hardly an unexpected bit of news, Iliana recalled thinking; her irresponsible, self-absorbed family matriarch almost made a game of entwining younger males. Easily attracting them, though, she could pass for being twenty years younger, with her well-retained model configuration, and help from a few minor cosmetic surgeries.

Iliana's father and Ivana lived in West End, Boston during his anesthesiology residency at nearby Massachusetts General Hospital. Three months pregnant with Iliana, and ready to begin a new life with financial certainty, Dr. Ilya and Ivana Gosnov moved to Los Angeles where the freshly Board Certified physician began his practice as one of six anesthesiologists at Five Palms Hospital, a well-respected 270 bed facility near L.A.'s Civic Center.

Shortly after the move, though, Iliana recalled with rampant distaste for her mother's selfishness and narcissism—at least so she heard later—that unrest began between her parents. Though pregnant, her mother ensnared herself in the arms of a young intern and the marital relationship took a dim turn.

Months after Iliana's birth in June 1979, her mother returned to Boston, and abdicated custody to her father. Ivana lived in the east since, and went through five husbands, of whom Iliana was aware, no telling how many suitors, she jested. Grimacing from the tormenting memories, she could not help feeling the same inevitable, expected and concomitant sense of abandonment and detachment, which so often recurred, as she grew older.

Through her formative years, Iliana learned of her mother's successes in *haute couture* modeling, via rare and curt phone calls from the woman, and occasional terse letters and cards. All the while Iliana angrily learned to cope with her malformed leg—the object of so much goading by young schoolmates—while living with her father's passive concerns. Whenever she pressed him, he reaffirmed, with notable indifference that her debility stemmed from the same genetic birth defect with which his sister and grandmother in St. Petersburg were supposedly afflicted. Specialists they consulted, given the half-truths regarding Iliana's birth, could only speculate as to cause.

All reported that surgical relief of the muscle strictures would be the only possible remedy and of that, there could be no guarantees. The ideas of massive postoperative scarring and dubious results were abhorrent to Iliana, so cope she did, as best she could, nonetheless insatiably curious, why it occurred. Why? She asked herself without relent.

The wicked bitch spoke only of her glamorous life and never asked me how I was doing. Patronized me, she did—begged me to stay with her and try modeling with my thin, lanky structure—was beyond torturous. She ignored my broken aspirations to become a model like her; damn her deceit, as if my ugly leg and grotesque stagger presented no barriers. Iliana quivered with the flashbacks, while she murmured continued distaste of the memories, until tears wet her cheeks, to ease her hurt.

Iliana turned toward the emergency exit door, brought her left knee to her chest while the right leg remained painfully extended. *How could Ivana have been so heartless? She knew I had no chance at New York runway work—a dead end road—for one as crippled as I. How cruel and selfish, to encourage me as she did.*

Returning thoughts to Ivana's phone call on her birthday as a budding teenager, Iliana remembered its purpose was mainly her mother's advisory that she relocated to West Concord, which, of itself was unmoving, until she added, "You know Concord, Dear; not far from the famed Walden's Pond."

Iliana was unimpressed. Walden's Pond meant nothing.

"Henry David Thoreau, the author, lived the life of a hermit out there in the mid 1800s and wrote his famous book about simplistic life in the wild. The dummy! What did he know of elegant living in the city, to reject it so harshly?" Ivana added.

Years later, her mother's ignorance and malevolent sarcasm that night became painfully poignant when Iliana entered college. During American Literature in her first semester, she delved into transcendentalism, finally read of Thoreau and his *Walden's Pond*, along with many of the poetic works of Ralph Waldo Emerson, one of Thoreau's mentors. At the age when independent thinking typically began, she took to heart the author's admonitions that his readers challenge themselves, seriously ponder, whether his or her life patterned itself in the way they truly wished to live.

Iliana recalled wrestling with the notion, when she finished the first year of undergraduate studies as an education major. Life as a teacher might not be that direction she wanted to take, as she considered Thoreau's caveat, and her quest for the cause of her debility. What could she undertake to help pursue explanations of her disfigurement? She began to wonder that summer.

Still uncomfortable in her fully reclined seat, Iliana restlessly shifted her position and ignored the attendant's announcement that they would be landing on schedule; to tighten belts, stow tables, and bring seats forward.

"Ma'am, please bring up your seat," barked a second flight attendant's reminder a few minutes later, and again Iliana stubbornly kept eyes closed to stick with the ruminations she so rarely visited. She was at the point where, in her distinct memory, she decided there could be more to the story of her disfigured leg than she knew.

A change in major to life science would be her next venture—her Thoreau-induced Renaissance. She opened to the idea of pre-medicine and, while so engaged, made the affirmative choice to explore the troubling leg disability on her own, as her scientific knowledge base increased.

"Miss, we do have an Air Marshall aboard. We are on final descent now and your seat will be raised. Must I call for assistance? They could detain you for interrogation. They may explore arrest at the terminal for your failure to follow instructions." The attendant did a quick about face and stepped briskly toward the rear of the cabin.

"Bitch", Iliana muttered loudly enough to awaken Kovansk, who snapped to partial attention when he heard the words, "explore arrest."

He turned to his left, toward the back, and saw the persistent attendant rush forward, followed by a heavily built black man in a dark blue suit, with cuffs in one hand. They did not look happy.

CHAPTER 7

PUGET SOUND

Aaron Greenleaf Concord, former Orange County business owner, born April 13, 1943, passed away in his sleep, March 3rd, at his home in Washington State. Retired senior partner of Concord, Stansbee and Fitch, a well-known medical malpractice claims investigation firm, his wife Peggy, two children, Beth and Robert, and two grandchildren survive him. Concord and his wife relocated to the Pacific Northwest from Laguna Beach when he retired three years ago. Often during his career, Concord was publicly noted for his involvement in many high profile cases against physicians and hospitals. No services are planned, according to family.

What a grim way to go ... such little fanfare, Aaron thought. Anxiously, he read the FAX as it ticked off his machine. Somewhat saddened by the brevity of the short news release covering his entire life in one column inch; his former partner, Ken Stansbee, chuckled on the phone.

Benign enough not to attract too much notice, the obituary Ken submitted to the *L.A. Times* that morning screamed disbelief. After all the terse article spoke of Aaron, whose feigned death sounded to him so real and macabre.

Aaron hoped few, if any, who knew him would see the unpretentious paragraph, but that needed segment of their investigative plan, for his ultimate safety—Step 1—was complete. Only if someone called Peg for consolation—which would soon be precluded by phone changes he would handle that day—might she become aware of the scam. Aaron and his old friend agreed to meet the following week in his former Newport Beach office.

High noon on the Hood Canal heralded bright sunshine for a change. Light rain earlier that morning drained saturated skies—turned them from varying bleak shades of gray to an unusual robin's egg blue, and portended a rare and welcome clear afternoon for that time in mid-winter. The freshly scrubbed, sweet forest scent, lush and inviting, tugged at Aaron's desire to fly.

A persistent southeasterly wind promised to hold low-pressure troughs at bay, and withhold delivery of moisture-laden cold air masses from the northwest, at least for the remainder of the day. Locals enjoyed the overcast break—ran, walked and cycled along Frontage Road where the Concords lived. Curlews bobbed their heads, poked and pecked for small crustaceans in the wet flats by the water. Snow-white gulls hovered and scolded, and two brown pelicans dove like bombs for small fish close to the surface.

It could have been the usual idyllic morning in any area but Puget Sound, with its otherwise perennial soggy blanket. Two kayakers moved north against the strong flood tidal stream, in close to the shoreline, swayed left and right in zigzag paths as each paddle blade dug into the choppy surface. They made little headway against it.

Those poor paddlers stayed down here too long … forgot to check the tidal bore, Aaron muttered to himself. He glanced at his watch and looked over the tide tables tacked to a cork bulletin board on the wall by the cabin's front door frame. *The ebb would have carried them at several knots over the bottom if they timed it right—no effort at all.* Forty miles north, the Straits of Juan de Fuca, the rough and tumble throat, drained Hood Canal's waters and the rest of expansive Puget Sound to the gaping mouth of the Pacific Ocean at Cape Flattery.

Aaron wished he could kayak in that direction himself, despite the extra work to fight the strong current, but there were things to do, most of all to finish what he began at dawn: clean-up the glass, prepare window frames, replace shot-riddled sills and cedar shingles, install a new window assembly in the bedroom, patch and paint the shot-pocked walls. He felt surprisingly contemplative, while he waited for putty to dry, though anxious, too, for the glass company to arrive, to complete the window work. They recognized the urgency in his request for help and promised completion by day's end.

November 165 Yankee Tango, his fiery red helicopter, out of the hangar and on the pad, nose to the southeast toward prevailing breezes, carefully pre-flighted, as Aaron always did first thing in the morning on a flying day; sat ready for airborne searching, soon as he set glaziers to work.

Aaron thought it wise to overfly the peninsula—look from about 800' above ground level at motel and restaurant parking lots—and search the myriad single lane byways and lumber roads that wove toward the Olympic Mountains and north to the Straits. Although he knew possibilities were slim, at least he would make an effort to locate the dark red van, which absorbed several of his rifle shots.

He could cover the equivalent of two or three days' searching by car in a few hours' flying time, at least two hundred miles or more of roads and stops, at a leisurely 70 to 80 knots. That airspeed range permitted adequate ground visibility, safety, also—plenty of time to see and avoid other aircraft. Flying more slowly, well under his routine 90 to 105 knot cruise speed, allowed more time while eyeing things below, to monitor high traffic areas he would encounter, or where he would overfly an air traffic control zone around an airport, which required tower approval before making a transition.

Though the distractions from such a search were many, he flew throughout the sound more than two years, knew the terrain, and radio call spots well. He'd have asked his flying friend, Jimmy Gibson, to be an extra set of eyes, but Jim served as a part time Mason County Reserve Deputy and would be too curious about the trip's purpose. Under the circumstances, for the present, he wished the incident to remain unreported. A private eye all his life, Aaron, while frightened terribly, was insatiably and irrevocably curious about why it occurred, and felt compelled to assemble the story himself.

Seated in an Adirondack chaise on his small front porch, rifle across his lap, he gazed lazily at the canal after he planned his flight itinerary, and began in his mind, a re-run of events the previous evening.

Had I not seen movement and the flash before the sound reached me, buckshot would have splattered across my face. Deader'n a damned doornail! Threw myself to the floor, as I did, probably an instant before she pulled the trigger, despite possibilities of injuring my back, sure as hell saved me.

The shot power and pattern fortunately dissipated with the distance and in that frozen moment in time, I thrust myself out of range, and took just the one at the top of my shoulder. Some sort of anticipation must have led me to fall back even before the flash. Whatever the urge may have been, it was a lifesaver, all right.

He winced from the mild pain when he lifted his left arm and swung it around. Only a flesh wound, bleeding quickly stopped with a butterfly bandage. Still, he considered, it could have been his head. *A valiant try at murder, someone wanted my tail in a game bag.*

Aaron summarized his recollections: *definitely a female shooter; the blast recoils nearly downed her. That decided right-legged limp, almost a scissor gait like cerebral palsy can induce, yet it's rare for the malady to hit just one lower extremity. Seemed her other leg was normal. A 12-gauge pump with those big loads, the shooter knew what she was doing. I was her twenty-pound male Canada goose, flying high, to be dropped from maximum distance.*

He cursed himself for failing to note the van's license number when its lights went on, instead of taking the last shot. The male driver's accent, though, he'd not forget. Thick, with a Russian, maybe Polish twist; there was a brogue wound into it ... East Indian, British, Scottish, maybe; he thought. "I'll recognize it if I hear it again—no mistaking that twang. 'Forget it.' The guy yelled. 'Get the hell in here and let's go before we get killed.'" Aaron repeated to himself, '*Let's go before we get killed.*'"

"I'll never forget those words," he said loudly, "never." His innate curious side raced with deductions. *The driver may have saved my life by stopping the first shooting session as he did. She must have done some intensive persuasion to bring him back for the second try; probably yelled at him over the entire time lapse until they returned. Something a wife or girlfriend could do, but not likely a professional accomplice, if the driver were the point man. Must be amateurs, not pro-hitters, I would guess.*

"Bet it's her grudge," he then continued aloud for more emphasis. "Not his; she roped him into it. She is likely a bombshell; he probably loves her, but his heart wasn't in it. Must be, oh, about 110-120 pounds, tops; five-seven, maybe; a tall one, all right, but quite slim, and that danged limp. What's up with that?"

Aaron pondered the two spent shotgun shells he found in the front yard by the yellow cedar. The others he picked up close to the road and placed in his ammunition drawer in the den, handling them all with plastic sandwich bags for fingerprint dusting if the opportunity arose later. He also found a paper matchbook with a printed logo and the words, "*Minsk*—L.A.," on the outside cover.

There were many fresh tennis shoe footprints on the dusty shoulder beneath the hanging flood lamp, castings of the three deepest of which he made using a watery blend of patching plaster, reinforced with dry grass— the best he could do given what was available in the garage. A careful search of the entire area revealed nothing more than a silvery button on the pavement, which appeared to have come from a pair of jeans, with the initials DKNY. He had no idea what that stood for, but vowed to find out, while he placed it in one of the plastic bags that contained the shells.

The sound of a truck slowing down in front sparked immediate trepidation. Aaron was still adrenalin-packed from the night's horrific experience. He raised the Mauser from his lap to firing position, fearing the assailants returned, and slid into immediate relief when the sign on the right door revealed the Two Brothers' Glass Company crew arrived. He exhaled deeply and relaxed.

Peggy called early to awaken Aaron that morning, more than provoked by his failure to phone her, or to check on his mother's condition. "It's not as though you have a desk full of cases to report, Honey, like the old days when work was always your excuse for not calling," she said. Peggy was glad she no longer had to complain like that.

"Thought you might have gone flying, given the pleasant pitch of brilliant weather that moved into the area today." She sounded a little miffed, he thought, but he quickly palliated the attitude. Admitting he wished to surprise her, mediated things. He boasted of a couple newly painted walls where Duke soiled the coating while he slept along the back of the couch and on the large cushion by the furnace vent in their bedroom.

Aaron smiled as he spoke, rolled in his palm, a few of the large shot pellets he extracted from the walls; and recalled Humphrey Bogart's similar and melodramatic moves in the 1950's era movie, *Caine Mutiny*. Bogart's character—mixed-up U.S. Navy Captain Queeg—rattled a clutch of steel ball bearings in his palm, whenever upset. Kind of ironic, Aaron thought.

After Peg assured all was well in Redmond, that she would stay a few more days, Aaron felt confident he would have ample time to masquerade damages to the house. If not, he cooked up Plan B: a few errant kids whooped it up with a shotgun in the middle of the night, took potshots at mailboxes—anything they saw along the remote road. "Probably still nursing their hangovers," he could say, naively. Even that would scare hell out of her, he quickly concluded, but it would have to do until he looked further into the incident.

A walk around the helicopter for one final pre-flight check, Aaron unscrewed both fuel caps on either side of the main rotor mast, stuck his finger in to confirm tanks were nearly full, and firmly twisted them closed. He negated oil and fluid leakage and surveyed both rotor blades for nicks or evidence of surface cracking. Before getting in the right seat, he reconfirmed that engine cowling doors were well secured. He always did that twice. During a training flight, he failed to check on the left side. *I was so terribly shocked by the tower's call after lift-off, that it was loose; flapping like a gull's wing.*

Strictly according to his initial flight instruction, Aaron habitually went through the full pre-start checklist aloud, before every flight. He finished with, "Altimeter set to Bremerton's level—29.93", manifold pressure limit noted for take off, seatbelt latched, master switch on, throttle and mixture closed." He looked to the rear with the door still open, assured the area was clear, and hit the starter button. The engine quickly took hold, and then roared.

"Mixture full rich, starter light out, set RPM to 55%." The rotor spun slowly at first, counter-clockwise, and quickly gathered momentum. "Oil pressure rising," he said, "clutch switch engaged, alternator on, avionics all on, clutch light out. Set RPM to 65% for warm-up."

While the operating temperature, oil pressure and other engine gauge needles climbed onto the green sectors, he double-checked each. Aaron set one radio for Bremerton's ATIS, the automated field weather information service on 121.2, for an update on conditions to the north, and the other to the field's Unicom, a non-tower, local communication frequency. He'd first pass near that airspace, would listen for traffic in the area, every few minutes and announce his position, direction and altitude on 123.025, the helicopter-to-helicopter frequency.

Flying low, he avoided busy Sea-Tac's airspace. Until he requested transition through Fairchild International's terminal control area around Port Angeles—on his way to Neah Bay, and the Pacific Ocean—he would not need further air-to-ground communication.

"Gauges in the green, gas is good." He ran the RPM to 101%, where the governor took over; completed the remaining checklist items and latched his door, re-checked his safety harness, adjusted his hat and headset. He applied pressure to the left pedal to counteract clockwise torque induced by the main rotor as he lifted the collective lever with his left hand, very slowly at first, to deliver power by the increase of main rotor blade pitch.

Just enough collective pull to get the aircraft light on its skids—as it twitched and joggled slightly—he assured directional stability with subtle changes in pedal positions and raised the collective for more power. That brought the helicopter to a stationary hover, five feet or so above the ground, for one quick, final power check. The windsock on the hangar roof—less than half extended, indicated the breeze continued from the southeast, his departure direction.

A further lift of the collective and an increase in left pedal pressure—nose down with subtle forward cyclic pressure—he moved ahead, rose above the trees, which he topped below pad level. Aaron dropped the nose slightly while airspeed climbed to 40 knots and gradually added more power to gain altitude. Banked into a gentle left turn toward the north, he leveled off at 800' and began to follow the coastal fringes along Highway 101, at 70-knot airspeed, boosted to about 80 knots over the ground with the tailwind's push from behind.

Aaron took a deep breath, exhaled and settled back in his seat, to begin a highway search. He orbited over each resort, parking lot, shopping center, campground, and the small roads leading to the west, into the Olympic Mountains.

Mt Olympus, a long extinct volcano, stood sentinel over the peninsula to his left. White-capped year round from its base upward, the summit reached nearly 8000'. He flew around it scores of times, with sightseeing friends. "One of the seven wonders of Aaron's Pacific Northwest," he reminded them.

Peggy's mention that morning—the inquisitive couple who stopped at his mother's home a few weeks before—gripped his thoughts as he carved a trail of lazy S curves along the canal shoreline. *Don't know any ex-army buddy with red hair; anyone for that matter living in San Francisco, much less one who speaks with a European accent. Girl with a limp ... too coincidental... had to be the frigging shooters. Damn, they looked for me there. A silver sports car at Mother's? What's the story with the beater Ford van the night of the shooting? Could they live locally?* He also kept eyes peeled for something sleek and silver on the roads below.

Marveling, as he always did when airborne, and unwilling to hasten the time from points A to B, Aaron never failed to be overwhelmed with the contrasts from aloft on a good day. Blazing skies, scattered high clouds, deep blue waters as far as could be seen to the north and east, and the greenest of velvet greens spoken by boundless stretches of the National Forest, riveted his attention. Aaron forgot, for a short time; he cheated death a mere twelve hours before.

Nearly every minute above *terra firma,* he'd lose himself—mentally whip his own behind, for not beginning flight training at an earlier age— yet he grinned gleefully at the good fortune to become a decent pilot at his age. Aaron accumulated almost 1000 hours by that very day, the bottom-line experience level at which some rotor wing commercial operators hire their professional pilots.

"Helicopter 111 niner zulu, over Brinnon, southbound at one thousand."

Aaron turned up the comm. radio volume, scanned the skies above and forward, and spotted the Bell Jet Ranger, a turbine powered helicopter, headed in the opposite direction above him, calling on 123.025.

He responded: "helicopter156 Yankee Tango, three miles south of Brinnon, northbound at five hundred; have you in sight, one niner Zulu."

"You, too ... no traffic behind us."

Aaron recognized the flashy yellow Sky-Top Tours aircraft, no doubt returning a few tourists to Seattle, and continued his survey of the terrain below.

Aloft for two and a half hours, Aaron spotted nothing even hinting of his objectives. Five miles out of Bremerton, he announced his arrival on 123.05, their Unicom channel—monitored mainly by those about to enter or flying near the pattern—and set down to fill tanks at the fuel pad, several hundred feet west of Taxiway Echo. Almost day's end, there was no time for customary coffee and his usual chat with the operators. He would be looking for the pad on the hill above his house in fifteen minutes, just before dusk.

What might be the story to explain a sports car one day and an ancient, smoke belching, stick shift van a short time later? He wondered, once airborne again. "I sure can't buy the San Francisco vacation story. Something, somehow, doesn't add up about those two. No, I'm thinking maybe L.A., not likely the Bay Area as they said to Mother ... probably not the Northwest.

All those phone calls after I fell to the floor, no doubt, to see if I was dead or alive. Tempted as I was to answer, no response must have satisfied them that I was gone.

While he couldn't determine the calling number on the hard line, it was easy to note the locale of those directed to his cell. All from a pay phone in Tacoma, he found—and one from downtown Seattle. Though he discovered the locales immediately after the calls ceased, he thought it worthwhile to rule out possible aimless driving by the couple with his aerial search along the northerly sector of the peninsula that day.

Aaron certainly would not answer the phone until he obtained new numbers the following morning in Bremerton. And then, there was the obituary. *Difficult things to reveal to Peg right now, I'll tell her for "security reasons," regarding one on my old cases; Ken called to suggest I pull off the faked demise, complete with obituary to sew up the illusion.* His former partner gave birth to the idea. Aaron needed to meet with him anyway about a few of their big cases that developed problems in recent months. He could think of no other connection to this clear act of attempted homicide but a player from one of his old files, with an unsettled issue. "I've got work to do...get to them before they try me again ... a few days and ... then ... then what?"

CHAPTER 8

SOUTHERN CALIFORNIA

A most inopportune time to be causing problems, to say the least: disguised, forged IDs, no legitimate credentials with them, and no pragmatic explanations at hand; real trouble approached from the rear of the aircraft. Kovansk roughly pulled Iliana upright from her slouched position, snapped her seatback forward, and, in doing so, thrust her against the seat ahead. The impact brought forth a growled, "goddamnit," unheard by the Air Marshall who stopped aside Kovansk's seat. He stood steady, hands on his hips, feet apart—a fighting stance, Oligoff thought—and wore an impatiently stern look on his face. He twirled the handcuffs around his thick right index finger, several times for effect, then folded and stowed them in a belt holster when he saw that Iliana complied. Curious glances toward Iliana and Kovansk; he asked them if they had a problem and if the flight went well.

Both responded with awkward smiles, genuine as could be mustered. The federal law enforcement officer shook his head, turned to the rear, and ambled back to his seat. He could go straight home, would not have to interrogate, make an arrest, and stay two hours overtime to complete requisite paperwork.

"Iliana, I'll have nothing more to do with this ... this vendetta, 'the mission,' as you say it." Kovansk breathed rapidly and knew the carotid arteries in his neck swelled with a sudden rise in blood pressure deep within. Anyone familiar with personality reactions could tell he was damned frightened, he worried.

"It is hard for me to believe you would act so defiant, like a Mongolian *svinya*, when we are so close to arriving home in one piece. He knew the Russian word for pig would cut through Iliana's crusty attitude in a flash. He guessed right. She let him have it with a barrage of whispered, but snarling, homeland cuss words, that stunned him to quietude until their plane rolled to a stop at the terminal, and disembarkation began.

Kovansk took the red duffel from the overhead locker and they merged with other passengers into the lobby. Two L.A. County Sheriff's Deputies walked toward them, and nearly sent the couple into patent unconsciousness. The officers passed by without interest—on a mission unrelated to their escapade—and left them to end their trip as intended.

Both wondered at the same time, as they walked the long corridor to the exit, how they would positively verify Concord's death. "We cannot call his house or cell from here, or a wide open lead would be broached that his—how you call—hitters flew, drove to, or lived in Southern California. Too boiling hot for my taste," Kovansk said, to which Iliana agreed. She reminded him and herself, once more, to make no further calls, as they did repeatedly in Tacoma earlier that morning. That they received no answers over a two-hour period seemed a safe enough presumption for the time being. Concord lay badly hurt, if not dead, by her final shot at the upstairs window.

The couple traversed through the main terminal parking lot to the opposite side and walked east to hail a taxi several blocks from the airport on the north side of Century Boulevard, for the twenty-minute ride to their Beverly Hills condominium.

Scheduled for duty at the hospital in the desert that night, Kovansk packed and poured himself over the pass right away, to catch up on sleep at the facility as much as possible before his shift began. Iliana had to spend the next few days in Beverly Hills, before resumption of her new schedule, in surgery, at work alongside Kovansk, as his assistant. An enviable team, it stemmed from two years' work together in surgery at UCLA Medical Center. Iliana grew to anticipate his every move—a surgeon's dream, while rarely visited.

Iliana sat up, rubbed aching eyes, flopped back to her pillow, shivered from the early evening cool, and pulled covers above her shoulders. She rolled to a more comfortable posture, and noted the time—close to 5:00 PM; not sleep enough, but nearly six hours. She thought about their condo's convenient access to Rodeo Drive, Beverly Center, and that immediate sector of Wilshire Boulevard proliferated with high-end shopping diversity she enjoyed. It would take some adaptive persuasion to feel similarly comfortable in the more barren, middle-class areas that surrounded the home they bought in the only gated tract near Mojave. Convenient, though, a few minutes' drive to the hospital they would own a part of together, when they married, the new locus bordered on the ideal.

For the present, and to her distaste, she lamented as she closed eyes once more. Kovi had to be the sole signatory on title documents. While capital input was largely her father's inheritance money, it was Kovansk's credulity as a physician, which allowed him into the medical partnership.

For the present, therefore, the share would remain in his name only, as were their cars and the condominium. When debt-free, and it was already going well that way, the strategically located facility could be retained or sold to a conglomerate and shareholders could retire or alter practices to suit individual needs. Later, the couple's dreams called for a move to stuffy Bel Air, to raise and school their children. For the present, that plan seemed a good a way to begin financial growth toward that end.

Iliana got up, drank a fast glass of cold Chardonnay and drew the drapes to darken the room from the closing afternoon sun that intruded through the plantation shutters. She collapsed into a deep sleep once again.

"Why does that phone have to ring at such an hour?" Iliana threw off the covers, reached to the small antique pine bench that served as a nightstand, settled back down, and checked the time before answering. *It's only 8:30 PM. It seems so late.* Tormented with horrifying illusions, nightmares transported her to unfamiliar surroundings where she killed people, lots of them, with an automatic rifle, indiscriminate in her aim or selection. She knew the source from which such figments erupted. *I shot a man this morning—killed a person I never met—on the strength of my father's contention that the man dirtied his hands in the evolution of my leg problem. How long is this apt to go on?*

"Hello," Iliana said, almost tearful as she placed the phone to her ear.

"It's me, Svetiia; are you all right, *devushk?*" Svetiia used the affectionate Russian nickname, meaning "little girl," for her friend. "I've had a terrible time of it this week, so overworked, and now my boss is taking more of my tips. I feel like slitting his throat sometimes; but enough of that.

"How are you? Did you and Kovi go off and get married? Svetiia giggled. Iliana did not. "I returned the cell phone to your mail slot, used it only a few times, but, thank you for it. Every dime is important right now. I am sinking into oblivion and cannot yet see my way out of it. The organization is so strong, Chernya so disrespectful, and demanding. Thankfully, though, he has more important moneymaking operations than the escort business to handle. He leaves me alone to work much of the time … unsupervised—or at times with one of his subordinates, Davidov. He's OK … drives me, waits patiently, but takes a piece of my earnings before they get to Bostovitch. I say nothing or he would erase me from the world … sink me in Silver Lake with so many others who toyed with them. How could this have ever happened?"

Iliana listened, unable to garner the harsh reality of Svetiia's predicament, yet she visualized herself in the same situation if something were to cause a split between Kovi and her—if she likewise became overburdened by debts. While a sickening thought, Iliana responded with some confidence, that her degrees and experience would always put her close to six-figure income potential, and that such a situation, in her case, could never occur.

Svetiia, a vibrant, natural blonde, slightly built but attractively buxom, was endowed with a beautiful face, Iliana always thought. A lovely Russian nose, she had sensual lips; gleaming, inquisitive blue eyes; and above all, an enviable set of comely legs. She stood nearly four inches shorter. Iliana found the woman, same age as she, almost sexually attractive when they lounged in their small apartment, wearing little or nothing before they dressed for evening dates. And, she had no hideous limp.

Why was Kovi so attracted to me? Why not Svetiia? Iliana could not help but wonder, while her friend continued to speak of her mob entanglement. Iliana took Kovansk for granted while she planned the trips to Washington, and committed to clean up her act when she went back to the desert.

Losing him after all of that would be a disaster. There were too many beautiful Svetiias in town, of whom Kovi could easily take notice; which persuaded her to give him what he needed once again. "I'm glad the phone helped a little. I wish I could get you out of this, somehow, but you borrowed so much … so long to pay it back. What will you do, Svetiia?"

"Keep up with the debt service and keep my life, if I can stick it out … no realistic options, nowhere to go. Now, tell me about your short flight and two quick days off. Was it fun to just get away on a whim like that?"

"We needed a little fix and now that we're home, I feel better. Problem solved." Iliana didn't elaborate and Svetiia knew better than to pry. Iliana did not often speak of personal problems and, above all, she quickly dismissed prying queries about her disabled leg. Iliana hoped she could soon feel the relief of vengeance achieved.

She still harbored nagging doubts about the remaining uncertainty, before she could finally relax with positivity that the dead man paid for what he did to her. "I have teaching days here; then I'll go to the desert and begin work in real earnest. I'm looking forward to a ten minute commute at worst, no more hour-plus drives to Joshua Trauma Center from Beverly Hills in the early mornings."

"Did the trip have anything to do with your leg … see a specialist; anything new with that, *devushk?*"

Iliana stiffened, kneaded her hurting right knee and thigh with both hands, and apologized. She had to catch up on her sleep. "You know what it's like, when you party for two days straight."

CHAPTER 9

After conversing with Svetiia, Iliana reflected on the need for a serious review of her posture, thus far, in Aaron Concord's suspected killing. "How did I get so hopelessly entangled in this act of revenge?" She asked herself aloud, while she searched for tangible answers. "This has come far closer to ruining my life than my spastic leg. Kovi will eventually have to know the full story. I might as well prepare myself to relate an orderly account for his sake, if for no other reason."

She got up, made a cup of instant coffee, and with notebook and pen in hand, returned to her spot on the couch to organize the past few months' activities. Compelled to explore again, the depths to which she investigated both Aaron and her neonatal hospital confinement, Iliana allowed her mind to wander, unrestrained. After her father died, she remembered, she found in his file cabinet at home, along with his will, a personal account of her delivery at Five Palms Hospital, contained in a manila envelope labeled:

To be Opened Only by Iliana Gosnov in the Event of My Death.

The handwritten notes—single spaced in his usual poor but unmistakable handwriting—wove an incredulous web she found impossible to believe at the first reading. Then, as she examined it more closely, the yellowed, dog-eared pages, replete with cross-outs and corrections, described a most disturbing and horrifying picture. A confession of sorts, it yielded the true story, she had to conclude, of events that led to her leg deformity. Expository of her father, Dr. Gosnov's theretofore-clear effort to distort the facts behind it, he wrote the missive in response to her endless queries for the truth, when he thought it important for her to know.

Finally, her suspicions proved true: her father's obfuscation of events that lead to her mother's' hypoxemia during her birth, was emblematic of the dishonesty Iliana always thought he nurtured. A cover-up of the worst sort, Dr. Gosnov did his best to protect his wife's anesthesiologist, a friend and colleague, from later attack. Dr. Raynes left his patient to assist Dr. Gosnov in the correction of intractable paroxysms of cough developed by his patient. Though reticent to subject herself to the displeasing narrative again, still filled with upset over the Concord shooting, Iliana retrieved the envelope, and its mind-fracturing contents from her dresser drawer. A few deep breaths to maintain composure and she read:

My Dear Daughter, Iliana,

You will not be proud of me, as you read what follows. I apologize for my cowardice all your life, as I blamed genetics for your problem leg. It was a lie, which tormented me each time I told it. Such mutations never existed in my family tree.

The night you were born, I tended to my own patient in the adjoining delivery room as I told you over the years. My good friend, Dr. Reggie Raynes, was to administer anesthesia to your mother. She broke her water and walked in that night while I was on my way to the hospital for a routine delivery. I never told you I was somewhat inebriated from a long dinner and too many cocktails at the Brown Derby, with a group of doctor friends.

Her OB and I anticipated an easy time of it. My patient was a healthy, multiparous young woman, with no history of problems, so he called at the last minute. About to deliver, however, and still a bit tipsy, I was not up to the challenge to safely handle the severe paroxysms of cough she developed unexpectedly. In short, I panicked and needed help.

I had no choice but to call for Reggie, and didn't realize your mother was so heavily anesthetized. I made a poor assumption and did not ask Reggie how deeply under she was, considering, I supposed, that she was just lightly sedated—50 mg. or so of Demerol—his custom and practice for a pre-op back then.

Since Reggie seemed unconcerned, I was not then worried for Ivana. Instead, she had been under thiopental sodium and gaseous anesthesia for some twenty minutes, with, I later discovered, an incompletely inflated, unsealed endotracheal catheter, that hissed like a snake when I arrived in Room #3 after my case was completed. Reggie was horribly inattentive to your mother, given the excitement with my patient, and his absence from Ivana for too long.

Only when you were delivered through the uterine incision; did your mother's very low oxygen partial pressure add complexity to the picture. It was worsened by an oxygen saturation level shown by blood gas analysis of only 52% as I recall. I regret, she was clearly hypoxemic.

Those conditions presented sufficient criteria for me to consider the strong probability of damage to your cerebral cortex, with ensuing cerebral palsy as a complication.

Your very poor five minute Apgar score, along with very noticeable diminutive muscle tone in your right leg, were strong warning signals. If your mother learned of the problems, no doubt, she would have retained counsel to sue; not to help you in later life, but to bolster her own meager finances. It did not seem right. I regret my silence, to protect Reggie Raynes.

I promised him that night; I would remain forever quiet. I removed the Anesthesia Record and the blood gas analysis report from the chart after Ivana's discharge, so all evidence of the crisis and Reggie's role in it, I thought, would disappear.

When you reached age twenty-one, I reconsidered, since Reggie had died by then, and I made a claim in your behalf.

I was interviewed by an insurance investigator, one Aaron Concord, with Concord, Stansbee and Fitch, in Newport Beach. I lied to him, though, about what happened, said nothing of Reggie leaving your mother unattended for so long, and denied we had the BGA done.

Concord told me he had copies of both documents. Hospital administration, recognizing their possible liability at the time, made an extra reference copy, before placing the chart in closed files. Then what was I to do? I painted myself into a corner, not only as an involved party in the care rendered to your mother, but as a conspirator, who tried to protect Reggie.

I did take you to specialists during your childhood, but led them to believe a genetic disorder was responsible, and turned attention from cerebral palsy I knew to be the real cause. I am so sorry I let you down, Dear Iliana. May your life be the best it can be. Hopefully, the meager estate I left to you will make things easier.

There may be trouble settling it; your mother will likely claim to be a beneficiary as she was in my first will. Good luck getting your share. I am and always will be so sorry for any distress I caused.

Your loving father

Iliana cringed at the final line, and with an angry outburst, hammered her fist on the coffee table, "Damn that horrible man ... called himself my father. How could he have done that to me, yet describe himself as 'loving?' He concocted such a cowardly excuse: to protect his cohort, for God's sake, in lieu of me, his own flesh and blood!"

Utter disbelief enveloped her like a dark shroud, birthed a new level of contempt she never before experienced. More than simple hatred toward men, she harbored deep physical pain—bled from a festering sore, imagined a wide swath across her gut that mimicked a stabbing, a scimitar's slice— that left her speechless, embroiled, and filled with more cunning than ever imagined.

That episode poured the foundation of her resolve to take down this Aaron Concord, who must have conspired with her father, she surmised. Quite likely, she could have moved similarly toward her father, Dr. Gosnov, had he lived through his short bout with inoperable brain cancer.

Iliana shuddered with the thought; that she could be capable of acting out such terrible fancies. Something else, too, fostered her contempt. Something, she could not grasp so easily, from her confused and hateful mindset, created this recurrent turmoil. Her consciousness could not be steered in that direction; despite intentions every time she reviewed her father's final written words.

CHAPTER 10

HOOD CANAL

Once again good weather beckoned a search flight: another aerial survey of the Olympic Peninsula, this time south of the Concord place, to cover as many subsidiary highways and parking lots as possible in that sector. *How will I tell Peg I had to disable her cell number and what do I say to throw the fear of God into Mother? For Christ's sake, 'simply hang up if someone calls and asks about me!'*

Aaron felt almost distracted enough not to fly as he steered the small tow motor and moved November 156 Yankee Tango outside its hangar to the pad. Proudly, he stopped to admire the mirror-like white urethane finish he applied to the building's floor, which gave it such a professional appearance. So clean, he could eat from it, he often thought.

"Pre-flight complete, tanks full … close to three hours' flying time. Everything, including the afternoon Terminal Area Forecast for Sea-Tac, looks good. Master switch on, strobe light on, area clear." He gave the pad one final look around, tightened his cap and adjusted his headset. "Throttle closed, mixture rich, prime 3-5 seconds, switch magnetos to both, mixture to idle cut-off. Start, mixture full rich and mixture guard closed." The rotor began with slow then deeper, and more rapid hissing slices as RPM gradually increased. Finished with his after-start checklist, Aaron was airborne within minutes. He turned after lift-off this time, to follow Highway 101 south, toward Shelton's Sanderson Field. Past Hoodsport, Potlach and Union, he tracked back, overflew the Wonder Mountain Wilderness area, and turned up nothing.

He listened first on 122.8, to find runway 23 was active. "Sanderson Unicom: helicopter 156 Yankee Tango, five miles north, inbound for direct set down on the city helipad. Confirm runway 23 pattern in use."

"Helicopter 6 Yankee Tango: wind 270 at 12; altimeter, two niner niner three; Cherokee on final, runway 23, no other traffic. Cross field at your discretion." The fixed base operator responded quickly.

"6 Yankee Tango: with traffic, thanks." Aaron adjusted the altimeter setting.

He began his descent, slowly dropped the collective, applied backpressure on the cyclic in his right hand to raise the nose, and reduce air speed. When at a fast walking pace, close to the field, he increased power to slow his descent, and set down, nose to the westerly wind, as close to the perimeter fence as he could. Once secured, he reduced rotor RPM and checked the parking lot—not a van or silver sports car to be seen. The fuel truck rolled close and stopped; Aaron opened his cockpit door when the driver ducked low and approached.

"Need gas?"

"No, thanks ... sorry for the trouble. Have you seen an older maroon Ford van or a silver sports car, maybe a Porsche, Boxter, Jag ... hanging around here in the past few days? Trying to track down some vandals who dissed my place, up north of Eldon."

"Nope, nothing like that this week, Last weekend an old Ford—dark red, it was—chocked full of U of Washington guys ... parachute club, piled out with all their gear to do a few group free falls in the drop zone northwest of here... had cameras ... lots of gear. Touch base with the manager later; he'll have a number you can call."

Aaron thanked the fuel truck driver, wound up the engine until the governor took over, checked gauges—all in the green—announced his intentions on the Unicom, and lifted to a hover.

Assured of no traffic, he crossed the taxiway, gained airspeed, and at 40 knots began a climb to three hundred feet with steady upward pull on the collective. He turned to his left across the field, and took a southwest heading to resume his previous flight altitude. *U of W kids ... can't be the same van, but*, he pondered further, *it might have been stolen. Have to check later with the jump school.* Shelton's field, he knew, was a favorite of parachutists in the area, who crowded the place on decent weekend days. No luck at Olympia Regional Field; he continued his effort southwest along the highway to Elma, a small, privately owned airport with few facilities, and very low traffic—thirty or so small planes based there. A fast turn around at Bowerman Field which served the coastal town of Aberdeen in windy Gray's Harbor on the coast; Aaron had enough for the day. He returned to Sanderson to refuel and, while there, introduced himself to Blair Goodman, the jump school operator.

Dressed in dark blue slacks, a light blue Oxford cloth button-down, and a leather military flight jacket, Goodman sported polished, laced black jump boots and a tan baseball cap embroidered with a Cessna 206. Horn-rimmed glasses that hung on the tip of his nose; he looked more like a CPA than a small town pilot. He checked his files and willingly offered the phone number of the university instructor who arranged three flights for his group, the Saturday before. They took but one, owing to a rapid drop of the ceiling from the west. By day's end, rain with snow flurries stepped in the shoes of earlier VFR, visual flight rule flying conditions, and closed the airport out until after nightfall.

Once back to his pad, Aaron carefully wiped down the plastic windscreen and side windows with non-abrasive cleanser, topped crankcase oil, and opened cowling panels for a quick post flight check. He turned the main rotor parallel to the fuselage by rotating the tail rotor a few turns, backed the helicopter into its stall, and up-dated his log before closing the electric roll-down door. Aaron rushed down the steep drive to the house and noted a card on the door from the phone company. His numbers were changed and unlisted replacements were in working order.

The parachute instructor answered after the third ring. "Yes, this is Rich; how may I help you?"

Aaron explained his interest in the van and learned it was owned by a student, Byron Redding, from Vancouver, Washington, a small town across the Columbia River from Portland. "A senior engineering major, and master jumper, he served two years' active duty in the 82nd Airborne. He'd certainly not be the type to vandalize property ... has a fiancé in Menlo Park ... goes to Stanford ... nice young feller. Why?"

Aaron demurred to further queries, got the student's number and called. No answer. Though he left an urgent voice mail and nervously awaited a return call, he received no response that night, next day, or the following night.

Finally, while washing dinner dishes, close to 11:00 PM, the student called. He just returned from a week in the Bay Area and seemed intently interested in Aaron's inquiry. He knew something strange happened. His van was not in the space where he parked it at Sea-Tac before departure and, to his delight, it was almost was full of gas. He left it close to empty. Continuing, Redding complained that the wind wing lock was broken. He reported bullet holes in the rear doors and left side. Aaron clenched fists, winced gleefully at his good fortune, and had to dodge a string of questions propounded by curious Redding, who had no understanding of his connection.

"I'm an investigator," Aaron explained, "and have reason to believe the van was involved in foul play. I strongly recommend you not report it to police, to avoid the hassle of becoming a suspect yourself."

"Of course ... yes," Redding agreed without hesitation, "where do we go from here?" He feared consequences if police were notified, when Aaron suggested it might have been used in the commission of a crime.

"I'd like a friend, a good guy cop in Shelton, to dust for prints. How soon could we do that?"

"If it clears, two buddies and I will be jumping again out of Shelton. You could check the car there—much closer to your house than the university. On second thought, so far, I am the only one who's been in the van since I picked it up, so any evidence is still going to be fresh. Someone may have used my wheels for bad stuff, but it wasn't me. I can prove I was down south almost a week during spring break ... Palo Alto, California, with my girlfriend."

"My mother lives in Redmond. If tomorrow morning would work, we'll combine a visit there with an inspection of your vehicle. I'll cover you a couple bills to fix the bullet holes and give you a full tank of gas for your trouble." Redding beamed; flat broke from his brief trip, he planned to junk the car at semester's end, anyway.

Almost trembling with excitement, Aaron knew he was onto something big and began to count the hours. Hardly capable of sleep, in anticipation of the morning's possible revelations, Aaron lay in bed and stared blankly at the hanging ceiling light. The smell of fresh paint still permeated the bedroom, however, repairs were complete, and the room looked normal. He left windows open too long for more air exchange, while reading downstairs, and cold air filled the void. The open beam ceiling and added interior volume consumed more heat from the undersized furnace than he would have liked. It roared in the hall closet downstairs, to compensate.

Saturated with unanswerable questions, he gnawed on too many dilemmas: would weather in the morning permit them to fly direct to Renton where Peggy could conveniently meet them? Would he have time to visit with his mother? What might Jim discover, dusting the van for prints; would there be other evidence? Will weather permit flying back to Hood Canal when they were through? Too many unanswerable queries for the retired mind to settle upon, he thought.

Aaron jumped up, stretched to extend his back, and turned on the computer. He went straight to the National Weather Service websites and looked first at the Area Forecast that covered the entire region—fairly reliable predictions for up to twelve hours. Prospects looked good for local VFR flight during the early part of the day; the high-pressure center expected to linger just west of the city ... likely, he concluded, for the next twenty-four. That should hold keep back the ever-present frontal movements for a short time, he pondered.

Winds expected from the northwest would be light, and the lowest broken ceiling, through which they could not legally pass, should remain at or around 4000', well above his intended flight altitude of 1000' or below. The Terminal Area Forecast and current weather—local conditions for Sea-Tac—reported expected visibility at plus six miles with a good spread between temperature and dew point, favorable signs to portend decent flying conditions in the morning. Light drizzles forecast throughout the sound in the late afternoon would be no bother. Thereafter a cold front that progressed south would lower temperatures and raise dew points over the area. Limited visibility could ensue with IMC—instrument mandatory conditions—along with increased precipitation.

Relieved the thirty-minute flight to Renton and short drive to the university would preclude a two and a half hour drive and the boring, hour-long Bremerton Ferry trip; Aaron settled back in bed, nudged to his right side, and jostled his body into the mattress to seek comfort for his ailing back. If Peg were there to wrap his arms around, he'd have been delighted.

Mind still bustling with confusion, he turned thoughts to the thousands of incidents he investigated from 1972, when he began his business, until retirement in 2007. Those he recalled lay together in a misty haze. Most were routine, especially clear cases of liability, which resulted in negotiated settlements with claimants or their counsel, or a lawsuit, if agreement on value was not within reach. His responsibilities often continued thereafter, when he assisted defense attorneys to develop trial strategies, found and refreshed witnesses, and collected medical records. Often, he located and interviewed knowledgeable experts to testify favorably for the client insurer.

The number of disputed liability cases he handled bothered him more. Many of those resulted in outright denials of liability. More frequently, the evolution of angered, vengeful patients who wanted doctor or hospital to pay, fostered incivility in the lack of liability or when compensable damages had not been sustained. Names escaped him, considering the long hiatus since he'd worked, but the gravamen of the more troublesome files did stand out in his recall. *Ken will remember more of them; between us, we'll come up with some possibilities. Someone sure as hell has an axe to grind.*

CHAPTER 11

LOS ANGELES

"So, how much might you charge to take this guy out and provide me with definite evidence, if I find my attempt failed? How would you prove success?" Iliana asked the short, stocky, and just plain mean-looking Russian-born mob *brigadier*, Chernya Bostovitch, whom Svetiia Kronoff introduced after her father's passing. Iliana did not yet see the phony obituary Aaron's old partner prepared, and sent to the *L.A.Times* for publication.

She tried to forget; Bostovitch sold her at inordinate cost, the false identification packages she and Kovi used for their Washington trips, that he failed to locate Concord, and steered them instead, to the home of his mother, in their first effort. Bostovitch knew he was on thin ice with Iliana as a result. "Let us first talk about it little more, young lady," Bostovitch said. He recalled her consternation and evident distrust when his, "intensive investigation," erred so drastically. "You did locate the man using much of our input; please remember." He reminded Iliana, too, that it was his report which placed Concord in Wasnington State as a good start.

He didn't forget that his group made $250,000 by taking the assignment to her father's estate in exchange for fifty percent in cash, advanced up front to Iliana. His eyes focused on a larger share of that pot of gold as he spoke again.

"Answer to your question—a few fingers, maybe a thumb would do to identify the dead man. OK?"

Iliana squirmed at the thought.

"We must get reacquainted, see if we can trust again, eh?" He rudely scanned her slender torso and hips, then peered straight into Iliana's eyes. Bostovitch called to meet with her at Svetiia's behest. Svetiia warned Iliana of the man's more bold callousness than before, and how deeply into his grip she worked herself while she tried to reduce her debt.

They sat in a small, black vinyl-upholstered booth, insulated adequately from the few other patrons in the South Robertson Boulevard bar called, "*Minsk*—L.A." Though dark inside, it lighted red and blue with color changes in the neon sign, figurative of the Russian flag that hung from a corner of the front window frame.

The dank place, in a crumbling multi-cultural area, reeked of stale beer and greasy fries and, Iliana worried, was hardly a friendly one for a female to visit alone. Pungent Russian and Turkish cigarette smoke hung in layers like stratus clouds, and tinny music—*hopak-kolom,* traditional Ukraine/Russian dance tunes—spewed from a worn out cassette player at the end of the bar.

She did not, but Kovansk Oligoff loved the homeland folk sounds and he danced well to them. He made it look easy to dip to the floor on one leg, while the other thrust forward ... arms folded straight out, followed by a kick and a quick rise and dip with the other. Iliana angered when Kovi exhibited his prowess at parties. Her malformed right leg would never permit such movement.

Out of her element, a hardy redhead female bartender served the all male *Minsk* clientele. An unsavory bevy of loud talkers, most stared longingly at Iliana and tried unsuccessfully to make eye contact as her gaze nervously revolved about the room.

Head shiny and clean-shaven, a full black beard of several days' duration, light tan suede leather coat, grey silk slacks, and shiny black shoes; the bar owner seated across from her looked like any well dressed business type, except for the shoulder holster that clearly bulged from his left side.

Bostovitch sported deep facial and forehead scars, too, which paled a prizefighter's by comparison; and a left cauliflower ear that looked as if hit by a 2" x 4", a rifle butt, crow bar—something heavy, and certainly painful, she guessed.

Bostovitch spoke fair English. Abrasive and guttural, though, he exerted little apparent effort to project appropriate grammar. He expressed relief that Iliana conversed in Russian and briefly volunteered—while he queried her, that he worked for the KGB after an Army stint in which he flew helicopters during the Soviet era's final years. He grew up mostly in Lithuania with Russian-immigrant foster parents. Both his mother and father, local government employees in *Rechnick Village,* a western Moscow suburb, were among thousands killed during the late Soviet regime. They tried in vain to accumulate capital, a concept then considered so abhorrent.

"Now," Bostovitch remarked, while he shook his head and chuckled, "forty some billionaires own most everything in the city and it's all right with regime. Capital accumulation? No problem; overnight a quick change of heart. One day, a new group in power will take it all away. Mark my words.

"I would slice them all to bite-sized morsels, if I were young and could swing the Cossack *shaska* as I once did." The inimical man, bitter as she imagined when Svetiia warned against contacting him again. He seemed so distasteful, she pondered, that she almost terminated the meeting when he arrived, just after she walked in the place.

"This er, gentleman, the investigator you describe; why is he so important to you?" Bostovitch inquired. "I asked you before; you declined to say. "What did he do, kill your baby puppy?" He grinned and showed two silver-capped upper teeth to the right of center. "I'm sorry," he said, when she flashed an angry expression with his self-induced belly laughs. "So, who is he, and why bitter vengeance?" He rubbed is chin and turned serious.

Iliana thought she could relate the upsetting tale. "I was born in 1979, delivered by Caesarean section, here in L.A." She asked for a straight-up vodka before going on, as she'd not unfolded to another soul, other than hints, from time to time, to Svetiia when they lived together. Certainly, she never went far with Kovi, she began to regret.

"I'm a nurse, learned too late in life to do anything about it. The anesthesiologist who attended to my mother in the delivery room was negligent ... inattentive ... they covered up his absence from the delivery room."

Bostovitch sat motionless, chin in cupped hands, elbows rested on the un-wiped table, sobered more than he expected with the outset of her story.

Iliana slammed the shot like a seasoned drinker, squeezed a lemon between her teeth, and gasped two deep breaths from the sharp bite of 100 proof Absolut Red Label™ before she continued. "My father, also an anesthesiologist at the same hospital, medicated another patient in delivery that night and, appropriately, left Ivana, my mother, in the hands of the colleague. The anesthesiologist was … ah, called. …"

Iliana burst into tears and blotted her dripping mascara with a soiled red paper cocktail napkin she took from beneath an empty coffee cup. "I cannot go on Mr. Bostovitch … just can't go there."

"Call me 'C', like my friends do."

She nodded. "Yes, yes. "We will have to continue this another time; I am too upset … first time to talk about it since father … his death bed … truth was told."

Iliana and her father enjoyed a decent relationship when she was a young child; he never stressed it with a second marriage, but she always distrusted the man when they discussed her debility. He seemed to hide behind his profession, as her queries became more persistent, especially when, in the midst of nursing school, she learned so much about childbirth complications while on obstetrics rotation.

"Papa became edgy, almost defensive, finally grew silent whenever I broached the subject. Eventually I quit … no longer asked him for clarity." Iliana struggled to relate more than small segments of the birth drama to Bostovitch.

"The bastard deserved to die and your father, the doctor; good riddance to him … his, ah, brain tumor," he concluded as they left the bar together with little accomplished. They stood a few minutes in front, where she parked.

Bostovitch lit a cigar, hesitated to put a price on anyone's head so soon, but asked for $ 50,000 without any sign of embarrassment, to finish off Concord if he were still alive. $5,000 to confirm his demise, if she did succeed, brought forward a violent flush of red. Iliana's quiet persona up to that point, turned to burning anger at such arrogant high binding.

"I'll think about it," she told him—barely able to withhold one of her outbursts, then left abruptly, burned rubber toward Beverly Hills, and away from the seedy Russian lounge. She broke every neighborhood speed limit in her black 2005 VW Passat GLX, and felt dirty all over again, in her rush to get as far away from the irksome mobster as fast as possible.

Another workday ahead at the university, Iliana walked to the nearby corner newsstand, bought the *Orange County Register* and the *L.A. Times,* and rushed home to look for news of Concord. She found no mention in the papers the day before.

Almost unable to believe, she saw it immediately in the midst of longer, more heartfelt, legitimate death notices: an obituary on page twelve of the *Times'* second section. "Damn, I did hit the mark," she said loudly. She shuddered with the real notion she killed someone with malice aforethought. First degree murder and life, or the death penalty, she knew, would be the court's mission. She then settled into a kitchen chair—sipped the latte she bought—and repeatedly read the release. She felt more complete, and practically guilt-free, by the minute.

This news offered needed, firm assurance that she could begin a new life, one that no longer haunted her with the unfinished business of getting even. It meant a level field with the person responsible for her failure to secure any compensation for the bad leg. Things could have been so much easier; she thought again as she did incessantly. Settlement funds, a trust in her name, her school years far less tenuous; little need for an outside job when funds from her father's estate flattened.

Died in his sleep? Iliana wondered. *Why did the release say that and not mention the shooting? It must have been such a bloody mess. I suppose his wife likely chose that route to better deal with family and neighbors ... much less upset. I must call up there soon, on some pretext, to make sure things are now quiet,* she thought. *Kovi and I will talk it over when I drive to the desert after my last day down here for a while. Maybe the elderly mother we met will be the easiest target for another covert inquiry. She unhesitatingly gave us all we asked for when we stopped by mistake at her house last month.*

"Damned Bostovitch, for that erroneous and potentially incriminating contact," she said aloud and gritted her teeth, "the old woman would most certainly remember us."

CHAPTER 12

PUGET SOUND

Jim Gibson wore an almost new navy blue flight jacket, crisply pressed denims, a white T-shirt, and a new pair of Aviator Ray Bans™. He lived to fly with Aaron, and anxiously awaited arrival of 156 Yankee Tango, when it settled down close by Sanderson Field's perimeter fence.

Aaron beckoned. Jim ducked beneath the whirling main rotor and approached. He held tightly to his cap, camera, and a briefcase with investigative gear; belted himself in the left seat and latched the door after he secured the equipment to the seat behind. Headed northeast, they lifted off while he adjusted his headset.

Retired from the force for two years, Gibson yet had access to the Sheriff's lab resources as a reserve officer and, after swearing not to mention the shooting to Mason County cop friends, would-be jurisdictional authorities in the case; Aaron related story details as they spun to that point. Gibson gripped the incident with shock and a nagging clutch at Aaron's sleeve. "Why? Who? He looked aghast. "Good God, Buddy; you had too close a shave there … murder one, ya know," was the best advice he could then render. "Glad you're still with us."

Renton's METAR, the terminal weather, updated just before Aaron left his computer that morning, all but assured VFR conditions—adequate visibility, sufficiently high cloud cover—as it did for passing over Sea-Tac: clear, ten mile visibility, scattered clouds at 4000' under an 8000' ceiling, wind 330 degrees at 8 knots. Concord quickly gained altitude with the light load and leveled at 1000'.

Hard as it was for Aaron's talkative and witty friend, Gibson learned to keep quiet at times like this. He monitored all air to ground communications; at his prompt, set the altimeter for Aaron and otherwise assisted by changing radio frequencies. He learned to do that and scan, too, for other aircraft during all the flying they did together.

ATIS-Echo, Renton's automated terminal information, reported current and favorable wind—330 degrees at 12 knots, and the altimeter setting at 30.02. Runway 34 in use, they would approach from the south. Aaron kept the Seattle Terminal Area Chart folded on his lap with the control area centered, and checked his morning notes ... frequencies in use, he scribbled on a 3"x 5" card clipped to it.

"Seattle Approach: helicopter 156 Yankee Tango over Vashon Island, at 1000'.

"Helicopter 6 Yankee Tango: Seattle Approach; go ahead."

"Seattle Approach: helicopter 6 Yankee Tango requests mid-field crossing, east transition over Sea-Tac, landing at Renton from the south."

"Helicopter 6 Yankee Tango: squawk 0276," Approach Control responded with a specific frequency for the helicopter's transponder. Thus began an immediate radar blip that identified Aaron's aircraft, for three-dimensional tracking on the controller's radar screen. Gibson repeated to himself: *0276*, and properly set the instrument's four knobs. Flying at 90 knots, Aaron's hands were full, with multiple radio transmissions, a close watch for traffic, and most of all, to maintain aircraft control. Accustomed to this level of congestion, he took it easily in stride.

Gibson, however, remained bewildered and overwhelmed with the concurrent activity required, which only hundreds of flight hours helped mitigate.

"6 Yankee Tango: Seattle Approach; radar contact, six miles west at 1000'. Confirm heading and altitude. Fly heading, 070 degrees." Aaron changed his heading slightly, to comply.

"6 Yankee Tango: indicating 1000', heading 070 degrees," Concord answered.

"Helicopter 6 Yankee Tango: Seattle Approach; contact Seattle tower, 119.9." Approach handed Aaron off to the tower as he neared the field, for closer control.

"Seattle tower: helicopter 156 Yankee Tango with you—1000'," Concord called after hurriedly changing to the tower frequency. He preset the second radio for nearby Renton's tower to prepare for that call, which he would make all too soon on 124.7, remembering to advise the controller he listened to ATIS - Echo, as required.

"Helicopter 6 Yankee Tango: Seattle tower; clear to cross mid-field at or below 1200'. Traffic is a BAC triple-seven on three-mile final for 34 right; Delta Airbus on departure roll; Cessna 210 at your ten o'clock, climbing through 1,700', heading 220 degrees—no factor. Scanning down, forward and up, using four busy eyes, Aaron and Gibson both saw the climbing fixed wing above and to their left, and the big airliners landing and taking off below. Concord read back instructions as required for confirmation, and reported all traffic in sight.

"Helicopter 6 Yankee Tango: clearing Class Bravo, radar service terminated, frequency change approved, squawk 1200; contact Renton tower, 124.7," the controller called and broke momentary silence, once Aaron passed over the busy commercial field. Jim changed the transponder frequency accordingly and activated the second radio after Aaron acknowledged, "Seattle tower: helicopter 6 Yankee Tango. Thanks, squawking VFR.

"Renton tower: helicopter 156 Yankee Tango."

"Helicopter 6 Yankee Tango: Renton tower; go ahead."

"Helicopter 6 Yankee Tango: five miles south with Echo, inbound for landing at south ramp.

"Helicopter 6 Yankee Tango: cleared to land direct, south ramp, altimeter 30.02, wind 335 at 5, departing traffic not a factor," the controller responded.

"Helicopter 6 Yankee Tango: clear to land, south ramp," Aaron confirmed, took a few deep breaths and descended quickly to helicopter pattern altitude. More slowly, then, he descended, neared the runway apron, cut to the left and sat down directly and neatly on a vacated helicopter pad, marked with a circle—a large white "H" painted in the center. Peggy waited by the fence and waved excitedly while he shut things down, and loped to the office to arrange temporary parking.

Aaron and Gibson carefully inspected the student's vehicle while he looked on with curiosity and interest. Laden with road dust, likely unwashed since he began school, Aaron thought, it was definitely the one. Gaping holes and slashes, remnants of the crisp snaps when his .30

caliber slugs tore into the van, shone in all their glory. Gibson shook his head almost furiously while he carefully inspected each impact point. He seemed more than passively concerned with Aaron's sloppy defense tactics.

"Somebody was definitely wearing gloves, probably latex," he remarked. Prints were not immediately evident when he dusted likely surfaces: dash, shift lever, steering wheel, door and window knobs, gas cap, even the stereo, head light, dome light, and heater switches, with delicate brushes laden with aluminum and graphite-based powders.

"Wait, yust ahhh minute," Gibson then whispered slowly, "just a damned minute, here; someone recently handled this without a glove." He held an unfolded road map with forceps, turned abruptly to Aaron and Redding, cocked his head, and flashed a wry smile. Before saying more, he pointed to several poor but partially visible, serrated ovals he discovered while dusting a corner of the document.

"Good enough to say they're not Mr. Redding's," he gestured toward the young van owner, "but for data base checking ... not."

Aaron and Redding were both inclined to ask, "Well, what then?" as Gibson continued.

"Paper and identifiable prints with dust are not a good mix ... need to use this ninhydrin spray. He removed a small perfume-type atomizer bottle from the briefcase, half-full of liquid, and lightly sprayed both sides of the opposite corner of the map.

"Got a steam iron in the house?"

Redding nodded.

"Go light it up, full of distilled water if you have it. We'll let this dry and then humidify it. Normally for strict specification compliance, we would use a humidity cabinet ... 50%, about thirty minutes or so, for the prints to show. We'll try it with the iron, though, and see what happens. Sweat glands on print ridges release proteins and peptides," he explained, "which form amino acids with atomized ninhydrin contact. "Left to dry and then humidified, we should get a bluish-purple print that can be lifted with my sticky fingerprint paper for preservation.

"There they are," Gibson boasted. The three of them stood in the fraternity house laundry room and watched multiple spots emerge beneath the iron's steam pattern. "Just what old Daddy wanted. These are good, solid ones," he said, "thumb, index and, with luck, a second finger—all over this corner. That's enough to try here. I have a couple other things up my sleeve for later: photos, using a green filter; examination under a special light, 530 nanometer wave length; and they'll show like lightning over Mt. Olympus on a dark summer afternoon. Yes, me boys, now we have something to talk about. Not much else to go on, but. ..." He held out his clasped hand, grinned as if it hid a gold nugget, and opened it. In his palm sparkled a shiny button with the initials, DKNY, smaller but of the same design, to Aaron's surprise, as the one he found on the road the morning of the shooting.

"Well, I'll be damned," I've got one just like that," Aaron exploded. "And you might want to do your routine on this." He pulled from his shirt pocket, a plastic sandwich bag containing the *Minsk*—L.A. matchbook he also found on the road.

Gibson noticed the rubber floor mat on the passenger side was replete with muddy shoe prints, and told Redding they would take it, after shooting several close-up photos. He looked, too, with a large magnifying glass at the wet carpet in the rear, picked up a number of what appeared to be red hairs, and several other fibers of different colors, which he enthusiastically stuffed in a small bag he labeled with a marker pen.

Satisfied with their findings, the two investigators—one the criminal specialist, the other, more an intellectual, less familiar with police procedures—thanked Redding. Aaron handed the student two $100.00 bills. They left the relieved van owner, enthused with possible discoveries, and more to come.

"And, remember, Mrs. Concord," Jim Gibson craftily admonished Aaron's mother as she lay comfortably and relaxed in her living room recliner chair, Peggy seated in close reach. "Now don't give out their numbers ... address or personal information to anyone, until I give the OK ... just a while, until we develop a warm trail to the vandals doing the trouble-making out there."

He glanced at Peggy, turned, and pointed west toward Hood Canal. Aaron and Gibson told both women of random pranks in the area, but revealed not a hint that Aaron was assuredly the object of a determined killer. Peggy would stay the following week, and provide continued assistance with his mother's transition to self-sufficiency again. Most important to him at that moment, that facilitated the trip south to review investigation files at his old office.

"We made some discoveries today. Let ya know, soon as I can," Gibson yelled to Aaron above the rising rumble of the aircraft engine and the hissing turbulence from downward main rotor wash. "Yup, we may really have someone's ID sooner than not, scream out from these prints."

Jim Gibson crouched away, arose when clear of the rotor, turned back, and waved. Aaron spun to full RPM, slowly climbed out, and circled once in the crisp country air before heading north to his hangar.

CHAPTER 13

LOS ANGELES

Almost beyond control, Iliana turned her Passat from the side street, dropped with the expected lunge over the sidewalk apron, bounced down the steep driveway, and then accelerated hastily through the sliding security gate once it opened wide enough to pass. She swerved into her slot in the condominium's subterranean garage and shrieked all four tires on the slick concrete pavement until abruptly stopped. Engine off—no effort to exit the car—she simply froze, with a blank stare through the windshield at the wall-mounted storage cabinet. Her hands and knuckles blanched almost white, so tightly she gripped the wheel.

A hectic afternoon at the Medical Center, she taught a group of six advanced nursing students how to handle themselves in neurosurgery. It didn't go so well, however, an especially late one, when operating schedules usually thinned out, and things got easier.

Not one of her better days, close to shift's end at 3:00 PM, an unusually grumpy senior neurosurgery resident scheduled a multi-level laminectomy and spinal fusion in a male patient's lumbar region, when, at that hour, he should have completed it. The procedure, routine for Iliana—a corrective measure for persistent sciatic pain, leg numbness, and encroaching immobility, designed to relieve spinal nerve root pressure—usually took several hours. Assured by the surgeon that she'd not be standing on her painful leg too long; Iliana opted in, with her clutch of curious nursing school seniors.

She used a spine skeleton that dangled from an IV pole, to explain how surgeons would remove sections of the vertebral arches, along with intrusive ligamentous tissue and errant bony arthritic growth, to enlarge the foramina, spaces through which nerve roots pass to the body from the central spinal canal. Hesitating while she described details of the pathological disc removal, and, with clear disdain, Iliana complained that such surgeries were usually set well in advance and for the morning schedule.

Nothing, absolutely nothing, in her view, necessitated the late hour procedure on this patient as immediately necessary; rather to provide relief of his long-standing, chronic symptoms. Earlier, Iliana perused the history to brief her clutch of eager learners and pointed out how frustrating it was that another day, an additional week, would have made no difference in the expected outcome. She angered more as the procedure's outset stalled while the three-man surgical team lazily assembled. Last minute inclusion of two junior surgery residents took longer than it should have and subtracted more from her Friday evening, with requisite participation until nearly 8:00 PM.

Iliana's most efficient protégé tossed surgeons into a fit early in the procedure, just after the ligamentum flavum, connective tissue that linked the vertebrae, was exposed. It happened well after all participants scrubbed, donned gowns and entered the sterile field. The student was to be the next handler of surgical tools, sponges, and the suction cannula under Iliana's guidance. She stacked the table neatly with the full complex of stainless steel and titanium instruments she was to dispense and keep organized. When subtly requested she firmly snapped the appropriate tool into the surgeon's hand, in the position in which he would employ it.

An outraged yell attracted Iliana's drifting attentions. Also scrubbed, she stood in the sterile field, next to the student, her right leg propped on a stool. Through simple inexperience if not absentmindedness, the student nurse contaminated her right glove by an inadvertent but inexcusable adjustment she made to her mask. Not tolerated, ever, and a cardinal OR sin, because of the immediate opportunity of wound contamination; she nearly crumpled from the explosive chastisement by one of the assistants, just before she would have rested her hand upon, and adulterated the sterile instrument tray.

Grateful for her mask, hair net, and the cap she wore, Iliana's' crimson blush went unnoticed. She was ultimately accountable for the *faux pas*.

Surgery skidded to a stop while new gloves covered contaminated ones, engendering anger, and intolerant head shaking amongst the operating trio.

Matters grew worse when the nurse-in-training did not relate the difference as Iliana relentlessly prepared her—between a Beckmann retractor, similar to a bent fork with sharp prongs and an Adson counterpart of about the same configuration and size, but blunt pronged. The operating team reached the fourth lumbar spinal nerve root on the left. "Adson retractor," the first assistant said, and reached out, eyes focused on the operating field. He wished it to pull back connective and nerve tissue deep in the wound to provide good exposure before lamina bone removal could begin. The Beckmann unit, instead, slid into his open glove before Iliana took notice.

Stalling the procedure a second time with multiple admonishments by the physicians, Iliana finally took the lead. "No more students today, Iliana; please," the senior resident pleaded. His eyes left the operating microscope to turn toward her. "You move in; please let this young woman go home. Let's rock and get this goddamned fusion done. My wife and I have a table for 8:00 PM at Boulevard 16 and we want to do some fancy dancing afterward.

"Three long jobs after rounds today. My feet are burning from immobility. I need to get the hell out of here; get fed, exercised, and eventually engage in some passionate love. It's been too frigging long, unlike you and my friend, Kovi, cuddling like mourning doves all the time, in your desert nest out there, away from it all ... lucrative private practice, you know." His self-absorption infuriated Iliana; she squinted to imply a smile beneath her mask.

She liked Doctor Finus Albers, a competent, emergent specialist in his field, personally and professionally, knew he would soon be on his own, and invited into a Beverly Hills partnership somewhere. Iliana felt unaccountably envious, though, of his marital relationship and their two lovely children. She didn't need the indignity, condescension, or any hostility, however jocular, at that hour. *His cuddly little stay-at-home bottle-blond wife ... always smartly coiffed and decked out in the latest designer togs ... no idea what's involved, what is given up, working long hours like this. Friday night: she gets to party while I hit the sack early, sleep off the long day, deal with chronic leg pain, an ugly deformity, and my absolute inability to dance. Damn my luck.*

Finally finished—a successful result despite the intervening tumult—both assistants closed the paravertebral musculature and overlying fascia. Albers left the suite. Iliana dutifully stayed behind until surgeons completed suturing, closed the skin with staples, applied pressure bandages and transported the patient to recovery.

Still seated in her car, ruminating over the trying afternoon, she pictured Kovi, absent clothing, never appearing even slightly less than sexually appetizing; healthy and young looking, fresh from the shower in their new house, probably curious what time she would roll in for the weekend.

As so often happened, though, offensive thoughts crept in stealthily, to displace otherwise pleasant wanderings. She never allowed more than dim candle light in their bedroom when lovemaking at night, always feared disapproval, if not Kovi's unrest, with her leg, and the muscular strictures which deformed it. Knowing how his curiosity got the best of him, when he would pry, pry, pry; she instinctively and impatiently shook her head and avoided answers to her well-hidden, strangely coveted story. It evolved into an unconscious drama in her mind for the many years she used it, unwittingly, to belabor or foster anger, to punish Kovi, and to keep herself agitated, so the self-motivated quest for a full explanation of her life's beginnings would never tire.

I'm not going to the desert tonight; too beat … head up early tomorrow. We will spend some quality time together, kick back around the house. She made the decision with little internal argument.

The basement elevator bell rang loud enough to echo through the parking garage and snatch Iliana from her musings. Arm in arm, a couple stepped out and skipped toward their car. She peered at them contemptuously, limped to the three steps to the elevator foyer, braced herself on the rail to climb them, rode to the second floor, and entered Unit 21 across from the elevator door. Iliana collapsed on the front room couch from intractable fatigue.

No sooner than eyelids fell closed, a stream of frightening and most unusual imagery filled her dreams—amazingly regressive pictures, as real as they had ever been. They spoke only to her subconscious, backdated to her pre-birth incapacity to exist on her own. She saw herself as vulnerable and helpless; an inviolate, near-term fetus, struggling for entry to the outside world. She observed her uncaring mother, still the safe harbor of her life, asleep, supine on the delivery room table, draped in green.

An endotracheal tube, positioned by the anesthesiologist to create a fully closed, positive-pressure breathing tract from her mother to the anesthesia cart, stayed in place by inflation of a small balloon that, when filled, expanded its terminal end against tracheal mucosa. Horrified in her dream, however, Iliana heard subtle hissing breath sounds, indicative of escaping air. Was it an ineptly placed tube leaking, that partially blocked the trachea, gateway to the flow of oxygen required by Mother's lungs? She tried to scream, attract someone's attention, but her utterances went unrecognized.

Iliana felt the umbilicus wrapped around her neck; to make matters worse, her mother's heart pulsed at a slower rate and with less power, owing to diminutive blood pressure induced by spinal anesthesia. Part of the sequence, and expected in those days, she knew maternal hypotension—errant low blood pressure—needed someone's attention, and could be countermanded by synthetic adrenalin added to the IV to raise it within normal limits. Was this important medication timely administered? She cried out the query to those who appeared to be present, yet no sound came from her throat.

Iliana helplessly experienced a very real encroaching weakness in her pre-emergent form, followed by abject fright, entwined with the raging anger of an educated nurse, and her adult views of the perceived omission.

Not knowing why, Iliana sensed the marked drop in Ivana's blood pressure, affecting maternal oxygen supply to the placenta—her unborn body on its other side. Did fetal hypoxemia—a corresponding and intolerably low oxygen level—step in without hesitation, she bitterly asked in her dream? She pictured the state as an indescribable, crawling, multi-colored monster. Could irreversible damage have occurred to the cerebral cortex of Iliana's brain? An unseen guide prompted her to inquire.

Still in deep slumber on the couch, Iliana grasped her head tightly in her hands while she endured the imagined horrific pain of oxygen deprivation. She saw herself writhing *in utero*.

The anesthesiologist was not in the room. The obstetrician who would perform the delivery was not yet present. Busy setting up drapes and instruments, oblivious, and involved in the usual pre-delivery routine while her mother slept, the scrub nurse did not notice. Stuck in these convoluted fancies, Iliana visualized an almost robotic, completely distracted circulating nurse, who hummed an old Johnny Cash tune. Sophisticated, alerting fetal monitors were not then available. Audio warning alarms, too, were then absent from every day use. The circulating nurse chatted with another in the main corridor from which four delivery rooms extended, each ceramic-tiled in blue, up to eye height, bright white above, their terrazzo floors polished and waxed to a high luster. 3:20 AM: two adjacent rooms were in use at that hour, lighted with recessed fluorescents and 36" diameter central, ceiling-mounted operating lamps on tracks. Adjustable by the circulating nurse to illuminate surgeons' fields of vision, they simulated shadowless daylight. Cabinets, with sparkling glass doors, contained all varieties of surgical staples, sutures, sterile drape packs, IV solutions, and infusion packs; shelves stacked with sterile sponges and instruments lined the north walls of each room.

Was there no doctor close to Ivana? Her model's body was taken into the silent world—initially induced sleep from intravenous thiopental sodium after regional spinal anesthesia by injection, while a mixture of inhaled gaseous halothane, nitrous oxide and oxygen, flowed steadily, inspired with each breath, to maintain unconsciousness through what would be a potentially difficult, though likely routine emergency Cesarean section.

Iliana's mind then conceived hallucinatory scenes in varying shades of blue, a part of her questioning why, while she succumbed to what she imagined or re-experienced without resistance, and with unexpected openness as to what next might occur.

Where was the anesthesiologist, she noted the chatty nurses also began to wonder? Iliana shrieked to stimulate their curiosity. Why wasn't her mother's doctor already scrubbed, sterile-gowned, ready to incise transversely across Ivana's protuberant abdomen to release baby Iliana, and relieve the problem?

She yelled in panic, imagined that red blood cells—carriers of life-sustaining oxygen bound to contained hemoglobin—might have been under-serving if not restrained by the leaking tube in Ivana's throat; if not, also, by the umbilical cord around her neck. Did conditions permit a heightened ratio of carbon dioxide to pervade, in lieu of a healthy level of tissue oxygenation? What physiological changes occurred as a result? What connection existed between her vision of low blood oxygen, and the deformed leg? Again, she demanded answers from those pictured in her fancies.

Spastic monoplegia, a variety of cerebral palsy involving one lower extremity, a rare yet devastating sequel to hypoxemia, crept silently. But

Iliana did not know that. She only felt directions to her leg musculature from oxygen-deprived brain tissue, become diffused and wanton. Right leg muscles went into spastic stricture. There was no way to know whether the imagery pictured was an extrapolation of what she garnered by review of the hospital charts, or, in part, what her father's letter had alluded. Or did all of this stem from regressive re-experience? Horror, she confided, underscored all possibilities. How many of her illusions were factual, her mind demanded? Iliana instinctively pulled her left knee to her chest, rocked to her side on the couch, and heaved in tumultuous slumber as though out of breath. She did not know, before those first moments in life, how desperately flexor muscles fought with extensors for equivocation— the result: irrevocable tension, sufficient compression on the yet supple long bones of her leg, to retard normal growth and neural function forever.

Rock still, Iliana feared awakening, unwilling to test reality of the scenes she fabricated. Slowly the colors merged from blues to dark shades of red. By far the deepest subconscious exploration she ever undertook, a pool of despair deepened as the surreal stream of events continued.

Incomplete segments of the delivery saga were related by her father—a tidbit here, and one there, over the span of many years—well after she learned enough to explore and understand physiological issues on her own, during nursing and pre-medical studies. Yet she faced strange, inexplicable, persistent, and repetitive queries: why ... why ... why? The dreaming offered no separation, no clarity, became increasingly confusing, more nightmarish by the minute, and eliminated more answers than were proffered.

Why did she perceive her mother's anesthesiologist administer general and regional anesthesia, then leave the room? Did he actually do that?

Then, it was usual for those practitioners in the art of maintaining a delicate balance between life, peaceful sleep, and death, to appear inattentive as they worked. Seated next to the patient's head, rhythmically and almost autonomically, they squeeze the supple, rubber respirator bag as it fills and empties and they might simultaneously read the latest *Field and Stream, Road and Track*, or *Reader's Digest*. Confident of the patient's status as they thusly breathe for them, they blend patient oversight and light reading with recordation of vital signs every few minutes, on the Anesthesia Record. That document becomes an integral and vital part of the patient's chart and forms a chronology of vital signs integrated with meds administered and pertinent events during the procedure.

Despite apathetic appearances, a delicate bond developed from the first IV puncture until release to recovery, that dictated an indisputable legal and ethical duty: the clear propriety and necessity of close patient watch.

An exit from the room? Was that ethical? Was it appropriate? Did it occur? Iliana questioned rhetorically in her dream.

Doctor Reggie Raynes, an old-school anesthesiologist, competent in his own right, induced Ivana to sleep, her father related, and as she learned researching medical records. He then responded to a frantic call for help from the neighboring delivery room. He left no log entry to confirm his departure. After all, Raynes must have reasoned, his patient was asleep; the obstetrician scrubbed just outside in the prep room; nurses were there, and Ivana was not yet incised.

Iliana recreated several intense arguments with her father, the man closest to her, but whom she grew to distrust, while she tossed and turned restlessly, tangled in an ever-evocative curiosity. There was so much more to the tale than the late Dr. Gosnov was willing to visit with her before his demise.

She reckoned unwittingly with the disturbing images. These events and what her conscious mind had known—what little her father said of them—sequentially filled a few blank leaves of a novella in progress. Agonizingly incomplete, though, it evolved to a story without plot, too replete with unrelated and incomplete segments.

The disturbing walking gait, persistent shortening of her right lower extremity long bones, and muscle atrophy equated sufficiently with Dr. Gosnov's claims of genetic mutation, to form the beginnings of her belief system that she inherited traits from which she would never recover.

Was there truly a brain deficit? The query rang loudly and repeatedly in her storm-tossed voyage for part of the night, as an excited PA announcement might have, at a university football game. Because of her father's blame on genetics, the hospital, obstetrician, and anesthesiologist were not suspected as culpable, nor attacked in her behalf, while the Statute of Limitations for a malpractice suit remained tolled by her minority.

She wondered about that as a teenager. Why did her father not seek the services of counsel to explore retribution then, which might have eased her coping with adulthood? She suspected correctly that he became a link in the conspiracy of silence.

Iliana woke with a start, to persistent chiming of her cell phone. Its cessation when voice mail intruded, kneaded her back to sleep, and onward with what seemed even more confused, while revealing wanderings, interrupted when she momentarily awakened. She always struggled with conflicting views of the events surrounding her start in the world, and became further confused after studying original hospital charts. How much of the unnerving dream, she continued to wonder, stemmed from a more questionable source: her possible fetal and immediate neonatal memories or even pre-birth imaginations?

Out cold in an instant, she relinquished once more to the resumption of that pathetic, sleep-breaking cell ring. Her spell of back-thinking completely lost its momentum. Iliana rolled toward the end table, grappled in her purse for the phone and noted the time at 10:39 PM. She raced through her formative times, pushed barriers aside like a bulldozer, and came to some startling discoveries, if based on fantasy. Resentful of the final interruption in this possible restructure of her life's incipient chronology, she massaged her eyes, and eventually answered.

Kovi worried. "Why aren't you here?"

He sounded angry ... if not demanding, she thought.

"What the hell are you doing, er ... a ... Love? Still at the hospital?" His quick temper flared but craftily shifted to a softness he could muster when persistence would lead to an open series of insults. "I called Finus, caught him and Rebecca at a club. His last op went slowly; he thought you left by eight o'clock. I worry about you and three big procedure days you endured. Love you; miss you; maybe you should drive to desert tonight." When she failed to respond, he said. "Better sleep then; come out Saturday, if you will."

For the first time Iliana began to understand—from tidbits dished out here and there by her father; discrete, carefully crafted, spuriously edited doses of information over the course of many years—the alarming events of her delivery night. She suddenly felt intense antipathy toward her father, with all males at that second, including Dr. Kovansk Oligoff, and his initial thoughtless, while gentle, persuasions for her to undertake the long drive. Rest and isolation seemed more welcome than companionship.

Rejected almost scornfully by her angry mumbling as Iliana awakened completely, Kovansk knew how demanding, what a taskmaster his former colleague, Albers, could be, and understood Iliana's peculiar attitude at the late hour. Like Albers, he, too, preferred to perform difficult surgeries later in the day, when senses heightened, despite physical fatigue. Selfishly, he did not bid that Iliana stay the night in L.A. to recover, instead finished with, a curt, "I expected you would be on road by now."

"Damned men and their needy, self-protective, fragile minds, encompassed by strong, agile bodies they wear as masks to belittle those around them when they please," Iliana said loudly, half of which she muttered before disconnect. What did she care at that moment, whether Kovi heard her words, lived or died?

Stretched out again; this time she rested her head until comfortable on a soft throw pillow; drew knees upward, her right one but half way. She folded arms across her chest and ardently tried to recreate the visions—however stifling—that arose Phoenix-like, over the preceding two hours, from the flames of distant, padlocked boxes in the recesses of her memory. She could neither sleep nor relate to what she believed she experienced, when thoughts turned to Aaron Concord. "That bastard…only one left in the picture with whom I can even the stakes," she muttered.

Ilya Gosnov, M.D., Iliana's father, re-entered her wanderings. A good doctor, always patient-mindful before himself, was un-athletic. He sat most days at work and nights at home, too, rarely consented to walking, however slowly she was constrained to do so, just to be out in the night air or early mornings on weekends. The Southern California sun warmed her bones, soothed her; she could never get enough as a child, to spite the abnormality she bore.

He encouraged Iliana to read as he did when he relaxed, always engrossed in those damned journals, she pondered, to keep up with new techniques, university studies, anesthesia product development, and most often, but never to her notice, cerebral palsy.

Balding by the time Iliana was a young teen, Gosnov used rimless, half glasses when nested with a book or magazine, and always wore shined dress shoes around the house. That stood out most poignantly in her lazy thoughts; foreshadowed the way he dressed, what kind of car he drove, or the occasional female from the hospital he might have entertained at home for the evening.

He always seemed so…so out of touch…defensive when I would pry for a better understanding of my crippled leg. How sly he became at changing the subject, yet how inquisitive it eventually made me, to find better answers. I learned to face the truth, not avoid it; that is how I found my target in Washington.

Ivana's obstetrician, at the twilight of his career when Iliana was born, died in the eighties, she discovered; while Reginald Raynes, M.D., her mother's anesthesiologist, worked at Five Palms, as a lifetime contemporary, and best friend to her father, until he sustained a severe stroke: barely breathed on his own, comatose, like his former sleeping patients. He vegetated in a San Fernando Valley rehabilitation facility, until he faded to slow demise in 1995.

Iliana wanted a piece of Aaron Concord, so concerned she became over his curious role in the obfuscation of events during her early breaths of life. Until she met and fell headlong for Boris Kovansk Oligoff, at UCLA, men were not a favorable part of her life. They deceived—covered for one another—liars, cheats, the subjects of her hatred and revenge.

Overtaken with despondence, more confused, and alone in her thoughts, Iliana's mind raced in an unbridled stream of consciousness. She took another hydrocodone pain reliever, her second for the evening, slid it down with saliva and, with a surprising will, put the entire bottle to her lips. What would she feel, were she to end it all, to know she finally won the chess game … no more responsible men to locate, follow and capture, to even a score? Maybe, beforehand, she mused, there would be time to scribble a short suicide note, to implicate Kovi in the Concord assault, for a nice, smooth conclusion to her bitterness. *He could dump me at some point anyway, now that he is so well situated with his own hospital … on my Papa's money.*

Suddenly she saw the colored imagery from her earlier nightmare streak before her again, but afraid to go back to that place, Iliana shook with panic. She propped herself to a seated position, grasped the open, blue plastic prescription bottle—almost full of the rough narcotic, lifted it with determination to her open mouth, and tipped the container, to end all ill thoughts of Kovi.

CHAPTER 14

LOS ANGELES

Ken Stansbee and Aaron Concord paused to regain perseverance; rubbed their foreheads, kneaded stiff neck muscles, prodded tired eyes, and stretched for the first time in hours. Piles of manila folders, accordion file pockets, and stacked temporary record storage boxes crammed with long-ago-closed files, covered the floor around their chairs. Together, they racked brains, reviewed old cases and files since early that Monday morning, until everyone left from Concord, Stansbee and Fitch for the night.

Ceiling lights over the cluttered, brightly finished wood conference table sent dimmed illumination through smoke-tinted partition glass, into the front office where the typing pool labored each day with dictation transcription. Almost dark, the reception area lay beyond, where four avocado and white, floral-pattern, upholstered wing chairs greeted clients who passed through double doors from the fourth floor elevator lobby.

Optimistic their efforts would spur memories, they pored over dead files, even indices, to help with possible name association. Files in which they found client compliments on their professionalism, gratified; while those occasional cases that contained threatening mail from angry claimants, whose cases they disproved or denied, sounded contrastingly vehement and haunting.

A hearty shake of his head to sharpen senses, Stansbee stood again, stretched nearly to the ceiling, and groaned loudly. Tall and lanky, a decent basketball player in college, he was still a member of the California Bar. He prosecuted felony cases as an Orange County Deputy District Attorney after law school, but never liked courtroom confines, which lead him to a lifetime of professional liability investigation. His skills, unusually valuable, were commonly employed in lawyers' malpractice cases assigned to the office.

Worn down, Ken rubbed his abdomen with both hands and again roared a yawn in his normally amplified, almost cultured stage voice. Time did not permit a noon break to eat or drink. He felt weakened from the absence of his normally large lunch, and one customary dirty martini for garnish.

Stansbee rolled his light gray dress shirtsleeves past elbows again, and loosened his tie another inch. He knew a long night, would surely pervade. He looked at Aaron. His pewter hair, far longer than he kept it before retirement, framed a high forehead, blended well with his pasty facial skin, and dark brown eyes. He worried that he, too, aged as did Concord, in the preceding three years. Glacier white, wide, and just covering the upper lip, Stansbee's moustache hid traces of dried instant coffee he rubbed briskly to remove with the back of his hand.

Comparatively carefree about his dress, and independent, Aaron wore a green plaid, flannel work shirt, khaki slacks, and running shoes, more oblivious than Stansbee to their surroundings: a top-end high-rise in Newport Beach's Fashion Island, filled mostly with opulent law offices, brokerages, and well-adorned occupants.

"Remember those early suspected fertility cases?" Ken asked, "kids born with teratalogical defects—the shocking absence of arms, legs or both, at birth? Their mothers, in perfectly good faith, followed medical advice … popped the new pills to improve chances of getting pregnant. Little did they know the drugs would be later be suspected as the cause of or a contribution to genetic mutation."

He pointed to the Roger Goodby file, first of many they investigated. Most cases presented similar histories: infants with analogous defects, newborn-Roger being one of the first to make newspaper headlines, and alert hungry plaintiff lawyers. "They came out of the woodwork like termites, didn't they?" Stansbee quipped.

Both remembered the drug company's Board of Directors in utter disbelief, and the terror that extended to their client, the manufacturer's huge product liability insurance pool. It stretched all the way to major syndicates in Lloyds of London in the UK, and beyond, to myriad underwriting groups across Europe, each of which assumed varying percentages of the company's first level and multi-layered excess insurance. Millions in reserves were exposed.

Their office received the first few, and then, later, many more claim files. A frighteningly suggestive relationship became manifest between many affected children, the fertility medication its mother took and what became a possible pattern of birth deformities, unmitigated, it was argued, by other common traits, such as medications, environmental factors or maternal physical similarities.

Those early cases filled their work lives while each family relationship they thoroughly backgrounded. Affected children were medically and psychologically followed, treated, died, or were relegated to institutional living. Settlements in some matters, slowly negotiated, were painfully accepted. Court cases were tragic. "Those, we will never forget." Aaron acknowledged. He remembered the torture of seeing, first hand, so many infants who suffered theretofore-unimaginable debilities. "They've been closed for so long, most handled by counsel after we did our investigative work; I can't see a one of them popping above the surface at this point. And then, the question: why me? Why not you … others in our office, and elsewhere," Aaron relented. "I wasn't the only gumshoe working those files." They both laughed.

"How about that 'jumper' north of San Francisco … houseful of young kids, recovering from a problematic surgery's aftermath … broke away from his bed restraints … jetted out the window? He landed multiple floors down in a shallow reflection pool. You were eaten up by the family lawyer—a university law professor and Bay Area political big-wig," Ken asserted. He shook his index finger as might a frustrated teacher toward an unruly pupil, "for the immediate appearance you made in behalf of the hospital's insurer, while handling another case up there. You photographed the broken cuffs, as they lay next to the bed after his flight out the window; I remember the shots well—proudly showed the manufacturer's ID labels ... the fabric failures. You then helped yourself to the restraints for safekeeping."

"Yup, the budding company turned out to be self-insured, filed for bankruptcy, and we got our client hospital out on a dime. How those threatening letters did flow from the poor fellow's survivors? Though we were damned scared for a while, I was just doing my job," Concord went on, with a shrug of his shoulders.

"No, that can't be the file. I remember the folks well; nice local people. I went to see them on crash day to break the news. It was more than painful. No, my would-be hitters were young, I think, not pros, worked off a personal grudge, not someone else's wish to get even. And both my assailants, according to Mother, spoke with pronounced accents."

"If I don't eat and we both can't have a drink, I'm going to take back that fine obituary I composed in your behalf, and put you back on the firing line. Damnit! I should be charging you our new hourly rate for this leg work."

A stop for an hour gave the men renewed vigor to keep up the search pace. Dinner and two doubles for Stansbee did the trick, while Aaron made sparkling water his beverage. He drank nothing alcoholic since he began pilot training.

"I've got one for you," Aaron said, spooning to his open mouth, the last morsel of a raspberry tart in the center of the table, before his former partner could take it.

"Go for it. What file is that?" Stansbee teetered his bentwood chair back on two legs and clasped hands behind his head.

"The infamous Hollywood shrink, Ervan Collier, MD, his last patient before policy cancellation, if I recall. Professional Medical Doctor's Indemnity, the carrier, gave members what seemed a 'real deal' and cut pending premiums more than fifty percent to break into the medical association market. They had a gimmick, a clever out, one their agents likely didn't explain adequately to insured physicians, who knew little about the malpractice policy language they dearly paid for, with heart and soul." Stansbee unconsciously swept crumbs from the tablecloth when the waiter cleared his plate, while Aaron continued.

"Prior to his current insurance contract, Collier's coverage was written on a discovery or 'claims-made' basis, as it was for years before, with the previous insurer; remember?" If claim was not made against the physician—not the alleged negligent act—but actual notice of a claim, did not occur within the policy term: whamo! No coverage. "Pro MD, though, left that market at the end of their first year, disenchanted with the poor loss ratio, and Old Franklin Group took over, with completely different language: an 'occurrence' contract. The negligent act, not a claim

93

made therefor, had to occur during policy terms, regardless of when notice was eventually given to the doctor.

"We got the file; the defense firm asked us to be innovative and especially clever," Aaron said. Our job: document Collier had absolutely no clue he would be a lawsuit or claim target during the discovery policy terms, when the decedent received his psychotherapy. Saying so before he suspected a possible coverage gap, got to the truth, knocked his protection out like the lighted tail of a swatted firefly on a mid-west summer's eve."

"I do remember that one," Stansbee answered. A wide grin burst from one side of his mouth, as if he snarled.

"You taped the doctor, with his chart before him, and did the same with both his office people; we transcribed the interviews late into the night, and they signed them next day, under penalty of perjury. Then you followed the same path ... re-interviewed Dr. Collier, thank heaven, with a Certified Court Reporter to confirm his story. Old Franklin got their money's worth on that one ... denied liability immediately."

Aaron puffed out his chest and exhaled proudly, well aware of his heroics. "The dead man saw Dr. Collier twice, got anti-depressants with the therapy sessions, and shot two people in his realty office before taking a mouth blast with the last slug in his partially loaded Colt 45. No mistaking; the doc had no coverage for the shattering incident. Collier's therapy and the shootings occurred during the discovery policy period.

No one thought him a possible culprit or made claim until well after the new policy incepted, offering coverage only if the negligent act occurred within its terms. In short, he got screwed, and was never kissed. He turned down the extra cost to endorse a 'tail' to the policy, which could have extended his coverage to cover the claims.

"Suits poured in the following year, named Doctor Collier a primary defendant," Ken Stansbee continued, "and he swirled down slope in a vortex of litigation. Finally drove his car off Mulholland Road near the Griffith Park Observatory in the midst of night, with an irrepressible motive to end it all, family said later.

Collier's heirs lost everything the doctor made during his illustrious career. The accusatory epistle one of them wrote to you was scary." Ken talked faster as more details popped up by association. "Then, one of the attorneys sued us for fraud, for the way you collected facts that led to claim denial. All the coyotes were looking for coverage, any source for a score, even from the drug company, for alleged inadequate package warnings."

Aaron grimaced. He gulped the last of his Perrier, as his recall loosened. There's likely some litigation still going on, that stemmed from your good work: getting honest answers from an honest man, while he hung himself out to dry in the process."

"Let's pull that file. As I now recall, Collier testified when I asked if he ever went by another name, that his family surname was originally Callieroni, Calloni or something like that. By God, I think he spoke with a noticeable accent," Concord continued, as the two re-entered the office after their late dinner. "So did one of his office girls."

CHAPTER 15

Fresh-brewed Brazilian coffee aroma and sweet scents of warm blueberry muffins wafted through the reception area. 7:00 AM—Aaron Concord arrived for the second day's work at his former office—used the key he retained, a symbolic gift given during his retirement party, to assure a perpetual welcome there. Though normal hours did not begin until 8:30, Aaron saw Stansbee when he entered the suite. He stood in the conference room: neatly pressed three-piece, dark-blue suit, red tie, and black loafers—a thick folder in his hands—already engaged with clerical personnel he bribed with future comp time, to help pull records for that day's perusal.

Gratified his former partner took the threat on his life that seriously; Aaron first stopped in the break room, poured a full cup of coffee, broke off a bite-sized piece from the edge of a muffin in the cardboard bakery box, and sat at the head of the table. Ball cap tilted at an odd angle, an inexpensive, olive drab designer T-shirt beneath his unbuttoned blue denim coat, Aaron looked, but did not feel, out of place.

"Well?" He asked, with a lazy grin at his ex-partner, "are you tired as I am today?"

"Found the Collier file," Stansbee replied without responding, "and there are two cassettes in there for you to listen to … see about those accents your mother remembered." Stansbee snapped the doctor's interview recording in the hand-held tape player and they listened:

"Today's date is Wednesday June 19, 1985; it's 10:35 AM. Aaron P. Concord is speaking with Doctor Irvan Collier in his office at 1780 Wilshire Boulevard, Suite 505, Los Angeles, California. Doctor Collier, are you aware that our conversation is being recorded?

"Yes, yes."

"Do you have any objection to our doing so?

"No."

"Will the information you are about to offer, be a true, accurate, and correct representation of the facts as you know them, to the best of your knowledge, under penalty of perjury?"

"Yes."

"Please state your full name for the record."

"Irvan Blanchard Collier, M.D."

"And, your occupation is, Sir."

"I am a Board Certified psychiatrist, in private practice, Los Angeles."

Aaron shook his head without hesitation, flipped off the player, removed the cassette, and dropped in another tape he made the same day—a recording of the physician assistant's interview.

He dialed his mother. Peggy answered the phone. "Hi Honey; sorry to call so early, but is Mom close by? Just need her for a second. Busy now … call you back a bit later. Yes, Ken's fine, looks sort of old since we last saw him, and the weather is … is lovely here." Concord winked at Stansbee. It just began to drizzle in Orange County.

Aaron's mother listened to the first few minutes of each tape and immediately negated similarities to the accents of the couple who, weeks earlier, stopped at her home in the silver sports car.

"Well," Aaron said when he hung up the phone, "I thought Collier was Italian. The voice I heard that night in front of the house definitely was not, confirmed by Mom, who is amazingly astute at those things. It sounded more Eastern European; at least he made an effort for it to sound so. Think we have ruled out that family." A look of pallor washed over his face. "Poor SOB; been dead close to fifteen years. Hung by his own, truthful bootstraps."

"I've got another possible source, here," Stansbee said. Aaron recognized the file tab immediately: *Chauncey Lieberman, M.D., City Orthopaedic and Rehabilitation Clinic.*

"Oh God, those guys ... the 'infection section,'" we used to call it. They performed record numbers of in and outpatient knee joint repairs, lots of shoulder jobs, and hip replacements, too. I remember the poor claimant, a middle aged chap whose life was ruined. Post-op complications ensued from a simple outpatient laparoscopic medial meniscus repair—removal of damaged cartilage in the right knee. In the aftermath, his leg blew up three times its normal size with a horrible wound infection in the joint. The doctor hospitalized him ... but far too late.

Nurses' Notes strangely made little mention, a clarion call for me to get into it. When I reviewed the chart," Aaron continued, "I was more than suspicious. Claimant's counsel said the knee drained a purulent exudate, plain frank pus, for, let's see here; it says three days post op. If true, it would have been obvious, not only from persistent pain complaints, but with abnormal fluid accumulation, an elevated white count, massive inflammation and pus leakage. The in-dwelling drainage pump would have required emptying at abnormally frequent intervals. Activity like that is always carefully charted."

Continuing his file review, Concord remembered. He asked charge and floor nurses, interviewed from each shift, why they made no mention of the swelling and drainage. "It turned out that Dr. Chauncey Lieberman, distracted by a pending divorce that ensued from a tempestuous affair, headed for his hideaway in Oregon for the long July 4th weekend. He knew of the impending problem and, before hurrying off, indifferently prescribed a broad-spectrum antibiotic. He left no orders for a culture and sensitivity. That carelessness eliminated the opportunity during his long absence, for identification of the bacterial growth, and a prescribed regimen of antibiotics to which it was specifically sensitive.

"Too late, it was finally isolated the following week as MRSA, methicillin-resistant *Staphylococcus aureus*—difficult and resistive to treat, necessitating a different med than the physician prescribed. Though on call," Aaron went on, "the doc never responded to iterative hospital pleas. When amputation was later required to stop gangrenous sepsis and potentially fatal clotting, Lieberman surreptitiously removed the Nurses' Notes. The old goat put the original pages that covered his long out-of-town weekend, with all the patient complaints, in his office file, and had the staff reconstruct them anew, according to his 'recollections,' not those of floor nurses. It was all B.S.

"For some reason, I caught the scent of a big rat. I asked Lieberman's office manager, when I went for the initial interview, to get me the 'other file,' after she pulled the one with the feigned notes to look over. Unaware of her flub, she innocently dug up a second folder, in which real-time complaints of pain, swelling, and overt symptoms of serious infection begged notice. The doctor was speechless when confronted."

"Sure," Stansbee replied, "that was the story. Because of the fraud you discovered, the carrier told us to deny liability, and they canceled him, *ab initio.* Two more serious claims while he was bare, the Committee on Medical Ethics suspended his license; his practice ended." Stansbee turned toward the growing stack of files when an office assistant came in with a fresh armload. "He called us with threats of hit men, arson, and so many other things for more than a year ... scared Harriet Browning, our office manager so much, she quit."

Lighting up with another revelation, Aaron remembered a problem case in Seattle as he spread the file on the table: a pre-teen female with chronic renal disease, staged for intravenous pyelography: X-ray studies with IV-injected contrast medium, to outline kidney, ureter and bladder anatomy. "The new intern thought he was opening a vein with a bottle of 5% dextrose and water, but carelessly grabbed the only bottle left on the shelf—one marked for a specific research project—containing a 50% sugar concentrate.

"This one left me with a horrible memory," Aaron said, as he opened the file to his preliminary report. When I answered the hospital administrator's midnight plea at home, he said reverse osmosis occurred almost immediately; the kid's brain shrunk, she began seizing, and didn't stop until death mercifully came the following day. When I reviewed the chart copy, I found no word of the erroneous infusion.

The cause of the seizures in Doctors' Progress Notes was 'indefine.' There had to be a reason. I went to the X-ray lab, plowed through records, and found the original notes, complete with Wite-out™ corrections and an over-write in the intern's hand. The guy threw away his life when he pulled that one, yet blamed me for his loss—'nine years' education and training, gone to hell in a handbag,' he said, while he cried like a baby, when he was fired. 'Some day I'll get you, and screw with your future in return,' he told me in multiple phone demands to cover his scam."

Stansbee added, "I think he was Egyptian ... educated there, so an accent was possible."

They listened to the young doctor's recorded testimony. With no hesitation, Aaron said his high-pitched voice was way off that of the male van driver's heavier, more coarse tones.

"Where is this search taking us, but in ever-widening circles?" Aaron asked.

They took a break and ambled out the ground floor lobby door to a patch of manicured grass between their building and the high-rise next door. Stansbee had to finish the disgusting cigar he began at dawn. Aaron spewed forth caveat after caveat in the down elevator ride, but Ken dallied with that foible too many years for Aaron's dissuasive remarks to work. He'd smoke them when he wished, until he keeled over, he always argued.

"There's another matter ... just occurred to me," Ken said, distracted by a twenty-something female who ran by in a short yellow skirt, while they sat on a misted concrete aggregate bench in the courtyard. He puffed deeply, exhaled enormous rolls of dense smoke from nose and mouth. "I should mention it, anyway."

Stansbee stood up, turned to the vast panoramic Pacific Ocean view, down grade from their perch, inhaled heartily again, and tossed the dying butt into a nearby trash container.

"A month or two ago, a female claims investigator from ... from, what the hell was it ... Manhattan Inter-Insurance Exchange, I believe, popped in unannounced. Cute, tall, slender, gorgeous thing: short black hair, milky skin, and a limp; she asked to review an old case, a claim made in behalf of a minor by the father ... some sort of birth defect. Cerebral palsy I believe ... may have been an anesthesiologist's error. I had to approve the review.

I called the rep's office; spoke with her Claims Manager, a thickly accented fellow, whose name I did not recognize. I knew the V.P. of Claims over there but no one else. We did no work for them recently. Her card had Manhattan's logo on it. I was unconcerned, don't recall her name, too damned busy at the time, as a matter of fact, and asked Kelly, my new assistant, to request the file be retrieved from storage. You help another carrier when you can."

"Jesus, Ken, did she have a right leg drop?" Aaron's heart rate jumped twice normal with Stansbee's remarks. His body turned rigid; facial muscles stretched, flattened wrinkles usually drawn upon his forehead by age, at the corners of his eyes, and across hollowed cheeks. He stood up, walked toward the building entrance, turned to his still-seated ex-partner, and impatiently motioned him to follow.

"Sure-er 'n hell did limp … can't say which leg … beautiful, though, and a very disarming young lady. Said the birth was in 1979, though first notice, she suspected, was in '89, '99 somewhere. I have the storage request ticket. The file should still be upstairs. She came back to look it over when I was in Arizona for a Mandatory Settlement Conference, and left after the girls made her a few copies."

Close to twenty years before, but Aaron's memory, and an immediate wash of guilt, quickly foreshortened the lapse. He ran to stop the elevator and thrust his hand between the closing doors, a long-standing bad habit of his to avoid the waste of time and wait for the next car. Those already inside displayed varying expressions of condescension and disapproval. The sliding brass panels retracted; the twosome boarded; Aaron nervously clicked the fourth floor button the entire ride upward. Stansbee smiled good mornings to several occupants but none exchanged words.

Aaron hurriedly scanned the Five Palms Hospital chart copy to assist his recall, before he reviewed the faded yellow carbon copy of his final summary report to the hospital's insurance carrier. *Reginald Raynes, M.D., administered anesthesia to a maternity patient, Ivana Gosnov, for emergency C-section, though confusingly, the claimant was one Igor Gosnov, M.D.*, Aaron read to himself. "Ken, we have something … something real hot here." he called to Stansbee, while he paced the conference room, their heavy file agape in his outstretched arms.

CHAPTER 16

LOS ANGELES

Saturday morning's light crept slowly into the condominium living room where Iliana lay, inanimate on the couch. Deathly still—it even smelled that way from disuse. Plantation shutters throughout the nicely decorated suite, tightly secured, windows closed, and drapes drawn; the eerie quiet spelled trouble. Traffic on busy San Vicente Boulevard already hummed, even vibrated the building from an occasional passing truck. Unit 21, though, could have been a mausoleum.

Iliana clumsily rolled to her left side, choked, took in a deep breath; yawned with open mouth, pressed index and middle fingers to her left carotid artery to assure it pulsed, and waited. Slow, probably in the low sixties, she thought, but at least her heart functioned. *I guess I am not dead. God, how I wanted to be through with all this.* Her voice inside heralded disappointment: another day to face, more worries, unrelieved recurrent vengeance, and renewed determination, all destined to restore upon her diminutive shoulders, an impossibly burdensome load to bear.

She turned to her right for a view of the wall clock. Blurry—too much so to see the hour hand—it was something twenty five o'clock, either nine or ten, she could not tell. She yawned again. A few sobering face slaps, and a second try, to focus her gaze across the nearly dark room, threw her further into confusion and disbelief.

"My God, Kovi will flip out; I have to get busy with things," she said, as if she conferred with a companion. "Soon it's 11:00 AM and the day will be shot. Maybe an hour and a half on the road with a double latte would help me recover. Kovie's arms will be open, I would hope. He will be anxious to comfort me." It dawned on her that her right hand held something within its tightened fist. She relaxed the grip, and looked with mixed emotions at the uncapped plastic bottle of pain pills in her palm.

She counted them slowly and deliberately. At least four of them found their mark. Tired as she was from the long workday, she knew sleep came, charitably, with their help, and saved her from consuming the rest. Cardio-respiratory failure could just as easily have been the sequel.

Ashamed at her indifference to Kovi—the evil thoughts she nursed while they spoke the night before—she fumbled behind the couch cushion, found the cell phone, and dialed. No answer; she called again, left a short voice mail, arose with a pounding headache, and poured herself a full glass of orange juice to quell her badly parched throat. She peered out the window, down toward the street, and squinted from the stark contrast. Cars below streaked by in both directions; each represented to Iliana, a confused idea, an unidentifiable feeling, an unresolved dilemma, a concept with no beginning, and no end.

This virtual impossibility, if not incapacity, to relate to her thoughts, pushed her closer to panic. A sudden chill ran from neck to low back, and she shook. Usually her clearest thinking times were the early mornings, but not that day. She closed the shutter as fast as she opened it. Her mind then labored on overload; a fuse sparked out, circuits went down, and she teetered on the brink of no control.

"I do not understand your attitude, Love; what did I do?" Kovansk Oligoff asked Iliana in an almost frenetically high voice. He had no idea know how close she came to ending it all, set to check out and leave him holding the bag.

Kovansk's glasses rested awkwardly above his forehead. He clutched his phone tightly, wore only shorts, and as he spoke, paced bare-foot from wall to master bedroom wall in his desert home. He looked down at the glossy floor while he spoke.

He stepped to the hall, paused at his study door. The high-luster, gold plate doorknob suddenly captured his attention. Round and oversized, its parabolic contour bounced back a distorted reflection, almost a mocking image of himself: large in the mid-section, disproportionly small legs, arms, and head, bespoke a new breach, theretofore unrecognizable, in his character.

An innate perfectionist dating back to his early years, augmented by decades of self-disciplined, conscientious study, hundreds of hours of tedious surgery, and almost limitless diagnostics; he could not view himself as he usually did: honest, confident, analytical, motivated, and calm. Lower than a deadly poisonous *Crotalus exsul,* the Red Diamondback Rattlesnake, whose sometimes fatal bites he learned to treat since his desert practice began; he felt serpent-like, demeaned by his own hands, and unworthy. If anyone needed consolation it was Boris Kovansk Oligoff, he thought.

The new, two story, tile-roofed house, far too large for him to occupy alone, he added, then asked what provoked the woman he loved so much to bring such sudden seclusion upon herself. Silence at the other end spawned more queries.

"Are you angry with me? Did I embarrass you when we operated together last time? You knew I was hitting bleeders with the cautery as fast as I could. The patient was fine when we finished. Thrown into the truck windshield, his lacerations, facial bleeding, and so many other injuries, were not near as life threatening as the subdural hemorrhage we found on CT scan. That we quickly decompressed. I knew you were worried about my priorities, but I did the right things, in correct order.

"Did I piss you off when we spoke last night? Something go wrong with our … our venture up north?" He was close to being more concerned over the trail they left in Washington State, than anything else for a moment. "Good God! You have not been contacted by police!" How he wished he were not a part of the shooting. Guilt crept his way again, slowly; but in its usual insidious and unrelenting fashion, it cut deeper and deeper into his consciousness since he returned to work at the week's outset.

Kovansk flashed imagined images of Aaron Concord, his face obliterated by the smashing multiple pellet impacts; at least three liters of blood, or close to half his total volume, probably pooled around the upper level of the cabin. Matters made worse, he drove the getaway car. How did his woman persuade him? He could not help but scream inside.

What would he do if faced with a patient so badly mutilated, yet still alive? It would take three surgeons to save him, and then, only if he were brought to an ER within minutes after sustaining such trauma. He quivered at the prospects.

"Iliana, my *popka ... how ...* why do you contain emotions like this? Iliana? Are you there, sweet *popka?*"

Kovansk's home remained largely unfurnished; most spaces vacuous and unfriendly, lacked a woman's penchant for warmth, supportive of the mind's desire to sit on something soft and brightly colored, surrounded by complimentary accessories, and mutually delightful objects d'art.

His roomy study, replete with a large medical book collection that filled one wall, and half of that adjoining, housed a Chippendale desk—cabriole legs with ball and claw feet—a fine example of antique cherry he bought on layaway while at Harvard and paid for in small increments whenever cash was available.

A contemporary tan leather chair, with brushed stainless steel arms, added eclectic appeal to the desk and a reproduction cherry secretary next to the hall door. Large sliding windows, spilled to a balcony that formed the east wall, allowed morning sun to flood the space with enviable white desert light.

Cream walls, dark walnut pegged and grooved flooring, and a medium blue, floral-pattern sleeper couch for visitors, helped keep Kovansk at home in off-work hours. Otherwise, his bedroom was the only other interior space even partly adorned. Absent any furniture but a new king—without head or footboards—the sheer drapes Iliana bought, which flowed like cascading waves with through-the-house breezes, offered a degree of dynamic aliveness.

"Sweet Iliana," Kovansk practically whimpered and evoked no response but faint sobbing. "You call me, hang up, and I am back with you again, Love; here to help with upset." Iliana dangled in a thin connection to her world, from the few pills she took after the loathsome dream. She listened to his words but was notably non-reactive. Detached and indifferent, she went there before with other men—listened, exuded empathy, digested their lies, misrepresentations, expressions of greed and want, while she heard nothing.

"We have done something we're gravely sorry we even considered. I can understand. I am pre-occupied, how you say, with regret, as you must also be. Please, however, let us not take it out on each other. It is our secret;

we can talk it through. We have an investment; we dreamed of children, raising them together, passing along some of our Russian culture, sharing our talents … maybe one a surgeon, and another, a good nurse like you."

"I am coming, Kovi." Iliana sensed urgency in her lover's voice. Her intuition called out; she had best muster whatever strengths possible and take the initiative to turn things around. Close to ending it all a few hours before, in her own case, coincident despondency in Kovi's voice generated the wake up call.

"Give me two hours. I will treat you to a much-needed night of love. We will watch the sunset from the bedroom balcony, feed ourselves, enjoy some wine, fill the tub with bubbles, and play in candlelight all night." She looked coolly and disapprovingly at her anomalous leg, and with some difficulty said, "I love you, Kovi."

Iliana packed, showered, dressed, and paused before leaving, to call, first to Svetiia, then Bostovitch, no idea what she would say to him.

CHAPTER 17

NEWPORT BEACH

Captured only by faint recall of the file he reviewed, Aaron tried his best to restore absent memories—fill in the blank spaces of his activities after the office received the case. Something not so funny, something he might have regretted, rang loudly about the case, but Aaron could not get a grip on it.

Anesthesiologist, Iliya Gosnov, M.D. wrote to Five Palms Hospital, Aaron's client, in behalf of his daughter, discharged after ten days' neonatal intensive care, nearly twenty years before, with an unexplained right leg deformity.

She just turned twenty-one. The father thought she had a right to bring action for what he described, in his first advisory of a claim, hypoxemia-induced cerebral palsy. Curiously, Aaron found no such diagnosis in hospital records.

Nervously, he tapped fingers on the table with his left hand. Aaron read with interest, licked his right thumb, while he turned each tightly pressed page.

Stored for decades, the file smelled and tasted, too, of a cold, moist, and musty warehouse.

Still on the prowl for the elusive clue to his assailants' identities, Concord flipped photocopied pages of the voluminous hospital charts for mother and baby. He meticulously read medical records, transcripts of his taped interviews and original notes contemporaneously taken, when he conversed with Dr. Gosnov, the only remaining medical witness when the investigation began.

Bland, full of, "I don't remembers, I don't knows," and completely unrevealing; recorded queries and vague responses during an interview with one of the former nurses then on duty, restored memory of a wasted flight to San Jose, in Central California, where the woman retired. Often valuable collateral sources of the truth, a witness such as this elderly RN, only one he found after so many years gone by, often expressed doubt that any of the charted notes were theirs. Almost impossible, Aaron thought. The aged woman's brief and dubious commentary contributed nothing to the unfinished pictures he tried to piece together.

Concord found himself intrigued, though, by the unusual chronology of events and the frank coincidences that defined problems faced by two experienced, attendant anesthesiologists at work in neighboring delivery rooms.

His memory began to thaw. Aaron finally drew the beginnings of independent recall of the Gosnov interview; when he analytically listened to the doctor's confused and guarded answers to almost every question. He sensed circumspect responses then, so reported to the defense law firm, which assigned the case, and thought the same while he replayed the conversation at the office conference table.

"Who is that clown?" Stansbee asked. He could not help but overhear the Gosnov tape playback as he perused his own notes in another file. "That saga has a twist in it somewhere, but time and fading recall just don't scream out anything else to me, at least for now. I'll reserve comment when I do my own file review this afternoon."

Gosnov left his wife, Ivana, at home, too pregnant to go out, and enjoyed dinner with doctor friends—in celebration of his child's forthcoming birth—at the famed Brown Derby on Wilshire Boulevard, a short hop to the hospital. Scheduled for an elective C-section the following week, and asymptomatic of any concerning distress, Mrs. Gosnov encouraged him to enjoy the evening break.

He admitted having consumed "several" Manhattans before, wine during dinner, and an aperitif or two thereafter, before taking two calls on the house phone, brought to the table by their waiter. A description of himself as sober did not add up, Aaron thought. *Doc must have been crocked.*

A 41-year-old, full-term patient expected to deliver at any time, compelled Gosnov to stay close to the hospital that night, per the request of the woman's obstetrician with whom he worked regularly. Epidural regional anesthesia for pain and light IV sedation were on the menu, and with good fetal vital signs, favorable fetal positioning recently confirmed, he could relax while she labored in the early stages. He expected routine, short-term, and shallow analgesia.

The first call, an alert by the patient's OB, brought him to his senses. The bar was about to close in any event. An ironic coincidence, a second call came from his wife, an alert that she arrived in hospital admissions, panicky from unexpected water breakage in bed, extremely painful contractions every thirty minutes, and no drop in the baby's position. Ivana's OB and her anesthesiologist, Dr. Raynes, were on their way for an emergency Caesarean.

Mind on his patient and worried over his wife, Gosnov raced to the hospital with two missions: to attend to his patient, and to be there for Ivana. He swerved into a slot in the doctor's parking lot, at around 2:30 AM, and went straight to delivery on the third floor. He donned scrubs in the doctors' lounge, and, assured Dr. Raynes was attending to his wife, he checked the contents of each anesthetic container on his cart, and the two affixed oxygen bottles, and found all with adequate fill levels.

Hospital protocol dictated, he reported, the practice of all staff anesthesiologists to assure containers on their carts were close to full at each day's end, to make last minute restocking adjustments unnecessary for after-hours' emergencies. He commented that Ivana's anesthesiologist headed the staff at that time and religiously adhered to the standards of practice he dictated.

As Concord read with piqued interest, he realized the possible Russian smack of Gosnov's name, and, when he listened to the interview cassette, it confirmed a definitive accent. Was he on to something, he wondered after he returned the first tape to its envelope? *So, what the devil was the problem?* Aaron asked himself, before reaching the interview point when Gosnov said his patient suddenly became restless.

After starting an intrathecal epidural—the needle is left in situ within the epidural space in the central spinal canal, for continuous administration—pain control was evident, and the patient became comfortable with IV sedation, Gosnov related. He charted medications used and vital signs, in the midst of which the woman recovered enough from the mild pre-op infusion to dive headlong into severe paroxysms of cough.

Aaron knew how the uncontrolled inability to get a breath after long episodes of exhalation coughing, panicked a patient; that the condition generally worsened without quick corrective reaction.

Owing to her heaving, thrashing and ensuing color change for the worse, Gosnov remembered that he called loudly to his colleague in the next room. He needed help. "Reggie ... trouble, come in here quickly," he remembered saying. Raynes arrived; Gosnov's partially sedated charge, struggled after each coughing spasm recurred.

"I asked Reggie to give my patient a quick hit of succinylcholine for immediate muscle relaxation and a pushed bolus of thiopental to put her back under, so I could intubate. With his help and the assistance of two nurses, we got the woman restrained again, and, eventually, I got her tubed," the Gosnov recording continued. Aaron listened intently for pauses, coughs or other signs of stammered, guarded, or feigned responses to his queries. "I remember, though, having trouble with the catheter. It took longer than I would have wished."

While working as a student employee at another hospital, Aaron saw paroxysms calmly countermanded by anesthesiologists many times, yet he sensed that Gosnov spoke with concern in his voice, even with the passage of so many years. The doctor went on to describe difficulty inserting the endotracheal catheter, deeply enough to anchor it by inflating the balloon when it passed below vocal folds of the larynx. Exhaustive spasms would stop as soon as he could artificially breathe for the woman.

"Why didn't he remember how long Dr. Raynes assisted him, while leaving his wife unattended?" Aaron asked Ken. "Why did he say, 'I am unsure,' when asked if he knew whether his wife was or was not anesthetized, at the time he summoned help from her anesthesiologist?

"I assumed not, or Reggie would not have come," the doctor opined later in the interview. Aaron ground his teeth and contemplated the veracity of that comment. *Gosnov must have panicked. Caught with his drawers down, the guy ignored the welfare of his own baby, soon to be born. Raynes, too, may have lost his bearings if Ivana Gosnov were already asleep, while a time bomb ticked in his absence.* Gosnov did testify that he knew his wife's OB was scrubbing, allaying fears of C-section surgery not progressing as quickly as possible. He saw him at the sink, through the glass delivery room window, scouring hands and arms with a nailbrush, soapsuds past his elbows.

Doctor Gosnov sent his own patient to her room after a quick and uneventful delivery, when she responded positively to catheter removal, and breathed well on her own without coughing. Then, he rushed to his wife's side. He described Dr. Raynes, his closest friend, as in control; his wife was out, intubated, breathing normally. The obstetrician opened the uterus, whereupon the cord was found wrapped around the neck of his soon-to-be-delivered daughter.

A hasty and appropriate extrication of fetus and placenta followed. Not until five fear-filled minutes passed, 100% oxygen and several throat aspirations to remove mucous, did Iliana, the newborn, respond, and begin to cry. Unnerving to Gosnov, but to everyone's relief, in spite of the low five-minute Apgar Score, the OB clamped and cut the cord; nurses cleaned her skin, treated her eyes, the baby was wrapped, and taken in satisfactory condition to neonatal ICU.

Uterine blood, darker than normal, signaled a stat blood gas analysis, high priority over other pending laboratory analyses under way, which showed marked hypoxemia—a concerning low oxygen level. Aaron knew pulse oximeters, to continually monitor maternal blood oxygen saturation, were not then in widespread use, nor were solid-state electronic fetal monitoring instruments.

Completely engrossed in what seemed a real-time narrative, Aaron understood the drama that pervaded the delivery room that morning. He studied the Apgar Scores—standard practice to rate a newborn's condition—in Raynes' handwriting, all in the grade one column—muscle tone, though, logged at zero. Serious findings, he knew. Ideally, they should all be twos, Concord considered. *This little one was in trouble, with clear signs, immediately indicative of a problem at or before birth.* Five minutes later, the ten-minute score showed improvement, though marginally. Muscle tone elevated to grade one. The other scoring factors: heart rate, breathing, color, and reflex reaction, doctors upped to grade two. Aaron knew those results still did not portend a strong chance of the infant's survival because of its first five minute scoring.

The OB's dictated and later-transcribed Delivery Report, part of the hospital chart, covered the birth narrative as Dr. Gosnov related it on tape, but it was notably silent as to Apgar Scores, all three entries of which appeared only on an otherwise and curiously blank Anesthesia Record labeled as "page-2," in the hand of anesthesiologist Raynes. As he perused the chart in the conference room Aaron could find no "page-1," nor the blood oxygen analysis report from the lab, after checking both mother and baby's records three times, page by page.

He stomped his feet, though, when he noted within Neonatal ICU Progress Notes, some evidence—though too early for pediatricians to diagnose but causally—of right leg muscle tone rigidity. "Hot damn, Ken, 'right leg muscle tone problems!' Now we're frigging getting somewhere. This may be our little girl … grown into a woman with a bitch to settle." An expansive grin peeled across Aaron's face and his eyes sparkled.

Ken nearly jumped from his chair; he stepped behind Aaron, peered over his cohort's shoulder, followed his fingertip and pointed to what should have been a graphic account of time—an hour or more—that documented initially administered anesthesia, medications, and serially handwritten vital signs taken every five minutes, if not more frequently.

Both men then gasped at what they simultaneously read. A curtain of gray toppled their pleased expressions to looks of disbelief and shock. Neither said a word for too long.

CHAPTER 18

LOS ANGELES

Less than usual traffic on the drive from Los Angeles to Mojave on Saturday, in lieu of a busy gridlock weekday, felt as a pain relief injection might to a suffering patient, thought Iliana, not unlike suddenly dropping into that welcome state of quasi consciousness—apart from the universe and its myriad vagaries. For a change, she did not grimace from the normal snail-like posture of the freeway.

A deliberate series of slow, deep breaths when she entered northbound 405 from the Wilshire Boulevard onramp, a quick sip here and there from her insulated coffee cup, and half the emotional load she housed after arising, seemed to migrate from her basket of woes. When she topped Cahuenga Pass, her mind felt clear, open to any fleeting notion, visual stimulation, and the the temporary relaxation that followed. Every conceivable shade of green erupted upon the Hollywood hills from recent rains. She caught herself with increasing optimism, then applied brakes and shifted to more negative ideations, the arena where her subconscious rested most comfortably.

Brush fires this summer will destroy the refreshing sight. The owners of homes hanging on the slopes like birds' nests will live in fear of fire for the next six months. The grass will soon be brown and summer construction—the incessant bull dozing of hilltops for new homes—will ruin it all. At least our desert won't burn. Return to earlier cynicism came more quickly than desired; she tried again to sweep the alarming voice from her canvas, though as expected, moved closer toward, not away from despair.

Why, she wondered, did Bostovitch brush her off when she called just before she left the condo? What that abruptness was all about, piqued her curiosity. *He's a tough, crafty SOB; skin as thick as tree bark, sometimes, and, completely without conscience. No surprise that he treated me like dirt once he got into my purse. This is a new project, though, one that will leave me nearly broke, and Bostovitch with freshly stuffed pockets.*

Unable to defuse nagging doubts about Concord's demise, Iliana again tried to use Bostovitch and his connections, which infiltrated the Seattle area as they did in California, to assure she met her determined goal.

"Keep up with your procrastinating, young and very pretty lady," he replied that morning, after trying to entice her in a demeaning way to work as an escort for extra income, "and the price could double. It will cost you more as time passes. You must understand risks, especially if he is dead. Accessories to murder one, if my people got caught nosing around his home. I do not need that for pennies on the ruble."

Anger cooked inside during their talk. She remembered with gnawing glee, undetectable from the surface, a little insurance she added to the mixture: the *Minsk*—L.A. paper matchbook she dropped at the shooting scene. Deep inside she chuckled at how that prop, if found, might suggest a link to the greedy Russian if ever it became necessary to frame him. *Maybe I'll use it ... induce him to remove his talons from Svetiia's life before she chooses to end it all.*

Iliana gloated over her craftiness while she drove, turned her steering wheel to change lanes, and noticed two buttons missing from the right cuff of her DKNY denim jacket. Where did I lose them? She wondered? Then thoughts turned elsewhere. She could not remember wearing the garment since their return from Washington.

"No doubt, the target's home is under surveillance," she recalled Bostovitch asserted, "and it probably has been since your possible bungling. Neighbors will be on alert; the man's mother will be under consistent scrutiny of lawmen."

Iliana remembered his every word, was discouraged by his new demands, and her lack of adequate funds—an even greater sore spot if Concord were alive, she pondered. Would Kovi understand, possibly contribute, to enable Bostovitch's further inclusion? She had no idea how to broach that one on her future husband, if things evolved in that direction.

Never, in describing acquisition of the IDs they used, did she suggest to Kovansk, the Russian mob as the source. All he knew, was what she reluctantly informed him: she, "obtained the falsified ID papers in L.A.

"Someone's incompetent investigative activity," she said to reassure, led them in error, toward Aaron Concord's mother. Iliana, poised for a kill at the time, not harassment, as she initially told Kovansk, was incensed at their close shave with discovery, a harmful witness, and the old woman's possible identification, when questioned. She saw and spoke with them both, and could likely pick them on a line-up, a most unsettling thought.

Iliana considered it an irreversible connection unless the mother, too, was eradicated. Kovansk put his foot down, however, was shocked and angered with her suggestion during the homebound flight, and responded with definitive negation at Iliana's suggestion that they push the project to that level.

"There will be no more violence as long as I am around. You wish to be single all your life, struggle to pay bills, never get out of debt; serve the Johns of Westwood like your friend, Svetiia; then you do that. Stay away from me, though, and never call; do not ever come to my home or hospital." She knew those words strayed as far as possible from idle chatter. Kovi screamed them with such frightening resonance, with the peeling of his characteristic deep forehead frown, and so convincingly, there appeared to be no alternatives but to regroup and back off that idea.

Iliana considered the risks of Kovi's absence from her life, but spiteful enough to ignore them as adverse blocks to their future plans, went on to reconnect with the mobster.

Vehicles on Northbound I-5 suddenly began to move slower, her route from the 405 Freeway to the Highway 14 junction that led northeast to the desert. More than a mile ahead, she saw red flashing lights, an accident; and curious rubberneckers who passed slowly around the mess to get a good look at possible carnage. Iliana's daily work life included enough of that, quelling even the slightest curiosity when she arrived at and traversed the scene—at a miserable five miles an hour, forced by the dragging traffic. Then movement halted completely; yet another collision loomed ahead, between a jack-knifed truck and trailer, and two SUVs. She found a few minutes to call Svetiia.

"Why would he be so angry with me?" Iliana asked her close friend. "I refused his offer to become a hook ... ah, an escort." Close to unnecessary condescension, she caught herself, and used the more charitable word to characterize Svetiia's impossible situation, one Iliana would never take on, ever; she repeatedly swore to herself. "I wished to employ Bostovitch's talents for some brief, ah ... undercover work and he thought me a short-changer? The filthy, slimy bastard!

"How dare he insult my intelligence, the choices I make, and destroy you as he is doing, my dearest friend, and closest confidant? "What else did he say?" Iliana inquired. She hoped Chernya Bostovitch did not speak of the shooting in Washington to Svetiia, another troubling dimension to the possibilities of unwanted exposure. *We left enough spots in the snow, as it is, and Svetiia ... no telling with whom she might innocently discuss it.*

Iliana rolled her window down part way to take in the drier air, and sensed the changing aroma of the desert margins: fresher, smog-free, and so much warmer. A tow truck passed, and churned a vortex of the endemic red-brown, arid dust in the center divider, a good indicator traffic flow would resume in a few minutes. Impatient for more input, though, and pounding with concern that Bostovitch could easily extort her, just by mere threat of exposing his involvement to Kovansk; she listened to Svetiia with interest.

"The slob has locked me into sexual slavery; it has become so bad," Svetiia sneered, "and he worries me with his contempt toward you. He said, 'Iliana, the little box of beauty, is a diamond in the rough,' whatever that meant; that you may be coming into some money ... some sort of malpractice action for your leg. Is that true?" Iliana remained mute. "He said ... boasted ... you may be, 'worth more dead than alive.' Tell me, Iliana, what did he mean?" Svetiia trembled with what Bostovitch might do to her friend.

Iliana's worst fear, when her search for the cause of her infirmity began, was the deal she made with the mobster—a Faustian contract with the devil she considered originally—then possibly running short of funds in the midst of his efforts, and his doing with her, what he forced Svetiia to do. She knew Bostovitch could easily sniff out her Kovi, and throw the carefully planned life with her lover into chaos, in the process.

"I ... I cannot discuss my employment of Chernya. It is not that I am unappreciative of your referral. He did, for the most part, what he said he would do. For now, though, let us just say he provided Kovi and me with some identification papers, for reasons I cannot now explain. I used them to do something terrible, something I felt compelled to do, so I could continue to respect myself and perhaps, even live another day."

Too fresh in her memory, as if the day before, she pictured the blast at Concord's upstairs window and what must have happened to him in the aftermath. It almost brought upon nausea as she continued. "Bostovitch seems to think there is more to do, more money to suck from me, I suppose. Where will this go next? I need your help to keep me closely advised, should he say anything about me, what he did, what I have done, or if he might remotely suggest initiating contact with Kovi. Could you do that for me? Svetiia?" She pleaded in a half-hysterical query.

"Bring ... please bring my name into conversation from time to time ... see what he says ... how he deals with it." I would be ruined in a heartbeat if Kovi knew I was still in touch with the man."

"Of course, you know I will. He will have me under his wing for at least the rest of the year if he keeps his side of the bargain. Chernya did tell me, and it felt scary, that he almost has you right where he wants you: short of money and needy. 'She's a beautiful little rabbit,' he laughed. 'Soon she will come to me, whimper one day for a carrot, ready to give old Chernya a good time for training purposes, before going to work like you did.'"

It became clear to Iliana that Bostovitch could soon make a play and then use every means at his disposal to entice her into his illicit organization. Iliana massaged her lower thigh with her thumbs, to temporarily increase circulation. She started the engine, and ended the call with Svetiia. Traffic slowly began to snake past the entangled wreckage.

Warmth from the early afternoon sun poured in from the west with the mild Mojave Desert breeze, and warmed Kovansk's face as he lay, a bit drunk, almost asleep, on the soft, green, double-width front porch chaise. He hoped, until their troubling phone conversation, Iliana would lay cuddled alongside after a night of closeness, but finally resigned himself to inevitable though unwanted isolation.

Blooms on the two native yuccas in his yard—dubbed, "Our Lord's Candles", by local dwellers, for their blanched, ovular blooms atop solitary stocks—added a pleasing fragrance. He savored, too, stimulating wild scents from the fresh, flowery bursts on spiny trunked Joshua trees, the yucca's close relative, several of which bordered the brick patio. Bees hummed at constant pitch, flitted wantonly from one native plant to another, and closed blank spaces in the stillness.

Pages from the first section of the *L.A. Times* flapped on his lap in the light breeze; beads of condensation dribbled down the sides of a tall pitcher of Margaritas on the rocks in the center of the glass top table next to his perch. He worked on his second drink, a heavy one, since he lay down in eager anticipation of his lover's arrival. *Is she coming?* He wondered. *Did I say too much? Did our Washington venture turn her away from the pleasant woman she was, before all the planning began?*

Have these proceedings and the sudden, increased distaste she developed with her leg, changed my sensuous little popka, *into an unpredictable, uncaring, and unaffectionate witch, filled with nothing but hate? Are we going to suffer interminable regret, as I think we may? When will we know of man's fate? I hope … really hope he was not struck, as I have pictured him.*

Too many imagined visual responses, some plausible, others purely speculative, he could proffer for each query his mind conjured. Partially unconscious from the stocky drinks, he allowed the disturbing thoughts to sail by, unaddressed. He needed Iliana's companionship above all. He thought she might provide more insight as time passed, however co-dependent he viewed himself for continuing the relationship under the circumstances.

Kovansk finally slipped comfortably into a light doze and was aroused within a quarter hour, by the unmistakable rumble of Iliana's Passat as it approached the *cul-de-sac*, swerved into his circular drive, and with a short tire screech, stopped just outside the low profile split rail fence that bordered the porch.

Late afternoon sun poured into the house, warmed the western exposure, while the temperature in the bedroom cooled their pleasantly perspiring and prostrate bodies. A lazy breeze swirled lightly around them. They lay nestled together, arms entwined, across the bed, heads hung slightly over one side, exhausted from unbridled love making which Iliana instituted the moment she arrived. She said little else, after leaning over him before he could arise from the chaise, beyond a whispered, "Hi, my love. I'm here to make you happy today, to relax you, make you forget your frustrations, give you loving you so much deserve, and to say how sorry I am for all this turmoil."

No hesitating; this was his usual Iliana. Kovansk was up in a heartbeat. He poured her a quick drink from the near-empty pitcher. The two left a trail of clothes up the stairs, where she surprised him with some new tricks Svetiia suggested she try when they spoke earlier.

Afterward, as they recuperated, Oligoff patiently massaged her right leg, a reminder of how indifferent he was to its partial dysfunction. Just what she needed: a dramatic showing of unconditional tenderness to ameliorate her near continual negative fixation with the extremity in recent weeks. Disarmed by his actions, she rolled over, faced him, and prepared, with a deep expulsion of held breath, to unwind with her side of recent events she theretofore refused to release. Quickly, she abdicated further defenses and energized by his light touches to her breasts, soft caresses on her flat stomach, and unstoppable romantic compliments, they loved once more before she continued.

Iliana reached to the floor for her purse and shamefully withdrew a page she tore from the newspaper. She unfolded it, and read verbatim to Kovansk. Aaron Concord's obituary startled him from his peaceful exhaustion. Shocked back to reality, his senses refocused; he smelled the fresh printing ink, a slight scent of her perfume as she flattened the page. His abdominal musculature gripped into a tight contraction. A surge of nausea delivered an immediate sweat, beads of which tumbled over the deep furrows that lined up across his forehead. He angered, instinctively placed his hands over his eyes, rubbed his forehead with fingertips, then sighed—relieved, in a way, with what appeared to be the evidence they sought of finality.

Kovansk pulled the paper from Iliana's hands, scanned it quickly to himself, eyebrows arched into decided crescents, pulled upward by his tightening forehead, and then read with deliberation, word for word— aloud, as if that made it true. Slowly, he bobbed his head in partial disbelief. Stripped of a comment for too long, Iliana filled the erupting silence.

"I wanted you to see this notice and found myself completely unable to relate the news over the phone," she whispered, then searched his obviously tear-filled eyes for a sign of empathy, approval, or any hint to indicate the article would not provoke one of his terrifying outbursts. "It's over, Baby, it is over. My teaching obligations, except for an occasional fill-in day here and there, are through.

"I can work with you at the hospital whenever you are on shift, and we can finally come home together, at the same time. It's all over," Iliana said again; though deep inside, after hearing the caveats espoused by Bostovitch that morning, she ruminated in sufficient doubt. She already began plans for the absolute verification of Concord's demise during the drive to Mojave.

Kovansk broke her musings. Stammering, he asked if they should not call the two numbers he repeatedly dialed in Washington the morning of the shooting. "Not necessary," Iliana replied. "I tried them both several times from a booth in L.A. They are disconnected."

"What about the mother in Redmond? She saw us in light of day … my Porsche, too, though with our disguises, and may have given police something, how you say, to go on? How can we be so sure that she did not record my license?"

"Bostovitch will…." Iliana clamped her mouth shut when she heard herself, but Kovansk who always listened intently, missed little whenever she spoke. He leered directly into her eyes for elaboration.

"Bostovitch … who is Bostovitch?" he asked with a penetrating glare, then turned on his furrowed frown.

CHAPTER 19

NEWPORT BEACH

Both were astonished at the discovery while they collaborated in the conference room of Concord's former office. Ken and Aaron turned to one another, said not a word, and stared back again—this time incredulously, with mouths agape—at the top left corner of the glaringly blank "Page-1" of the Anesthesia Record. Tucked in at the left margin, close to the clasp, and nearly hidden from view in the dog-eared, photocopied Ivana P. Gosnov hospital chart; Aaron found the square, yellow Post-it™, twice stapled to the page, that cradled scratchy, handwritten notes:

> *Per defense counsel, A.C. removed Raynes'*
> *Anesthesia Record for alternate storage.*
> *"Not to become part of investigation report*
> *or claim file ... very heavy liability exposure,"*
> *said McHibbin. "Lose the original ASAP! It*
> *never existed." Destroy this note if file is*
> *subpoenaed. See my personal file.*
>
> *—A.C.*

"For the love of God, A.C.," Aaron's former nickname at the office, "what the blazing hell does this mean?" Ken looked nervously toward the typing pool area, saw no one within earshot, and whispered close to Aaron's ear as he bent toward the curious entry for closer inspection.

"That's your handwriting; I'd recognize it anywhere. You quoted attorney Mike McHibbin's caveat. That slimy. … His entire group, except the two new guys they recently hired away from Baltomer and Doncier, would lie about anything for a fee. Lausine, Grippi & McHibbin—unscrupulous as they came, back then.

"They won so many of their cases by cheating … ignoring; completely obfuscated medical records … conduct far below good standards of practice. I hated those bottom-feeding, smooth talkers." Stansbee flushed almost purple just thinking about several close shaves they had when they covered for the shady attorneys. He took a chair next to Concord and continued, "Facts were facts, far as I was concerned. If they were bad, we said so, and we easily got the settlement authority we requested. Good, strong defensive position and we'd recommend denial or pound the claimants for a drastically reduced settlement figure. That's how we commonly worked it."

"Unfortunately, I got talked into 'losing' a couple pieces of paper that might have served as the stage to explain an innocent newborn's right leg strictures, even properly diagnose the malady so it might have been treated, instead of accepted as a genetic anomaly," Aaron replied, embarrassed beyond belief at the transgression gone wrong. *How the hell could I have allowed that lawyer to talk me into it?* he asked himself. *I vaguely recall talking to McHibbin before going to the hospital. No one at that point, beside possibly Dr. Gosnov, copied the file or reviewed it, so McHibbin thought removal of the Anesthesia Record and any telling blood gas analysis reports, would mitigate the very prominent potential liability and high-dollar stench of the case.*

Stansbee yawned, stretched perfunctorily, and replied, "That outfit had you earmarked for the kind of character, who, when occasionally asked, could be induced to keep injurious facts in medical records from being discovered by plaintiff attorneys. They could skate by liability when dangerously revealing records of the client were requested through the usual processes: *subpoena duces tecum*—a court order to produce them—medical record release at the patient's written direction, or voluntary surrender by their office.

What never made it to the defense lawyer's file or to the insurer, items taken from the original chart, didn't exist in McHibbin's eyes, and would never appear as evidence in trials or depositions, so long as we got to the chart first. Regrettably, though it was an unusual M.O., it obviated top-drawer legal thought, or memorable defensive strategies."

Aaron's recall, clouded at first, then blanched into a sheet of emergent white that lifted like a window shade—along with a blizzard of biting regret.

Tightened body movements ensued, indicative of shame and dishonor; coupled with shallow breathing, and an irrepressible pounding in his chest. He sensed an acrid taste in his mouth and reached for a sip of the last bit of cold coffee in his cup. In and out of stunned consciousness danced confusing imagery of the late evening when he stopped at Five Palms Hospital, his insured client, to review the Gosnov chart while he worked another case.

Originally there to meet with night shift nursing personnel on that matter, he arrived at the hospital armed with a strict mandate from attorney McHibbin to, "Get the Anesthesia Record out of the file if it's devastating, and pull lab reports on blood gases, if any, at the time of delivery.' Aware he was asked to compromise all legal ethics he could imagine—to cleanse the chart of vital evidence that exposed a breach of duty—he stooped to the lawyer's plane after twelve new files were offered to their office by McHibben earlier that day. That batch of new business was enough to keep several men busy for weeks. Things were slow, he remembered; several investigators were laid-off, temporarily. The insidious circle of non-disclosure, fabrication of facts, and obfuscation, potentially relieved the hospital of some exposure and brought in needed work to Concord, Stansbee and Fitch, as a sideline.

The hospital administrator left work hours before, and placed the Gosnov charts in her unlocked file drawer for Concord to review and copy. He vaguely remembered: he found the Anesthesia Record—a most offensive one at that—far more than a simple embarrassment. He began to recall that a quick study told the story of too long a time lapse within which anesthesiologist Raynes was absent from the delivery room.

During the critical period, implied by Iliana's father when he presented the claim, no vital signs were recorded. "Something about that rings new bells. What could I do but follow McHibbin's instructions, when I saw that?" Aaron asked. He turned palms up, and shrugged his shoulders.

A look of disdain moved across Stansbee's face and he sighed deeply.

"It's beginning to come back." Concord admitted, he succumbed only rarely to that level so long as they worked together. Aaron knew Ken was aware of the shady law firm's practices; that he went along with the few times they bent rules, and failed to disclose the existence of a damaging record.

"McHibbin always said, 'just this once,'" Aaron muttered, "when he needed to keep something from a file that screamed heavy-duty legal exposure. The Gannett case is another I will never forget. Heating pads left under an elderly male patient's back and legs, not wrapped in a towel or blanket per normal protocol, caused the old fellow to suffer horrible burns on his sweat soaked, friable tissue. That led to full skin thickness decubitis ulcers they couldn't aptly treat with his poor peripheral circulation—bed sores just waiting to happen, so large and exfoliative that he died in a few days. I distinctly remember taking the Nurses' Notes from the chart. They 'disappeared,' McHibbin specifically told me to conspicuously remark in my preliminary report. From then onward, the damaging evidence never became manifest.

"We did let that occur, when we darn well shouldn't have," Stansbee replied, "and then we got smart, refused any more files from those clowns—ordinary crooks, decked out in three-piece designer suits. By the way, what did you mean, 'personal file,' where you wrote that the Gosnov Anesthesia Record would be retained, after removal from the chart?"

"I haven't any idea," Aaron said, "maybe personal financial stuff, I don't know. "We've got to find that file now. I have a feeling a few other "lost" bits of records reside there, too, for old time's sake, outside the claim files where they belonged, and not technically subject to subpoena with the files, so McHibbin claimed.

The girl who came in to review the file could be our shooter, but we need to verify. If she is the one, her prints were left in the chart, as she fumbled through the pages during her review.

"My cop buddy and I lifted some good ones from a map the duo likely used in their getaway van. The shooters may have seen the obituary but are apt to use collateral means to verify I was nailed, as they must have assumed when they sped away from the cabin. What happens when the cat's out of the bag? They find out the shot missed me, except for this? Aaron pulled the neck of his shirt aside and showed Stansbee the superficial wound in his left shoulder. My life won't be worth two cents. And that moment could be coming soon."

"I've got her card, I think, in my desk drawer … left it when she reviewed the file. Do you think she saw the note you inserted?"

"That may be the reason she's after me, for all I know."

Ken rushed down the corridor to his office and returned, smiling, with the business card given him by the woman. He dialed the number of her purported Claims Manager, that she wrote on the back, and turned to Aaron with a perplexed look when a man with a deep foreign accent answered.

"What's up with the weird look?" Aaron whispered.

Stansbee covered the mouthpiece and replied, "A guy just answered: '*Minsk*—L.A.'"

Ken hung up, redialed, and again the same voice said, "*Minsk*—L.A. Who the hell is this?"

CHAPTER 20

NEWPORT BEACH

"It's coming together, Ken. I picked up a matchbook that morning, printed with a *Minsk*—L.A. logo, in the area where some of the spent shotgun shells lay. Couldn't help but wonder, at the time, why or how paper matches from such a place could appear so far out on Puget Sound. My cop friend, may have pulled prints from it at the Sheriff's lab in Shelton. Should they match any of those taken from the map in the van; it will be all too interesting."

"We've got to take a drive to Los Angeles and check out this *Minsk* outfit," Stansbee replied. "Why did the young lady give me that number, unless she was a phony ... set it up beforehand, and wanted you instead of the file? Who might be the stand-in 'Claims Manager,' she said was her boss? He must have waited by the phone when she alerted him we were about to meet. A female answered for the supposed carrier; I'm sure of it. I assumed her to have been at the company switchboard. She transferred me to the 'boss' ... I thought. What a scam."

"Kenny, my friend, you were duped, tossed a wild one by some folks who played their game quite well; don't you think?"

Stansbee blushed; they both assumed labored looks. The woman pulled a perfect con; more importantly spoofed a seasoned private investigator, trained to be observant and suspicious of nearly anything. "Am I getting old, soft, or just plain negligent in my duties, A.C.?"

"I think you're simply aging. Maybe you should consider retirement ... a move up north near our place."

"Not with shootings going on like this. I'd be safer walking the streets of downtown Los Angeles at midnight."

Past the hour for the office staff to leave, Stansbee and Concord, still hard at work, felt, and looked exhausted from the long siege of file reviews. Many they checked from front to back after the Gosnov matter turned up, just in case the prime suspect—who labeled herself as a claims rep--was not their objective. Nothing else during the long day sparked more than idle curiosity, other than the big problem: where was the "personal file" to which Aaron referred in the note he left in the chart? Both considered the missing Anesthesia Record of great materiality.

"At least we have something to go on, in the interim, if we assume the woman's current name is Iliana Gosnov. No name appeared on her business card, the reason I called for the department head to verify her position. No idea," Stansbee continued, "what she threw at me when she came to the office the first time, and I was out of town when she returned for the actual file review."

"Well, let's run her through a few databases and see if she's around," Aaron replied, while he downed a half can of flat cola in three noisy gulps. "That's easy now. Thirty years ago, we'd have foot-pounded for days through the Hall of Records, all the municipal courthouses around the area … a few calls to law enforcement friends ... lots of follow-up door knocking. Now we hit the computer with a few keystrokes and, voila!. We have leads no end."

Stansbee's personal assistant and the firm's office manager entered the conference room, purse in hand, expectant she would leave for the day. Her plans quickly changed with whiny pleadings from both men to help with the computer search.

Stansbee left the cluttered conference room to search for Aaron's old, private financial files for starters. He kept them in a secured drawer in his office since Aaron retired, and hoped they'd not been culled to provide space for files of more recent vintage.

Ken exhaled deeply, wished for a deep drag from a fresh cigar, but the rule against smoking in the suite was his. He could not indulge. The lanky investigator looked longingly north toward the Santa Ana Mountain profile, through undraped floor-to-ceiling corner windows his desk faced.

Enshrouded in early evening mist; they looked far away, but still beckoned. How he would rather hike through the upper reaches of Trabuco Canyon, as he often did on weekends, than stand on the front stoop of identifying a possible murderess, he thought; then turned with resignation to unlock the file cabinet.

Aaron anxiously peered over Pamela Manners' shoulder while she tapped into a countrywide system to which the office subscribed, and entered, Gosnov, Southern California. Though the father called her Iliana when interviewed by Concord, the hospital chart only referred to her as "Baby Gosnov."

At least they had a possible first name, and a firm date of birth, Manners noted. The latter permitted far more focused retrieval possibilities than would otherwise have been the case. Still, without confirmed given and middle names or a last known address, she would have to take several approaches and use two different programs. The clock ticked too slowly for Aaron. He twitched nervously and tapped his feet noisily on the hardwood floor, on the forefront of his shooter's identification.

Nothing interesting turned up in the first search, other than Ilya Gosnov, M.D., Iliana's deceased father, and his last known address on Los Feliz Boulevard in Los Angeles. More than twenty years old, it would be of low priority, though, eventually that old locus and four other Gosnovs the first search revealed, would require checks. One of the young upstarts in the office could easily hit those in a day or two, Aaron thought, armed with a description of the woman from Ken, and others who saw her in the office.

Pamela Manners straightened her back, adjusted her cheap reading glasses, moved her head closer to the monitor, and with piqued attention, scrolled down the page that appeared. Aaron followed her lead and did likewise.

"Hmmmm," Pamela whispered, "looks like we may have something from the Department of Consumer Affairs—Board of Registered Nursing—RN license application in the name of Iliana O. Gosnov ... Santa Monica residence address. That what you are looking for?" she asked, while she proudly pointed to the entry on the computer screen. She looked with a questioned frown at Aaron, for an OK to go home for the night.

"You take off, Sweetheart; thanks for the help. Could well be our girl ... same name as Dr. Gosnov's daughter, in whose behalf he presented the claim that precipitated our original investigation. I'll take over from here." Aaron slid his chair closer to the table and tore at the keyboard with renewed gusto.

"Ken, I think we found our over eager trigger finger!" he yelled down the corridor to Stansbee, with hopes afterward that the office was otherwise vacant. Nothing had yet been said of the ordeal to the staff. The men wished to keep their efforts under wraps until they made their next move. "Her DOB is the exact date of Ivana Gosnov's admission to Five Palms. This is our shot gunner, without question!"

Locating nurses was basic Skip Tracing 101 for the firm. Aaron knew, after initial licensure, state requirements mandated reapplication every two years, with proof of thirty hours' continuing education. *We would soon be able to get a current address if the listed one is out of date,* he mumbled to himself. *Think I'll take a drive to Santa Monica tonight, to see if my little crippled friend still lives at the license address. I'll stay up there tonight and give myself plenty of time to make morning cold calls, too, should the need arise.*

The chances of a nurse working night or graveyard shifts were good, Aaron knew, so the extra time he might have while he waited around between shift ends would permit calls on some of the other Gosnovs listed as L.A. area residents. *11:30 PM would be good for Iliana Gosnov, and a second stop at 7 to 8:00 AM as a back up. That allows room to size up the* Minsk *place, as well. Guess I'll just walk in there, innocently ask for 'Iliana,' and see if that query generates any notable trepidation.*

"What are you doing A.C.?" Stansbee asked when he emerged from his office, to find Aaron in suspiciously deep contemplation. "If you're thinking what I think you are, No! You're not going alone. This smells of real trouble; we're driving together, like old times in tight situations. We'll use our phony IDs, my pickup truck, and phone company uniforms, if you can still fit in yours. I'll pack my .38 snub nose and we will watch each other's backs; right?"

Aaron stammered for words. "This is damned serious stuff; you're right, if we have our mystery female identified as it now seems."

Stansbee waved three files marked: *A.C.–Personal,* then slapped them on the table in front of where Aaron sat, still on the edge of his chair. He gleamed with pride at having discovered them so quickly. That the folders were where they should have been was an uncommon rarity around the busy office.

Concord opened the thickest one first, which covered the period 1998 through 2002. Right away he discovered an Anesthesia Record, "Page-1," stapled to a blood gas analysis report. Each bore the name, Ivana Gosnov. The documents, absent in their earlier chart inspection, screamed for explanations, and filled the gaps in the Gosnov hospital chart.

"Sure enough," Aaron said. He shook his head, lips pursed and eyes glazed, and regretted the reality that, years before, he must have removed the important components precisely as asked by defense counsel.

"Why the hell did I allow myself to be prostituted by that flake lawyer? The presence of those records would have been keys to the establishment of hospital liability and that of Doctor Raynes—Ivana Gosnov's anesthesiologist. I do remember the telling papers, now that they're in front of me again." Not proudly, he held them up for Stansbee to see. His ex-partner sat quickly; both carefully studied the critical notes entered by Raynes, contemporaneous with events that transpired before and during the C-section early that 1979 morning.

Penned lines on the crosshatch-printed background, connected dots from left to right. Each represented a point in time—every few minutes, from the start of medication administration. Some systolic and diastolic blood pressure levels, pulse and respiration rates, and general status checks were appropriately charted, but only early in the chronology.

What stuck out like sore thumbs, however, were unusually long spans with no time reference marks. These lines formed a glaring hole—the investigators knew, if critiqued by an expert witness—which could open doors and explain an undetected hypoxemic episode.

Shocked by a sixteen-minute hiatus in recorded vital signs, it was clear to Concord and Stansbee that Raynes either left his patient for that period, during which she was fully anesthetized, and required one-to-one surveillance, or that, very negligently, he was there, and simply made no record of vital signs for the significant period. Either way, the lapses called out to any onlooker that Doctor Raynes was grossly inattentive, and did not perform in accord with common anesthesia practice standards.

Such a breach of duty defined malpractice per se, both men agreed, and might have dictated initiative for insurers, with that information in hand, to accept at least some responsibility. Supported by the blood gas analysis report that confirmed a dangerously low oxygen level, any defense attorney with integrity could not have looked the other way, and would have characterized the case as one with potentially high-end exposure.

Aaron sensed the urgency expressed by the carrier's unscrupulous attorney those many years ago. Absent the important file components before them, to confirm ostensible reasons for the baby's contraction of cerebral palsy, a soft look at liability would have been taken.

"No wonder the woman might be less than happy. Her lawyer may have turned his hands ... palms up." Stansbee gestured accordingly. "She was likely told it would be too speculative to invest a lot of time and expense prosecuting the case, without more tell-tale proof of neglect."

Aaron replied, "her father as the initial causative factor, and a dead, culpable anesthesiologist, putting forth a defense would have been an uphill climb. That left me, Aaron Concord, as a suspect ... larger target, better said. I was the only one in the picture still alive and vulnerable, for having obfuscated facts by slipping out material chart components. But could that precipitate murder?"

"It sure might, from a psycho's perspective," Stansbee snapped. "I wish you didn't do that, if we did get a handful of new cases in exchange for the gesture. You could have been six feet below the grass right now ... and for what? To save our insured hospital client some money ... make a crooked attorney look good?"

Traffic on the 405 Freeway, stop and go as ordinary during evening rush hour, delivered 300,000 thousand workers from their jobs in Orange County to homes in Los Angeles, the San Fernando Valley, even points beyond. Concord and Stansbee, off to the big city in Ken's white 2003 Ford F-150 pickup truck, idled in the center lane, dressed as telephone servicemen. Both wore tool belts with phone receivers, disguised walkie-talkies for fast one-to-one communications.

"Just like old times," Aaron quipped, "as we often did when engaged in difficult subpoena service, when we located recalcitrant witnesses, or conducted surveillance on claimants we thought exaggerated debilities. I did enjoy those days. Remember that night I was chased by that big hulk of a fellow along an upstairs apartment building balcony, angry as hell after I served a summons. You were the getaway driver. I lost the toss and had to hand papers to the big ironworker at the back end of his apartment building ... after local bars closed—the only time he was ever home."

"Never forget; I watched you knock. He opened the screen door a crack, looked at the cover sheet, then pushed the door off its hinges and bounded after you with a vengeance. You took a desperate leap at the front staircase … must have cleared ten steps and he did the same, but somewhat drunk in all probability, missed his landing. The poor SOB went ass over teakettle, into a pile on the front sidewalk.

You jumped in the car; I was already on the move, and we hauled tail out of there. A look in the rearview mirror, I saw no movement in the crumpled mass you left behind." Both men laughed heartily. That experience typified so many similar and memorable close scrapes that became routine for investigators after a few years in the field.

Minutes later, Stansbee emerged from the restroom with no moustache and a razor in his hand, light designer shades, and the black wig he often employed when activities required an appropriate ruse. Hunched forward, he appeared remarkably shorter and bore no resemblance to the tall, healthy basketball player type he normally presented. "Iliana has never seen you; so you'll be the straight one, use your Boston twang. I'll speak with my southern drawl, in case she's there or should the current resident describe us to Iliana in later conversation. I don't want our subject to know I am the Stansbee she met, or she'll freak and consider taking me out, too."

More than an hour of stop and go, Stansbee and Concord merged onto the westbound I-10 Freeway; then sailed at seventy-five toward Santa Monica, where, at 1016 Brixton Avenue, Iliana lived, according to data base information. Once they confirmed her name, they negated other leads from collateral sources like phone listings, post office boxes, and police R & I, before they left the office. Curiously, Iliana Gosnov left few trails around the city, as would most residents living normal working lives.

"Good evening, ma'am," Stansbee said to the young woman who answered the door. He used his well-rehearsed accent.

A small porch lamp above the doorbell threw just enough light to illustrate her features. "Hello, wh … what is the problem?" the thirty something female responded. She looked over both investigators from head to toe, clearly tried to discern whether they were cops, the men thought. Earlier she donned white shorts and a pale yellow cotton blouse, unbuttoned low enough to reveal the upper curves of alluring breasts—a

European pulchritude if ever there were one, Aaron thought. Along with long blonde hair, naturally lustful lips, and an almost perfect face, her subtle accent barely betrayed foreign extraction. He flashed a glance toward Stansbee who implied by his quick responsive expression that she was not their suspect.

"We're in the area checking lines … ah … we have some confusion in names and accounts. Now, this is 1016?"

"Yes," the woman answered, more suspiciously this time.

"And your name, Miss?"

"Svetiia … ah … Kronoff." She replied guardedly, only after evident hesitation and notably nervous shifts in her gaze.

"Might you know an Iliana Gosnov?" Aaron asked with a straight face.

The woman turned red, then shifted toward ashen gray. Lost for words, her eyes dropped to the porch. Her cell phone chimed, an excuse to end the encounter. She said nothing in reply and slowly closed the door.

CHAPTER 21

MOJAVE DESERT

Kovansk and Iliana sensed the awkwardness that suddenly dropped over the room like a stage curtain. He looked at her more than curiously, with sufficient serious concern that she felt exposed and frightened, when she carelessly unleashed the name, Bostovitch. Iliana could tell by his demanding expression; she would have to provide her lover some details, plausible explanations to outline some, but not all, of the mafia *brigadier's* involvement, in order to quell Kovansk's growing apprehension.

How far do I go? she asked herself while she gathered wits. *If I told him everything—the money I paid the mobster, and what we have recently discussed—it would throw Kovi into a* grand mal *seizure. Should I say Bostovitch was hired to verify Concord's death and if I did not succeed, to finish the job, Kovi would be through with me. I would have few assets, and he ends up with most of Papa's money tied up in the hospital partnership. Where would I go? Drop fast, I would, into* Dante's Inferno, *the way of Svetiia, with no means to climb out?*

Kovansk persisted and cut short her musings. "I asked you; who is this Bostovitch? I want an answer, now! His forehead flattened, then the typical rippling began again and, harrowed it into a field of wrinkles. Iliana knew he could soon fly into a rage and did her best to concoct hurried explanations that might temper his impatience.

Self taught in the art of distracting men when their thinking diverged from her intentions, Iliana rolled toward Oligoff, pulled back the sheet to expose his body and purred softly. Her fingers crawled over his face and neck while he spoke. Her lips found his. She whispered while she nudged him, "Kovi, you know how deeply I love you, how I wish to be your wife, a devoted mother, and bear your children. Let me show you again how much you mean to me."

He turned his head in protest; his complexion reddened, and he tried to continue with more determined interrogation. His words were muffled, however, by the gentle brush of her cheeks, lips, and finally her breasts, when she slowly swayed them across his opened mouth, for him to savor. Iliana slid her nude body over Kovansk, and with little additional encouragement, sent him into starry oblivion, for the third time that evening.

Still panting from expended passions and close to delirium, Kovansk closed his eyes, then lazily opened them to find Iliana peering deeply, primed, she hoped, for continued discussion. This time on her terms, she prepared to deliver a unilaterally self-serving report in partial response to his earlier-expressed concerns. *Maybe now Kovi is supple enough to absorb only what I wish him to know,* she uttered to herself. *He should be satisfied for the present. We can move forward, make dinner, and love again thereafter.*

"Bostovitch, an investigator and the head of a finance firm," she lied well, and without conscience, "was an old acquaintance of Svetiia. Of course, you have not forgotten her. Too often, I used to watch you drool, study the anatomy of her lovely legs and bottom, as she waltzed in skimpy clothing around our apartment like a seasoned ballerina. She always eyed you similarly.

Kovansk said nothing, though he pictured the diminutive woman and recalled the innumerable fantasies he enjoyed, mostly about frolicking in bed with her. While tempted, and even teased close to his tolerances, a few times when he and Iliana had their differences; he never made a move.

Yes, it was Mr. Bostovitch," Iliana went on, after the brief jolt of jealousy, "who arranged the location of Aaron Concord. Also, he advanced funds against the value of my father's contested estate, which allowed us to immediately extract $250,000, most of which we used to acquire our interest in the hospital. All the confusion after Papa's departure and my mother's efforts to get her hands on estate funds, I avoided a drawn out probate case that could have taken forever to settle. Bostovitch's lawyers, took an assignment from me to pursue the case in my name thereafter, charged me half of the potential recovery, in exchange for the immediate partial disbursement. It was an unconscionably large portion for them, I know; but you needed the money right then, to act on that narrow opportunity. They agreed in the process, to take what remained, that they might recover, and you got your hospital partnership.

"I know … should have told you this before, but I feared you would never approve such a large compromise in my inheritance. It got you into the hospital, didn't it?" She'd throw him on the defensive and he might back down, Iliana craftily pondered. "Weren't you pleased that happened?"

Kovansk said nothing, remained fist-clenched and shocked.

"Bostovitch is involved in … ah … many business enterprises, is very successful, and I trusted him to deliver on his investigations, also. He did so, given the temporary hitch, when he mistook Concord's mother's residence in Redmond, Washington, for his home on the Hood Canal. At least you and I eventually found the man, based on most of his investigation."

"He sounds like someone less than legitimate, Iliana. Is this man, how you say, above the board? Can he be trusted never to reveal his activities? I cannot have this hanging over my head for the rest of my life—always wondering if he will want more money as time goes on, and he sees our affluence grow.

"I want to know," Kovansk demanded with increasing fervor, "have you … is this full story? Is there anything more going on, which I do not know? Are there others you wish to harm? What was the reason behind your anger with this Concord fellow in the first place? There is still too much secrecy between us."

Kovansk's worries flowed more rapidly than Iliana grasped them. She stared vacantly toward the ceiling, barely tuned into to his queries; her hands fidgeted, fingers interlocked, then relaxed, and her respiration rate almost doubled. It concerned Kovansk that more should be said, and he would have it no other way. This time he wished all the answers, not simple palliative responses, half-truths, or blatant lies, he told her. He insisted he would continue to press until she stepped forth and told the truth.

The sonofabitch, she lamented silently; *so typical of a man who takes, control. He gave me no leave to deal with issues this important to me, in my own way, and at my own pace … no appreciation of the degree to which I planned to stop Concord from further dishonest screwing around with medical records.*

The mobster, nothing more than a paid thief, had to be halted, repaid for his intrusion, that cost me so much, if not my ruination. It possibly precluded a life of normalcy without this foot dragging behind me like a ship's anchor.

"All right, Kovi, I paid $2500 for Bostovitch to find Concord and to assist me in crafting a ruse to gain access to the file in his former office in Orange County. There I confirmed it; the Anesthesia Record was missing from my mother's delivery chart, as it was from the original. That and a BGA report were extracted by Concord at the outset of his investigation, when Papa made a claim against the hospital in my behalf—just after I turned twenty-one.

My mother's anesthesiologist died shortly before. I played the role of an insurance claim investigator, on the advice, and with the assistance of Bostovitch, who was well versed in such *sub rosa* activity. He … ah … set me ah … provided me a phony ruse, identification for the caper, as he did for our trips to Washington State … cost me close to $5,000."

Kovansk Oligoff could tell the forging of documents and undercover work advocated by Bostovitch suggested he was not the head of a legit financial firm as she contended earlier. "Sounds like a common crook, *popka* … does anything below legal, for inordinately high fees. Is not true? Knowing of Svetiia's current illicit occupation, I suspect mafia connections. Are you headed in that direction, too?" he inquired with an icy, inquiring stare and turned away.

"You have murdered this Concord and it was with my help. Said before; I am in jeopardy along with you; stuck, not only with that but possibly becoming a future hostage of this common thug you introduced into our lives. Jesus Christ, Iliana! What the hell are you doing to me?"

Kovansk raised his voice to a harsh yell, then thought of her incredibly sensitive and recently lustful sexual proclivities. He did not wish those qualities compromised, he settled back to the pillow, exhaled deeply with resignation, and shook his head as might a father with a teen-age son who just wrecked the family car.

"Iliana sat up, perched her body on the bed's edge, and cradled her head in her hands to prepare an appropriate retort. Kovansk studied her irresistibly good looks, near perfect body: the way her porcelain white breasts, with large nipples, were firm, naturally up-lifted, and robust. His critical survey dropped to beckoning hips and then to her right leg, malformed and partly dysfunctional, never before the object of his disapproval. However, that night, for the first time ever, it seemed anomalous to him; aberrant, if not almost disgustingly unattractive, quite unlike her friend, Svetiia's alluring lower extremities to which Iliana unconsciously directed his attention with her earlier sarcastic reminder.

He remembered how Svetiia, a most unusually lovely Ukraine woman, dressed in a revealing teddy around their apartment in the evenings— sheer, open-backed, and low-cut in the front—designed, he thought at the time, to titillate and taunt. *Damn, he thought, I'm stuck with a killer and Svetiia, always a picture of sensuality, as smart as Iliana, though broke, is serving sentence, for some reason, as a hooker. Where is my taste, 'in my mouth,' an American might ask?*

"*Popka,*" he called toward the *en suite* master bathroom, where she went to bathe, "I cannot go on. We will discuss this further in the morning."

"Tomorrow then," Iliana answered while she turned on the steamy water. Her cell phone rang. Outside her view, Oligoff withdrew it from her purse, noted Svetiia as the caller and, before the signal repeated, he turned off the power.

Lovely as she is, and as good a lay as she must have become with all her practice, she should not be in contact with my Iliana. Same goes for this Bostovitch character ... two sub-culturals we do not need in our lives.

He rushed downstairs, quickly entered her number into his cell contact list and discovered Bostovitch was not listed. *Somehow, when I call Svetiia, I will be obtain that man's phone contact and get on his case like a stubborn osteosarcoma tumor infiltrating a lumbar vertebra.*

CHAPTER 22

LOS ANGELES

"Sweet Svetiia Kronoff," Stansbee said, when they reached his truck, parked across the street from the woman's triplex unit. "She knew the name, Iliana Gosnov; for sure." They rounded the corner, turned into the alley behind the deteriorating, 40's vintage, lap-sided structure and, three lots from the intersection, identified the open carport behind it. One space pertained to each residence. The slot marked, *1016*—occupied by a 1999 Honda that bore vanity plate, "NO SVET," they presumed belonged to the recalcitrant informant.

Stansbee called a source to identify the registered owner and confirmed it was the young woman's car. Earlier, they ran Iliana Gosnov through DMV records and, while no vehicles were registered in her name, her driver's license also traced to the Brixton Street address. If not living there now, both were confident she certainly did in the recent past. "C'mon," Stansbee said, "let's go back and press her for Iliana's whereabouts. A second try may produce better results."

Aaron moved to the door, knocked hard six times in a rapid staccato. He heard bare footsteps approach on the hardwood floor and muffled one-sided conversation. Kronoff spoke on the phone. He pressed his ear to the peep hole, but could not discern her words. The door opened with a surprise. Concord pulled back and excused himself for bothering her again. Svetiia rudely answered, "I have never heard of that woman. Don't fricking bother me again." She tried to slam the door, but Aaron caught it with his shoe, and left a four-inch gap to forcibly extend the conversation.

"We know she lived here in recent years; where is she now, please? We don't wish to bill you for her recent long distance charges. It's very important we speak with her." Aaron smiled to allay fears they might be cops, but it didn't work. This time the door closed with a harsh bang. "Leave me alone," the woman yelled. The deadbolt clicked shut. Curtains in the window next to the door snapped closed and lights in the room dimmed.

"Looks like I spooked the girl," Aaron said, seating himself back in the truck cab. He snapped his seat belt. "This one covers for our subject or I've lost my intuitive touch. Let's drive around the block, park a few houses up the street, and stake the place until 11:30 to 12:00 or so, just to rule out Miss Gosnov won't appear after working a night shift close by." Iliana never showed. Stansbee and Concord, with little time to complete their planned work, departed immediately.

Southbound on Robertson Boulevard, thirty or so minutes from Santa Monica, the investigators slowed and began to look for *Minsk*—L.A. when they approached a deteriorating area, replete with small body shops, liquor stores, creepy spaces for lease, and Persian restaurants. "Let's just amble in, order beers, and after a few minutes, pop the question," Stansbee remarked. "We'll see if we get the same indifferent response as we did from our tight-lipped female informant in Santa Monica."

"There it is," Aaron said a few minutes later. He double-checked the address copied from the matchbook, and surveyed the locale. It fell far short of instilling comfort; men of all ages wandered aimlessly along dimly lighted sidewalks. Some staggered; some carried paper-bagged bottles in one hand or beneath an arm; sleazy hookers loitered on corners, and police patrol cars were conspicuous by their absence.

A blue and red neon banner identified the lounge, visible from the street in a corner of the back-painted front window. Tough looking, a large man with the build and appearance of a wrestler stood stoically in front of the open door—arms folded, feet spread apart. He appeared ready for most anything. A bifurcated red velvet curtain dangled across the opening and further impeded easy entry. Hardly a tavern that beckoned two well-heeled martini types from Orange County, both wondered whether this inquiry showed good judgment.

Stansbee parallel parked a few doors away, turned off the engine and spun the cylinder of his loaded .38 Smith & Wesson snub nose revolver. He replaced the pistol in its holster, concealed in the small of his back by the bulky jacket he wore. Aaron hesitated, thought again that they might have erred, when they opted to handle this aspect of the chase themselves.

"Please, Ken, go easy with that thing, only if we need a life saving distraction and a quick exit," he warned. His cohort simply smiled, though a terse one that required a bit more effort than usual. Ken left the truck doors ajar to ease their quick escape if required, and motioned Concord toward the blue and red lights.

The men brushed past the bouncer, ignored his imposing look and casually pushed him aside. He followed them part way in and turned to reestablish his watch, when he saw them confidently walk to the rear of the room and approach the curved bar.

"Two drafts," Aaron said gruffly once they seated themselves by the register on chrome-framed, backless stools with crudely sewn, slip on, black vinyl covers. While the red head female barkeep slung overflowing glasses to the bar, they both noticed being under the curious scrutiny of a heavy-set bald man in a booth behind them. Attired in a black dress shirt and knit tie, suede coat, and light gray slacks; shades rested on his shiny crown. It took but a few minutes for him to take the stool next to Aaron, and to size him up with a steely head-to-foot survey. Leaned forward, elbows on the bar, Stansbee's holstered piece popped into view; he fast realized, when he sat up straight to take his first sip. He pulled his jacket down again.

"What I can do for you boys?" the glossy-domed leather coat asked Aaron in a loud accent—Russian, Concord presumed. When the stranger nudged him as if an old friend, their host grinned, and showed his two silvered upper front teeth. "You boys from West or South Bureau? What you look for? You know we run clean shop, right? No hookers, no dope here … *nyet*. You from vice, narco, some new crime unit? They send you to me for training, eh?" He laughed with a gut shaking, deep wheeze.

"Not fucking cops, just wanted a quiet beer," Stansbee answered, all but ignoring the man and his query. After a blank glare toward the bartender, he interrupted what would have been an unpracticed, if not incredulous response, if from Aaron.

"Well, then what are you?" the intruder asked more softly.

Stansbee looked at Aaron, briefly back toward the inquirer and replied, "Looking for Iliana … you know her? Gosnov, as I recall."

The Russian leaned away from Aaron, again looked cautiously at them both, dismounted his stool, stepped quickly behind Stansbee, and drew a husky Glock pistol from his shoulder holster, assured that none of the few patrons, who remained at that hour, observed his move.

He whispered to Stansbee, while he pinched his neck in a vice-like grip. "Now, why not just pass me your piece without fuss, and let's take a walk outside ... back door, if you please. He motioned with a nod of his head for the bouncer to accompany them. Stansbee complied without looking back.

Oh my God, here we go, thought Aaron as Stansbee dismounted his stool, followed by the bald man. *We're done for, I can feel it.* Aaron followed the two and the bouncer brought up the rear, in a single file column past open, musty smelling bathrooms, a stockroom overrun with empty beer bottles, and outside to a small, unlighted parking lot in back.

"Now, who the hell are you two and what do you men want? And, why this sweet little .38?" the bald man asked before frisking them. He dug the phony identifications from their pockets, looked them over perfunctorily, and gave their wallets back. "Eh? Why the sudden silence from talkative telephone men who ask for ... er ... ah, some ... ah, Iliana?" You are not the law; they call me before they come in ... always. So, who are you?"

Stansbee responded when Aaron fell mute. "We have a thing for her, met her at the hospital. She said to look her up here if we ever wanted to reconnect. Svetiia said, too, that we might find her here these days."

How the hell did Kenny pull that one from his hat so fast? Aaron wondered, when he noticed a clearing expression on the gunman's face and relaxation of the hand that held the deadly Glock.

"Goddamned Svetiia, ah, er, who might, ah ... this ... ah, Svetiia be," the shaved head asked with a sneer, but more insipidly. "Sure," his eyes shifted side to side, "Iliana used to come here for drink and some Russian chatter from time to time, but she has moved ... don't know where she went."

"And your name is ... Mister. ...?" Aaron asked as if he were a cop.

"They call me, 'C.' I, Bostovitch, own this dump—a touch of old Moscow, do you think?" He stashed his pistol and nodded to the bouncer who returned to his post. "I should be concerned but you clowns seem more dumb than curious. If I were you, I stay far away from *Minsk*. Ever read the *Vremya Novostei*? Eh? It is Russian news medium and I, Cheryna, am often mentioned—not so nicely—in write-ups. They are not good to

me, though I run clean shop, always careful to go with law. Between three," Bostovitch went on, with a wide yet ominous smile, "I am lo *Bratva* boss. Look that up. You might not wish to fuck with our *vo zakone*. Very rough bunch."

Stansbee and Concord, petrified on the inside, realized they struc cord with the Russian Mob, and that, likely, their host was a higher-up the L.A. sub-organization.

"We can part friends, can't we? All big mistake? I buy you beers : say to you: 'do not come back again.' Now ... go on ... back inside all big misunderstanding, eh? You do not want Iliana. Right? And Sv ... nothing but a commoner. Stay away from her. A raving beauty, smart, oh yes; we would all like her for arm candy; but she became working girl."

He patted Aaron's shoulder, hard enough to show he was far f weakened by his approximate fifty-five years. Concord noticed the l of his right hand—covered with a large green and red bear head tatto looked gnarled and strong. The left bore an eight-point star. A face de marred with scars, both quickly concluded by nervous glances at another, that they more than met their match. Escape with their became a new objective.

Stansbee and Aaron held their cool throughout the harro experience, though, as if they did not take the situation seriously. aura of cockiness likely saved them, both pondered as they re-entere lounge, C in the rear this time, his semi-automatic beneath his coat pressed it against Aaron's low back as they passed the filthy restroom: cluttered storage alcove, and returned, unsteadily, to their stools.

While two fresh beers sloshed their way from the scantily clad barr Stansbee set down a ten. They left minutes later with vacant smile: salutes to the gunman who watched them from the same booth which he emerged. "Goodnight gentlemen and do come back," he y "Next time, perhaps, you might think twice, though, before you ask : Iliana. She was friend of mine, too, you know. Should you see her, sa C wished her the very best, eh?"

After the duo exited the bar, Bostovitch told the bouncer to get vehicle plate number and, more seriously, taught lipped, and with a expression, to, "get it goddamned right!"

"Well, that was enlightening enough for me, for one night," Concord quipped, still shuddering, when they reconnected with the I-10 Freeway, back toward Santa Monica. "Let's hit the Brixton address once more, just before 6:00 AM, and stake it until 8:30 or so in case Iliana shows from a graveyard shift or leaves for a day job somewhere. No doubt she's our girl; we can scrub the other gum-shoeing we had in mind, and chase her down in earnest."

"Ties to the Mafia don't excite me. We have to clean this up, find her, and get out of town. All I need is for them, not some ticked off amateur, to be after me."

Stansbee nodded and replied, with a comparatively unworried expression, "my thought for our next plunge is a phone canvass of local hospitals and the larger medical clinics. Odds are, we'll catch up with her that way. The office can start on that bright and early."

Close to 1:30 AM, they nursed two drinks at their boutique hotel, and settled in for the night.

CHAPTER 23

MOJAVE DESERT

Oligoff rushed back to the master suite and resumed his posture on the bed before Iliana finished her shower. He would soon have heart-to-heart talks with her off-color cohorts; he promised himself. *I will be as tough as I used to be on Moscow back streets when I was sixteen—seventeen, and worked in the inner city after school. Scare hell out of anyone, was my mantra ... with my voice and angry expression. Confident I was; I handled myself in any challenge, once I learned* Sambo, *our Russian-style martial art. Those two are as good as out of the picture, if I wish them gone.*

He remembered disabling scores of aggressive youths—even adult criminals—who roamed the streets in the old country, during robbery attempts, when he used his well-practiced craft for protection. While his silent words stirred and self-assured, Kovansk had no concept of Bostovitch's broad underworld connections, or what he might be up against, if he dealt threateningly with the man.

His attention diverted to Iliana when she stepped from the shower. He stared, approvingly at first, at her glistening and shapely body.

"I am clean again and feel wonderful, Kovie dear," she said, stripped of all accoutrements, save the rose towel wrapped around her dripping hair. "I'll cook a nice dinner, nude as a Grecian statue for you, in the kitchen. You may play with me while I work."

Tantalized as he always was, by her spontaneity and the immodesty she often displayed after sex, this was the old Iliana, Kovansk thought. When she limped awkwardly toward the bedside to embrace him, however, he felt alarmingly and inexplicably repulsed by her deformity, and emotionally withdrew with a start. Oligoff became increasingly perturbed the more he considered Iliana's earlier remarks. He needed more input to assess their exposures, and the risks of visibility so close to their old home in Beverly Hills.

"*Popka,* we have to talk; just a quick dinner if you please and then further conversation about your friends. I am troubled over your continued contacts and associations and what we should do about them from now on."

Iliana pouted, donned her robe, and trudged to the kitchen. She slipped her phone into the pocket, having heard its chimes while showering. "You stay there," she turned and said over her shoulder, "I will bring our meals to bed, and iced vodkas to wash them down."

While she microwaved frozen pasta and *katletky,* their favorite left over Russian meatballs, her phone vibrated. Svetiia sounded incensed.

"Svetiia, love; what is wrong?" Mixed with troubled sobs, her friend's words were garbled, a confused product of English and Russian, spoken too rapidly for Iliana to aptly comprehend. "Just slow down and speak to me, *devushk;* what is it?"

"I … I think … I … believe … police are trying to find you," Svetiia answered. Iliana stiffened and turned gray-white with the news. "Two men in telephone company garb came by the house, asked about you, where you lived … too much prying. I thought at first they wanted me … maybe a John informed on our escort service, but no! They wanted you. I knew they were not phone men. I … I called when they left … found no such vehicle registered to the company, nor were there records of the curious one who gave me his card and asked so many questions.

"I spoke with Cheryna today. He said two men posed as phone company servicemen, who fit the same description, came in the *Minsk* late last night, and asked about you … said you met them at the hospital, whatever that meant. Both denied they were cops; one carried a pistol … loaded. What is happening? Bostovitch is angry with you for steering them to the bar. You didn't do that; did you, or direct the men to me?

"Of course not! Please, you must calm yourself," Iliana retorted. "I did nothing of the kind and have no idea what they wanted. We have done something which could bring down the law, but we were so careful in its execution, our identities and activities were so well concealed. Next week I will meet with you, at the bar, and we will talk this out and include

Chernya; so do not worry. They must be after me. What did they look like … quickly now?"

"One was medium height, the other a bit taller and slender … wore shades so I could not see his eyes. Both white, pale, and clean-shaven. The shorter of the two did less talking, seemed nicer, stooped a bit when he sat down, and got up from the couch. The tall one, maybe six-three, with jet-black hair, no moustache, tougher and demanding, forced himself in the door at first. Any thoughts … sound like anyone you know?"

Iliana shook her head and said, "Not at the moment, no. You told them where I live, did you?" She looked toward the stairs to assure Kovansk would not overhear. Her blood boiled with the presumption.

"I said nothing to them, not the slightest hint … nothing at all. They do know you are a nurse. Bostovitch said that."

"The three of us must meet. Oh, oh, sorry; Kovi is coming … must go. I shall call later."

Iliana dropped the phone back into her robe pocket, but not before Kovansk, in bare feet, slipped down the stairs—soon enough to see her act suspiciously.

"Who was that," he growled, as the forehead scowl worked across his enraged face. "Who the hell was it? Svetiia? A damned intruder! She called for you thirty minutes ago. What does she want and why the circumspect conversations? She is not good for you. I tell you the little vole spells trouble for us. How, I do not know; but she is problem."

"Kovie, she is my trusted friend," Iliana pleaded. She faced him, arms opened wide, "A confidante like no other, loyal to the end; she would never divulge what we did … that is … er, anything we might have done."

"You told her, didn't you? Damn you, Iliana Ona Gosnov!" Oligoff walked from the stairwell to Iliana, grabbed both her shoulders, and shook the woman so violently that her reading glasses dropped to the floor. She bruised her left hip when he pushed her into an outside corner of the granite counter top. "You are a fool with mouth so wide; it could destroy my medical position." His shaking did not cease until Iliana went into hysterics. He relented. She dropped to the floor, sobbed loudly, then blubbered what, to him, seemed a vacuous and patronizing apology.

"You told her, I know it, and I will get it out of the woman. There is no possible excuse for you to inform Svetiia … anything we did. Sit down, now, and relate to me all you two discussed." He pointed to the breakfast alcove with built-in, dark gray upholstered seats.

Iliana, more frightened by his explosive anger than ever before, complied, and sat without argument. "Really, I have said so little to Svetiia about Washington State, Concord, or his demise. I said only that I did something regrettable … no details. Honestly, Kovi, she knows nothing unless Bostovitch spoke of it to her." She hesitated, took on a fearful expression, and shook her head as if helpless, "I am still worried about what is happening."

"Why would Bostovitch know anything of our venture in Washington? Answer me that, Iliana."

Ignoring his earlier admonition, she related what Svetiia just told her. "Two men appeared at Svetiia's apartment, where I used to live, and the same night at one of the bars Bostovitch owns in L.A. They looked for me … may be police detectives. Nothing was said of our activities in Washington, only that they wanted my current phone or address." Oligoff looked mystified and was shocked with the news. He began to tremble as the implications became evident. *Where did Iliana leave a trail they so quickly followed,* he wondered? No apology nor further explanation, he dressed in shorts, T-shirt, and boat shoes; stormed from the house, and drove away, unleashing burning rubber until the tires found traction on the bone dry pavement.

Terribly worried of repercussion from Bostovitch, Iliana called him as soon as Kovansk sped out of sight. To her amazement, the Mafia *brigadier* first related happenings the night before at the *Minsk*. While not concerned at the time, he thought further, and opined to Iliana that his visitors could well have been disguised police investigators. "My little beauty," he said in conclusion, "the price to verify your target's death or to extinguish him, if still alive and kicking, just increased another notch.

"Oh yes, police, this hot on your trail already, will have you tracked to your desert home in very short time. You can count on it. If I were you, I would disappear for a while … best advice I give you," Bostovitch went on. "In meantime, let me ask around … press a few of my inside contacts at P.D. Central. What I pay Watch Commander monthly for … ah … services beyond, ah … call of duty, would more than cover a few complimentary sniffs from within their walls."

Never surprised with the way Bostovitch could put his hands on anything he wanted in the city, Iliana shivered with the thought that she and he were merging closer and closer to the same tangle in which Svetiia unwittingly succumbed, to save her own life.

The organization would snuff either of them in a heartbeat at any time they felt it prudent; she knew. *What am I going to do? I have no one to protect me. My only out may be to point the finger at Kovi. He removed his gloves at times when he drove the van; I remember. Mine stayed on the entire time and the weapon is gone ... lost at the bottom of Lake Washington. Any lingering fingerprint evidence should point his way, not mine.*

Long ago, powder residue on my hands and clothes has washed away. His prints and my denial could tie him into a defenseless knot. The trooper stop on Highway 5 ... a log note, possibly a video, will verify he was driving when the two patrol cars pulled us over. I could say, and they would believe me, that he had a pistol trained on me. He threatened to shoot if I said or did anything provocative.

Iliana, however, always had a paradoxically difficult time blaming males in her life, at first glance, for her problems—a frustrating, troubling and self-limiting paradox—that commonly arose when they most deserved her wrath. Never did she understand that weakness in her personality, often followed by extreme delusions of killing them to break even, when she grew angry enough to project fault in their direction.

Returned to the bedroom, she lay back, relaxed, closed her eyes, and sauntered too easily to past memories. Those she did uncover, however, were very rarely visited. Twelve years of age, going on thirteen, a new entrant to puberty; lips became full and pouty, hips began to form, and breasts were well into lady-like development.

Late at night, she remembered with great attending pain—when he thought her asleep—she heard her father approach her bedroom door, opened just a crack and back lighted by a bright sconce in the hall. The floor creaked with his careful steps, and for a moment her room brightened, then darkened as the door behind him quietly closed. The stench of his fresh cologne sickened her.

How ... how could he have been that crude, that willing to tempt my sanity? Even my father, like all other men I have encountered since, was bent on sabotaging my life, and my battle to find happiness.

Feigning slumber, Iliana remembered the intrusions as though they occurred yesterday. He breathed deeply and slowly as he sat on her bed's edge, and, inch by inch, pulled her blanket and top sheet below her knees. Eyes open just enough to see Dr. Gosnov's silhouette and close to a state of near panic, young Iliana felt her oversized pajama top opening, button by button until she lay completely exposed. Her father lustfully took in the new experience with gruff breathing she would never forget. She was cold, wanted to shiver, she recalled. Alarms went off in so many directions, she chose the path of least resistance.

Damn him! I kept quiet, rigid, and dared not yell. Warmth from his lips lightly dusted her throat, chest; then applied pressure when they found her youthful breasts. Why, she did not know, but it felt relieving, even sweet, and loving, as she reflected on what she later realized was an unconscionable and horrible assault.

Time stopped. She remembered feeling like a movie actress, the object of unrequited love her male costar showed. Cleopatra must have felt that way—deeply adored, she remembered thinking—when Antony moved toward her with romance in mind. Was this real love, young Iliana wondered? She challenged herself to resist, but her new school friend, Lucas, she imagined, instead of her father, touched her in that special place school girl friends talked about, never to allow. It felt good. She felt alive and loved.

Memories, though clouded by many years of denial, abruptly cleared when she arose to a seated position, and considered halting the injurious wanderings. *Better to fester, and face the hate I can cook up for men, whenever the mood strikes. Such opportunists they are.* She stretched back to continue her explosive musings.

By fifteen, fully developed with all the proportions of a grown woman, again her father came on to her similarly, always late at night, opened her to his perverted world, with invasion and contrasting closeness she was not yet able to define. Was it love or was it wrong?

Older by then, the level of excitement increased each time Gosnov entered her space, and finally culminated in a state of relaxation she never imagined could breach much stronger feelings of fear, resistance, guilt, and doubt. The result: Dr. Gosnov removed his clothes, slowly divided her good leg from the deformed one, and inserted his manhood when her excitement wetted his target. Resisting somewhat, she fought to decipher good from evil, but beset with years of teasing activity, and feeling a sense of obligation upon which he prayed, she relinquished as usual—frequently exploded in ecstasy, to join him in the purge of forbidden desires.

Iliana's senior graduation formal ... two days away; she could never forget or let it go. Her father's covert appearances increased, with the number of liberties he took, and the time he spent with her. Again, he approached, unclothed, lay against her naked body, and began his wanton caresses. She felt the usual warmth and desire. That night, however, she was in love—not with him, but her teenage boyfriend of four months—from whom there was never a single serious sexual overture.

Amidst her father's passion, not hers by that time—and indulged with sufficient, what she misinterpreted, as deep care—she screamed, pushed her jarred father aside, and called him every vile name she knew, in both their languages. There would be no mistaking her intentions. This was it; she decided. Her body was for someone she loved, not a repulsive, lying, inhumane male who called himself a loving parent.

No further physical contact occurred, by her choice. Given the obvious bitter anger that soon enveloped Iliana's consciousness, Dr. Gosnov ceased the lecherous behaviors. The confusing and guilt-ridden molestations that spanned six years, were never discussed, and she moved out shortly thereafter, to begin college. *Never so glad to go away somewhere,* she pondered, *anything to stop what I thought for so long was reasonable and proper. I could actually have killed the poor, sick man, my Papa or not. May he rot in hell!*

Iliana finally settled into what became a peaceful rest, having once again faced her most frightening demons and prevailed, she thought. Manifestations of her earlier childhood pulled her away, took her unconsciously closer toward bitter hatred, and distrust. *Is it any wonder I feel so vengeful toward Kovi and seem to wish him harm? Is that why I included him, to take Concord out ... the perfect scapegoat?*

CHAPTER 24

NEWPORT BEACH

Aaron and Stansbee returned to the office after the revealing meetings with Svetiia and Bostovitch. It would not be long, both agreed, before their quest would turn up somewhere locally—that they would stumble upon Iliana Gosnov, positively identify her, and inform local law enforcement.

Who was the van driver, they continued to wonder? Did he live in the Pacific Northwest or in California? Alerting both informants the way they did, was sure to reach the elusive assailants. Time, therefore, was of the essence: find her before she found Concord was alive, and tried again.

"OK, OK, Peg," Aaron replied in response to his wife's pleadings that he return home, "I know I'm wearing out my absence, and I'm sorry. You know this is serious, though, Sweetheart, and how much I appreciate your caring for Mom at the same time. So glad to hear she is back on her game. Now, I've got to get back on mine."

Peggy Concord wished to return to their Hood Canal home. Fearing a possible renewed attempt on his life, though, Aaron felt uncomfortable with her being there alone. On the cusp of discovery, he was unready to leave the area in which he believed the shooter lived or recently resided.

No question; they clearly defined her motive and opportunity. Now they had to find the trigger finger and her accomplice before presenting probable cause to the law for their arrest. To do otherwise would expose

Aaron to a renewed attempt on his life, he worried, and that he was loath to do. For the present, he continued to assume they thought him dead.

Not wishing to unnecessarily frighten Peggy with a full story of the assault, Aaron successfully deflated her admonishments that he return home, to allow for a few more days of detective work. "I'll make it up to you with a little flying vacation," Aaron promised. He missed the freedom of flight. He knew she would be anxious to go with him for some barnstorming, and cozy nights in a few of the peninsula's quaint, small-town bed and breakfast inns. He could not forget the importance of Peggy falling for their lifestyle change, which brought them north in the first place.

"I've got some heavy news, Aaron, so hold on to your seat," Jim Gibson, his retired cop friend enthusiastically reported, not long after Peggy offered him the reprieve for more investigational time. Aaron could hardly hold the receiver to his ear, anxious as he was for news.

"Remember the prints I lifted from the road map in the van, and that matchbook you found? Well, the same pinkies pawed on both. They appear to be female, I'm almost sure, and eventually identifiable, I would hope, though not through our Washington database. That was a dead end. So, I'm expanding search efforts as we speak. U.S. Customs and Immigration requires prints for green card applications, FBI clearance, and for citizenship, too.

"Given the strong evidence of the fearsome twosome being foreigners, I'm pursuing that. Since his prints haven't been found in our state's files, I'm thinking Idaho, Oregon, California, and maybe Nevada. Shouldn't take too long, but we're up against the old problem: no ten print, sequential patterns for comparison, as would be the case were our subjects fresh arrestees. Most of the lifts were partial, not all fingers were available. They were not rolled as they would have been if taken by law enforcement in an orderly fashion … so much easier for the Fed's computer to compare that way.

"FBI records contain close to 100,000,000 criminal and civil print records from most states, federal job applications, and so forth. While they can process more than 150,000 submissions daily in their facility, some within minutes; the problem arises if they are random like ours, taken from objects touched by a few digits, in the field, and clumsily extracted at best.

"It will take longer than usual, if ID is even possible by the FBI. No prints on the shotgun shells you picked up; shooter wore gloves when handling them.

"I did find with a little sniffing; the matching buttons we both discovered were likely from the same women's jacket. I took one to a couple Washington clothing outlets; both advised it was from a women's black denim long sleeve, vintage this year or last. Suggests our female gunner is in a decent economic position, afforded expensive clothing, and is conscious about her looks. DKNY™ is a big seller to young women, so keep an eye out for a couple missing buttons if you personally confront a slippery little lady with a bad leg.

"She's a nurse; the designer clothing idea fits," Aaron said, and then contemplated the fingerprint news to himself.

"What did you find out about *Minsk*—L.A.? Gibson asked.

Concord related the results of their efforts, how they identified Iliana, established probable reasons for her contempt, and that it seemed an unarguable presumption the two culprits were Russian. "Strangely, our DMV has no record of her as a driver, so she may have married and applied under another name. Ran her through national databases, however; and no marriage license record has popped so far."

"Let's get you back up here to take me flying real soon, before you get too old, for chrissakes. I'll call if you're not home by the time I receive possible or positive IDs from the prints, or when FBI responds. Otherwise drop down to Shelton and we'll catch up with progress."

"Mr. Concord ... Mr. Concord," Pamela Manners, the firm's office manager spoke in a whisper to Aaron from the conference room door, "there's a call for you. The woman wouldn't identify herself or discuss the reason for calling." Knowing we're not to say you're here or to give any information whatsoever, Jennifer placed the woman on hold and advised me. Do you wish her to say anything? Perhaps, that you have not worked here for over three years ... something like that?"

Aaron lifted his head from a light doze. He finished reading a stack of reports by several operatives in the office. Neighborhood canvassing they did the day and evening before, provided nothing but negative results. Concord took a brief break in view of the late night Stansbee and he spent in Los Angeles. Deep in thought, to consider their next moves, he reacted sluggishly.

"Just hang up; that would probably be best when I'm not here," Concord said, "Otherwise, I'll use one of my dialects and be Roger Henry, the General Manager. You can buzz me to get on the line. Keep up the good work, Pamela. By the way, how did you make out with DMV vehicle registration?"

"The search turned up Iliana Gosnov all right—owner of a VW Passat—but the address was only a PO Box in Santa Monica, four years old. Tracing that through the Post Office revealed the Brixton Street physical address you two staked out yesterday. No other leads, I'm sorry to report. This woman, it seemed, went out of her way, for some reason, to make her location obscure as possible. Now, the call, Sir."

"Roger Henry, here, eh?" Concord answered in a distinct Canadian accent.

He heard enough chatter from a close friend raised in Vancouver that he sounded more than legitimate. "I'm the General Manager, eh; may I help?" The female caller spoke with a tinge of a European accent, though higher pitched, and sounded somewhat like Svetiia Kronoff on whom he and Stansbee called the day before. "May I ask; does a Mr. Concord, an Aaron Concord, work there? I need to discuss an old file with him."

"And what file would that be, eh?" Aaron responded. The caller stammered, was silent for too long, and finally asked once more for Concord. He felt sure it was Iliana Gosnov, if not, someone calling in her behalf.

"I am so sorry, Mr. Concord passed away at his home in Washington State some time ago. He was not in good health." Aaron could not help sneering, though he realized, too, that he might be speaking with his would be murderess—a determined psycho hunter with a deep grudge—still on the prowl.

"I am so sorry; might I have the number for any next of kin I could call to express my sorrow for their loss?"

That was too much for Aaron to digest. "Sorry, no information may be released to the public and he had no relatives, at any rate. If you cannot state your business, I'll have to answer another call. He dropped the receiver back to the phone when a dial tone filled the void, and casually swept doughnut crumbs from the papers before him.

"Damned little urchin ... still at work. We have to stay away from the Hood Canal a bit longer, that's for certain," he muttered.

Stansbee entered the conference room and sat across the table from Aaron.

After being informed of the curious phone inquiry, Stansbee said, "A.C., I think we need to hit that Svetiia once again, this time below the knees. She has a weak spot, if I'm not wrong, that we can get to if we're tougher this time. Let's try to scare her by asserting we're private dicks being highly paid to find Iliana Gosnov and that we're prepared to harass the hell of her until she relents. I got from her shyness that she might be vulnerable to high pressure. Try it tonight, then?"

Concord nodded. It sounded worth another attempt. Steering clear from the *Minsk* bar, though, he asserted to Stansbee, would be a must, for self-preservation. Ken quickly agreed. He heard tales about how the Odessa Mob and the *Bratva* strongly ruled subterranean gang activity in L.A., with openly admitted murders, insurance fraud, tax avoidance schemes, extortion, and even killings within their own ranks for no other reason than "respect" paybacks. Disrespect a member, you die; was his understanding of the rumors around town that pervaded police departments, civic officials, black and Latino gang leaders. The Russians were a large and expansive team, tough as nails, and not to be reckoned with, he knew.

Late afternoon traffic build-up closely followed them as they breezed along, ahead of the mass exodus from Orange County, on the 405 Freeway, at a consistent seventy, toward Los Angeles. Just before the off ramp to LAX it thickened and remained so until the I-10 Freeway transition west to Santa Monica, which put them less than fifteen minutes from Svetiia's residence.

"We'll be kind of obnoxious to the little weasel this time ... 'slut,' I recall Mr. Tough Guy Bar Owner called her before he changed his tune, and all but said she was a worthless unknown. I'll take the lead, be the bad cop; you be the good one, and we'll quickly disable her. What a beauty; but she will be on edge. When you see her shaking, come in to me with a gesture to cool it a little … get her back on your side. You taught me most of these tricks, Pal; don't look so surprised."

Aaron felt like a newbie with Stansbee, as if he'd have to grapple too deeply to find his lost touch—the special and easy use of spontaneity and craftiness that makes a good investigator great—with the lapse of three years as a retiree. Stansbee was just at the point where his edges, honed to fine perfection, were sharp, rapidly mustered, and amazingly disarming.

Ken rang the doorbell once, twice and again, then knocked loudly with his fist, just below the peephole, where the door was the weakest, and reverberation the loudest. The pounding resounded but at its cessation, they heard no inside activity. Knocks resumed; still no response. He and Aaron returned to the pickup, drove through the alley, to note the absence of Svetiia's green '99 Honda in the marked stall.

Disappointed, Aaron suggested they park at a discrete locus where the back alley was visible, to await Svetiia's return. Boxed dinners opened, they ate Chinese, sipped bottled green tea, and planned their approach with the woman, while they waited.

6:05 PM: "There's the car turning into the alley at the end of the block. She's driving," Ken barked loudly, and excitedly pounded the steering wheel. He tossed his binoculars on the seat and drove quietly to the cross street, then to a green curbside parking zone three houses north of the triplex. He looked at his watch. "We'll give her five minutes to relax."

He knocked hard, as before, but this time omitted the bell as a friendly precursor. Evening TV news blared within, bare footsteps approached the door, and both men stepped aside when the peephole snapped open. The deadbolt squeaked, the front door swung inward a crack, then fully. Svetiia stood a few feet away, awkwardly wrapped in a sheer black robe she fumbled to close with a tie. Realizing her silky legs were fully exposed, the subjects of two appreciative stares, she looked up, blushed, and straightened the garment, startled to see the same twosome as appeared on her porch two days before. Svetiia reached to close the door.

Stansbee said, "No! Not this time, Baby," in such an assertive, take charge way, that she paused. Her pool blue eyes fired and a grimace slid across her face.

157

Shifting her startled gaze back and forth between the men, she squinted to exact details, collected herself, and said loudly, "You men again! I thought I clearly said I did not know anything about Iliana … er … a … the person you asked about."

"Look here, Sweetie," Stansbee said, "no more B.S., if you please." He strode straight into the sparsely furnished living room, and lightly shoved her aside. Concord followed more shyly, but slammed the door behind him with a bang. Svetiia shook her head, lifted her natural blonde, shoulder length hair from behind the robe collar, and tucked both sides behind her ears. She stepped back—looked horrified when Stansbee moved two steps toward her—and asked if they were there for entertainment at Bostovitch's behest. "If so," she said while blushing, "I am booked for the night, and could not see you until after 2:00 AM. I do not know why he does this to me; it happens all the time. Won't you sit down and we can call him to arrange a new appointment?"

Stansbee and Concord glanced at each other. Ken looked at the lovely figure before them and realized she was a hooker, *probably an expensive one at that, given her unbelievable beauty,* he concluded. *At least we're inside and our informant is hardly difficult to look at … certainly a rare one.* Stansbee collected himself before she could react further to their forced entrance, stood tall, and looked down at her. He thrust his right hand into his front pants pocket, jingled change for a bit of distracting drama, pulled out a quarter, flipped it, and slapped it to his wrist.

"Heads says you know Iliana Gosnov. Tails says you don't. How about that?"

She met his eyes with a more relaxed though puzzled glare, opened her mouth but said nothing, then turned attention to his cupped hand as he lifted it. "Heads, it is, Miss Kronoff. Time to fess up. We want that woman and will write up the issue in our report if you don't tell us what we need to know. Then what will your pimp, Mr. *Minsk*—L.A. do about it? Tell us that." She pictured being contacted by vice detectives and Chernya or Davidov later teaching her another lesson with a brutal beating. The last one she received landed her in the emergency room. "Miss Gosnov has lived here," Stansbee continued, "we know that, and she may still use your place as a crash pad. We can all agree you know her, right?"

Svetiia's hands shook. Nervously, she crossed one leg and then the other, each time allowing her robe to creep higher up her thighs, her only approach to possible distraction. She saw the men glancing and reached to the coffee table for the phone. Stansbee clamped his hand to her wrist and pulled the instrument from her grasp.

"Not so fast."

Damn! Aaron thought, *that could be a frigging felony.* Intervening aloud, he said, "Hey, Henry. Go a little easy; just ask her nicely. She'll help. I can feel it." He forced a kindly smile, looked at Svetiia, and nodded for her to say something.

Stansbee sat back in a bucket chair next to the small couch, as if he relinquished, just as they rehearsed.

"Are you cops? What's the crime here? Why do you need Iliana? OK, she is ... was ... a friend; so what?"

Quick winks exchanged between the men as she twisted her hips, pulled the short robe down, and closed its lapels to preclude their views of alluring cleavage. "What is the crime and why must you dicks press me farther than you know you can. I need a lawyer, don't I? Would your shift commander approve these tough guy tactics with a hard working escort girl, charged with nothing, and innocently resting at home?"

Stansbee jumped up again. "How does murder one sound, Sweetheart? Does that resonate with you in any way? Do you really think our boss would listen to you under these circumstances?" Aaron squirmed with that one; *Ken jumped in, up to his neck. Holy Christ,* he thought, with mouth hanging agape, *why did he have to go there?* He almost cut in again for some good guy amelioration when Ken continued.

"Yes, murder one, in fact—that's why we want her. You know where she is, and we all know that. We've you both chitchatting like schoolgirls, by phone. As a matter of fact," he snatched her cell back, and scrolled to the contact list, "here it may be ... yes, right here it is." To her dismay, he continued to scroll, and turned the screen toward Svetiia when he found Iliana's number. He called it out to Concord who scribbled it in a small spiral booklet, pulled from his shirt pocket.

Svetiia began to cry and through her uncontrolled blubbering replied, "I ... I do not know what to say. I ... honestly ... know nothing of any murder; truthfully, I do not. She's never ... never said anything to me about killing someone. If her father were alive, she would probably kill him for what he did to her as a child, but he died years ago.

"Kovi, is he all right?" She clammed up, instinctively placed her hand to her mouth, and realized she said too much. She knew immediately that she suddenly piqued her questioners' further interest. Poker faces were not mustered soon enough. Who was Kovi? She knew they'd want to know.

"Now, this Kovi, who might he be?" Aaron asked predictably. "And what's his connection with your friend, Iliana?"

"I have revealed enough; get out," she screamed while continuing to sob into clasped hands—so loud, she could alert a call to the law. They had the number. They got what they wanted. Staying any longer would tempt fate. Both stepped to the door, Ken closed it softly, and they cut across the front lawn at a semi-run, in a short cut toward the parked truck.

The front curtains parted as they drove away. Svetiia wrote the license number on an envelope she picked up from the floor beneath the mail slot, and called Bostovitch. He would grow angrier the longer she waited.

Ken and Aaron reached the I-10 Freeway and ramped up to the speed of other traffic. "Damned good thing I hung the dead license plate on the back before we arrived, as I did when we paid our visit to the *Minsk* bar," Ken said with a grin. The plate, taken long ago from a totaled vehicle, lay on the seat between them.

CHAPTER 25

LOS ANGELES

Aaron wasted no time when they stopped to fuel at a gas station near the La Cienega Boulevard off ramp, and dialed Iliana's number from a pay phone. "Damned voice mail responded," he complained. "No doubt Svetiia Kronoff alerted her or she didn't recognize my number on the screen, became suspicious, and elected not to answer. I couldn't leave a call back number, so I just said, 'We know you did it and we'll find you soon.' There will be no doubt, what I was talking about, when she listens.

"This cat and mouse chase is getting to me, Ken; it's almost ridiculous. We're practically on top of her, somewhere locally, but can't quite make the connection. The only new lead we have is some guy named, Kovi—if Svetiia wasn't purposely misleading us with that tip. To top it off, we've unwittingly included the Russian Mob, which poses a greater threat to me, to both of us now, than an inflamed and avenging claimant. Step on their toes and we are good as dead meat right now."

"Kovi, eh? Sounds, maybe, like a Russian nickname; doesn't it?" Stansbee retorted as he signaled, and entered the right lane of eastbound I-10. We can do some searches for that one, but it's unlikely any nuts will fall from the tree with nothing more than a nickname. We need to turn on the heat with repetitive calls from pay phones all over the place to Iliana Gosnov, loosen some screws, get her wired up, guessing, scared, and on the run." He swerved left to find a space in the diamond lane. "At least her attentions will divert from you in the meantime, when she's on the defensive for a change. You can go home. We will both flood her with threatening voice mails. How 'bout that for openers?"

"Good as anything I can think of for now," Aaron replied. "We should throw this Kovi and also our mob friend, Bostovitch, into some of the messages we leave—create some intriguing infighting, and interpersonal accusations. Each will think the other has spilled the beans. That could create some inside strife. We may get some leads to bounce in from the feedback. Also, let's try that phone company contact you used to have, for a billing address, if we should be so lucky. You can get Pamela on that in the morning."

"I'd like to speak with Iliana," Stansbee asked the woman who answered Iliana's phone. He called from the pay phone in his building's lobby while Aaron anxiously eavesdropped.

"This is Iliana; who is calling?"

"I know it was you and Kovi who killed the man in his home on Hood Canal. I will call Kovi next if you don't turn yourself in to the Santa Monica Police immediately. As an alternative, I would accept one hundred thousand dollars in cash within the next two weeks to forever hold my tongue."

Aaron, awestruck with Stansbee's brazen approach, quickly realized the woman would be swimming in fear and worse, new confusion; with mention of an extortive motive. Twisting the name Kovi into the picture, just from Svetiia's inadvertent mention of the name, was a long shot, but the brief monologue rang loudly to the stunned listener.

The long pause before she responded, gave her away. "Who is this. For heaven's sake, what are you talking about? What do you mean ... Kovi? I know nothing about any Kovi." Iliana looked at the phone screen again and didn't recognize the number. "Why would I pay you one hundred thousand, whoever you may be? Are you calling for Chernya?"

That bastard, she cursed to herself, *he is at it again ... blackmail this time, just as Svetiia and I suspected might happen. Soon as I trip, he is ready to catch my fall, but always for a price. He wants to own me, take over my life as he did with her.* It took a few deep breaths before she could continue. Stansbee heard the gasps and knew her pulse pounded.

"Who gave you my number ... Kov ... er, ah, Bostovitch or Svetiia ... who?"

Stansbee covered the mouthpiece and whispered to Concord, "She's already slipped, lost her cool, clearly let on that she knows this Kovi, whoever he may be."

"Bostovitch had you call, didn't he? He asked you to do some of his dirty work, to generate a little more money for himself. Not from me, he won't. I will call him myself. Don't bother me again, you meddling SOB."

A dial tone broke the ensuing silence. Stansbee leered with the success of their first harassment effort. He redialed, but this time called the *Minsk*, hoping to beat Iliana to the draw. "Put C on the line, please," he directed the female who answered. *Probably the stocky redhead behind the bar.* "Mister Bostovitch," he drawled in the same deep voice used with Iliana, "I just spoke with your Russian nurse lady friend who says you participated with her and Kovi—took out an innocent man up north a few weeks ago.

"I want you to know my lips can be forever sealed. Money could keep you out of the mess she has created. Conspiracy to commit murder is not a small deal, and with testimony from Iliana, Kovi, and others, you could rot in prison like dead carrion in Moscow's *Bitzevski* Forest." Bostovitch knew of the wooded hills outside the city, which Stansbee researched on the net, for added authenticity.

Ken heard conversation in the background—glasses clinked as they were washed, and the sound of running water—but not a word from Bostovitch. He clearly struck a chime. "Think about it; have a decision in mind when I call you again." He disconnected before Bostovitch could reply.

"That's enough for now, A.C. Better to let him boil with curiosity for a while. We must have stirred up a real bee's nest. Someone may be roughed up for it. Perhaps the group will start some immediate self-destruction. We still need to get this guy Kovi identified, though, and include him in our harassing phone chats. He may have been the driver that night."

"Let's do a drive-by tomorrow or the next day and have another talk with Svetiia to keep things agitated for our next move," Aaron answered. "She may be our most talkative informant as this unfolds."

The phone at *Minsk*—L.A. almost exploded with activity after Stansbee stirred the pot. "What do you mean I had someone call you, Iliana; have you been drinking today? Are you crazy?" Bostovitch said in response to an immediate call from Iliana. "Why would I volunteer myself to be in the center of murder plot, mixed with extortion? I already did one thing too much, to involve myself when we located Aaron Concord and prepared your false identifications. There was not enough, I told you ... not enough money to get excited considering the risks, so, my dear price must go up again." Someone put me in the circle with you and Kovi. I do not like it, not at all; nor will the big boss if he hears of it."

Though with difficulty, he talked above Iliana's rampant curses and shouting to make his point. "Stop for a minute," he said. We do not yet know if the man is truly dead, remember? These men could be police or hired dicks, doing lots of work ... dangerous work, too. If you failed to waste the man, you face little more than a charge for attempted murder, at worst a plea to assault with deadly weapon. Keep that in mind. Our next task, in view of the heat coming on so fast, must be to verify whether Concord is or is not gone."

Bostovitch listened closely this time to Iliana's pleadings. "No, I will not do it for ten thousand," he eventually responded. "The price for any further investigation in Washington is now $20,000, and for execution, if he is not now dead, will be $150,000. Either that or you come into my arms ... one long weekend, maybe two or three," he chuckled, while half serious, "and very soon. Give me as much as I can handle of your very best, and if you are half as good as sweet Svetiia, you go to work immediately as escort in your spare time ... pay it off like she does." He finished his point with a deep guttural laugh that shook his head. "You do not wish Kovansk to hear ... ah ... know of, er, find out ... hear details of our, ah ... past and possible future working relationship; now do you?"

Though incensed at his suggestion of blackmail, Iliana cast far too many epithets his way. It angered Bostovitch and she did not need him angry. Not when she needed his help, was so alone in her tenuous situation, and on the defense. "God, no!" she cried. "He knows so little of this; we have no such cash. Papa's inheritance, the portion you forced me to take, has left us strapped since Kovi bought into the hospital.

"You must understand. I need funds to live on; Kovi is very close to cash broke. We're almost upside down on the condo in town, and it is not selling, even with drastic price reductions. Payments on our desert house are high … so little left at month's end, Chernya. Don't you understand? I am not made of dollars.

"No! I did not say anything to the caller about you," she went on, after Bostovitch interrupted with a fuming query. "You know there is no chance I would cross you or the *Bratva*; you can trust me on that. I do not wish cement boots. I have no idea what led those two men to your business." She nearly forgot; she dropped the matchbook to the road as she and Kovi drove from the scene. If found, it could save her from direct finger pointing. It might have been the best thing she did to shift, or at least, share exposure.

Bostovitch remained mystified and wondered: *who did what, to open my name to the public, police, or a private investigative agency … the family, Concord's wife? Maybe that small county department handling the local investigation gave up, with no leads,* he thought further, *leaving family to do it on their own. I will have little talk with Svetiia. She was the mouth … must have been. Best go there alone … no Davidov or Yakal for watchdogs. I should push in the face of that little filly … stop the gossip now and use her as a fresh example—why we do not tolerate dishonor.*

Svetiia Kronoff lay on her bedroom floor, partly propped against the double bed. The white cotton coverlet—stained with her blood, disheveled, a corner of it twisted into a rope-like coil—wrapped tightly around her neck. Semi-conscious, eyes swollen, and bruised about the arms and torso, both hands pulled down on the garrote, which almost precluded breathing. She gasped desperately for deep inspirations, tugged at it more than twenty minutes, and eventually loosened its constricting grip.

He kicked open the door, surprised her in the bathtub, unrelentingly slapped her, and left the woman sprawled nude, and bound on the hardwood floor. Until she was speechless from his facial slaps, Bostovitch admonished her to keep her mouth shut about him, Iliana, or Kovansk.

Hysterical and wounded, Svetiia lay weeping and in pain when Stansbee and Concord arrived for another try at extracting information. Front door ajar, they looked about the neighborhood, saw no one, and helped themselves to the living room. They heard faint sobs, found her bedroom, and the gruesome scene. No doubt existed; it fit the work of a man without conscience, someone like Bostovitch or one of his cronies, both opined in muffled whispers.

"You poor girl," Aaron said; he shook his head, covered her, and lifted Svetiia to the bed.

"Who did this to you young lady," Stansbee asked. We need to know. We'll try to help you."

"C … C … can't say more … caught me by surprise … in the tub … slapped me and with the bed covers wound tightly around … so tightly around head and neck. Thought he would kill me … didn't resist. Why are you here again?"

Both men worked hard to maintain their feigned accents as before. Stansbee could not chance identification through Svetiia's possible description to Iliana. He still sported his black wig and sunglasses. Aaron's appearance remained unchanged.

"Do you wish us to call an ambulance, the station—for a report?" Aaron asked, while he sponged the abrasions with a moist washrag, and cleaned her face.

"Oh no, I would be killed if there were a next time. No, I'm locked into their escort operation, where I must work until my debt is paid … maybe six more months of this. How I will manage to survive the rest of the year, with things like this, I do not know."

"You need to get out, young lady; leave while you can," Aaron replied. His look was stern, borne of Svetiia's beating and possible infiltration of the Russian Mafia into Iliana's murder effort. "We may be able to assist but you must help us. We need to find Iliana Gosnov and this 'Kovi' person, as soon as possible. It's about murder." Aaron purposely omitted the "attempted" part, not wishing to expose his survival at that point. The longer Iliana truly thought him dead, the less energy she would expend trying to verify it, and then hunt him down.

They could see Svetiia, torn about releasing added information, would talk no more. What she already gave them, led Bostovitch to the reprimand. A clear warning, she knew it unwise to say anything further to anyone.

"I must keep things to myself," she said, while she feebly tried to regain her composure. "I let something slip, must have, to anger Chernya so much. Iliana, my dearest friend; I do not wish her to get in trouble. Yes, she can have a thing for men. Her attitude … anger, toward males in her life has always escaped me. Why, I have asked her? But she cannot explain. Iliana is not up to killing any one.

"She gets impatient, and sometimes does so with me. I can feel her hurt, but never know where it comes from, exactly. We can do or say things to each other, which are hurtful yet unintended, but we always resolve our differences, and never through violence."

They left, to beat the mass of southbound traffic headed to Orange County.

Stansbee gave Svetiia two pre-paid "burner" cell phones to use and avert caller ID, if she needed to call out. Svetiia suffered enough trauma for one day. The two felt it appropriate to touch base with her the following morning, to see how she fared, and then follow up at least once more, personally; to fish for hints that would enable them to find the shooter, and her driver. At that point, Svetiia held the keys to further discoveries.

"Svetiia, this is Brinks Rogers from yesterday, just checking to see how you're feeling. Hope you are better. Any questions, call me at the number we left. We're both terribly sorry our intrusion might have caused any of this." Aaron finished his voice mail message with, "*Spasibo,*" a Russian thank you he found on a language website. "She'll return the call; I can feel it," he said to Ken. "We have to drive out there one more time, right away, while she still feels our compassion, and before she holes up somewhere, to hide from Bostovitch. What do you think of our setting her up with temporary quarters in Laguna for a short time ... maybe my vacant apartment? It's out of the way, and she'd be safe from the mob for a while."

"I think it's not so good, Buddy; she's a danged hooker. Basically a loser ... cute little thing all right, but what's Peg to think if she hears about it from your old gabby next door neighbor she still talks with from time to time? Bad idea, me thinks."

"You're right, of course. How about a few days during which the three of us could go out for breakfast, dinners ... we'd treat her right, and maybe break this open. I don't have forever down here. I'm getting more than frightened with developments and especially with the closer intrusion of these *Minsk* folks. Maybe they financed the shooting ... have a vested fiscal interest in this Iliana. They're a damned mean crowd at best."

"We'll try tomorrow. How about it?"

CHAPTER 26

MOJAVE DESERT

"Those two detectives came back a second time," Svetiia rambled, almost aimlessly. "They gave me their number in case I needed any help, anything, I guess … very kind. I'm not sure they're cops—never showed their badges, Iliana—kept repeating that you are wanted for murder. What on earth did you do?" She spoke from bed, aching but recovering from the tumbling she received at the hand of Bostovitch. She felt she owed the investigators something more, a night with her, perhaps, if not just some friendly conversation.

It seemed to Svetiia that sex was what any man would wish before all else, a side of herself with which she only recently reckoned. Already, she stereotyped all males into one slot after but a few months in the escort business. She wondered where she might be in six more months. "I could have allowed Kovi's name to slip into the conversation, *devushk*. I am sorry if I did. They may have obtained your number from my cell phone—definitely nothing more. I cannot be sure but they could have," she hedged.

"They took care of me after Cheryna beat me terribly. He thought I sent the investigators to him. I swear I said nothing to involve him with you … your … ah, whatever you may have done. They got the *Minsk* address from someone else, not me. I am positive. How could they have known of him … the bar, Iliana?"

Seated on the office balcony porch, she absorbed the coolness of the tile floor, and the balmy breeze from the southwest. Iliana wore nothing, shielded by a three-foot parapet that precluded visibility from ground level. Early afternoon sun crept over her body; toasty and relaxing on her dry skin. She flew mad at Svetiia's almost unbelievable availability to the police or private eyes, whoever stopped to see her ... more than fearful that anyone might be so close on her trail.

"How the hell could you have allowed them to get my number? You are completely *nevmenyaemyi*," Iliana screamed. She told Svetiia in their mother tongue, that she was insane ... an imbecile.

Insulted and beaten down, in spite of having done her best to protect Iliana from discovery, Svetiia crumpled in sadness. Anger then ensued, along with a new and heavy feeling of detachment from her long-time friend for linking her with the other players. *Enough abuse for one day; I do not need that wicked woman. She can fend for herself for all I care. She's angry at the wrong person. She needs to look at herself, Kovi for possibly helping, and likely, the injury her father imparted to her as a young teen.* Disconnect was Svetiia's next move—in the midst of Iliana's misdirected rants—before she retreated to her more serious concerns.

Iliana threw the cell phone across Kovansk's office, while she cursed at her predicament, and obliquely, at Svetiia. Unable to accept responsibility for her vengeful actions toward Concord, her fury flamed by the minute. Iliana's ill feelings swerved then focused on Kovansk, the nearest male. *Where is he?* She wondered.

Kovansk Oligoff sped toward L.A. on Highway 14, after he left Iliana abruptly; frustrated with her lack of candor and determined to seek answers from Svetiia, even Bostovitch if he had to reach that far.

The rumble of his high-powered Carrera awakened Svetiia from a light doze when he pulled to a stop in front of her apartment—easy to find, as he spent much time there with Iliana, before they moved in together. He pictured Svetiia's comely legs, and almost glacial white skin while he collected his thoughts; her youthful and lovely face, enormous soft blue eyes, natural blonde hair, and alluring breasts. He remembered her as a raving beauty ... smart, too, despite nursing career intentions that ended abruptly. A surprised pluck in his stride, he almost hopped up her four front steps and knocked lightly on the door.

Svetiia felt better after the roughing up she took from Bostovitch; she recognized Oligoff when she pushed the front window curtains aside. Barefoot, as she was most of the time around home, she slipped on light aqua shorts and a revealing white bikini bra, absent the dregs of modesty to curtail her sudden frivolity and surprise to see him. Kovansk on her porch spurred excitement ... a pleasant surprise and welcome sight. Svetiia swung the door wide open and greeted him with an excited look, a hearty hug, a peck on both cheeks, and then a tender kiss on the lips. Enthusiastically, he returned the gesture.

Casually attired himself, Kovansk grinned uncontrollably, was whisked into the front room and met with another embrace, not knowing how then to respond. "Kovi, Dear, wha ... what ... why ... are you here?" Svetiia looked around him to the street. "Is Iliana with you?"

He shook his head.

"I am terribly angry with her and the wild accusations flying around that I was involved in an incident with her ... you, too. I think it was said, 'in some shameful activity,' she called it."

He stared helplessly into her sensual eyes, for a moment uttered nothing but, "No, I came, ah, alone," almost inaudibly. Kovansk blushed when she stood on tiptoes and hugged him once again. She smelled fresh and pleasant from rose scented body wash. "That is why I came to see you. I am not getting full story from Iliana. You know her better than anyone. I thought you might help."

"Come, sit down, let me pour you an iced vodka and we will talk all you wish. Yes, it seems I am included in an ongoing police or private investigation ... a murder, they say, for which they want Iliana ... man killed in Washington State. These investigators will find her very soon. They just got her cell number.

"Is it true; has she done this? I was so worried when they told me, with thoughts that she took her hatred for men out on you. My first question to the investigators ... 'was Kovi, all right?' You will never know how I have dreamed of you, making love to you, brightening your day with kisses, sweet notes, phone calls; traveling together, completing my nursing training and working with you. All fantasies, I know, of course; but I wanted the reality even if she did get to you first.

"It hurt me so, when I saw you together at our place … sleeping in her room, the noises you made during lovemaking … all of it … so unpleasant. My God, what am I saying?" Svetiia asked, while she blushed, and covered her mouth with her hand. Then she laughed lightly. "It has been bottled far too long, I guess. Dear Kovi, what can I do for you?"

Kovansk inquired about bruises on her forearms and chest and some remaining swelling about the right eye.

"Yes, I took quite a beating the other day from Cheryna Bostovitch, a *brigadier* in the *Bratva* … Russian Mafia … commonly takes liberties like that with me. She brought him up to date with Bostovitch's clutches on her life, at present and into the future, for a period not finally determined. Thereafter, and painfully, Svetiia described the events that led to her abduction as a near-slave.

"Can I do anything to ease the hurt, dress that spot on your shoulder, throw a stitch or two, at least a butterfly, to close the cut in your thigh?" Oligoff could not help but notice as she fidgeted next to him on the couch, that Svetiia's bikini straps slipped from her shoulders, allowing her breasts almost complete exposure. His near-hypnotic gaze gave him away. "I apologize to you for the problems that have come up, for your beating, if Iliana had anything to do with it, and wish you to know she did do something terrible. That is at root of all goings on right now.

"If you are in firing line because this place was her former address, it is sad spin-off. She surprised me with an act of violence to settle old grudge of hers and I, too, am now unfortunately and most uncomfortably exposed." Kovansk sipped the last of his vodka, as did she.

Svetiia poured another from the pitcher, for each of them. A warm glow swept across her numbing forehead. *I would do this man in a heartbeat if he made even a hint of a move*, she asserted to herself. *He is irresistible, strong, kind hearted, and brilliant, and I have cared for him for years. Iliana struck out at me, without provocation, one too many times. It's time I gave her a legitimate reason to complain.*

"Svetiia, did you have anything to do with locating Aaron Concord, for Iliana?" *She is the picture of beauty, such lovely skin; peaceful, understanding, no strangely penetrating, vengeful eyes. She seems so content with herself, absent Iliana's hatred and contempt, which trouble her, and me, so much. She is picture of sensuality the way she moves—that beautiful body, her silky long hair—and she looks kindly at me when she speaks. She would have to do little more than make a pass, with a couple more vodkas, and that would be it.* "Did you prepare the fake identification we used in Washington?"

"Absolutely not. I have nothing to worry about. I have always worked on the straight and narrow. Because of the association I was forced into having with Bostovitch, though, I did lead Iliana to him when she asked if I knew anyone who could advance cash for a portion of her father's unsettled estate. Bostovitch and his other … er … capabilities were made known directly to her." *He is looking better and my temperature is rising by the minute. Quite amazingly, my bruises no longer ache.*

"What exactly did Bostovitch do for Iliana? *Her painted toenails are beautiful and her French fingernails, exquisite. Lots of class underneath it all.*

"Far as I know, she received around $250,000 from the father's estate, the phony identifications for you both; but beyond that, she said nothing. You could ask Bostovitch if you wish more detail than what Iliana has shared with you. She kept me in the dark, too, and I think, now, I am glad she did."

Svetiia poured the last bit of vodka for Kovi. Her hair brushed against his forehead as she did so. Kovansk grabbed her locks, gently pulled her toward him, and when their cheeks touched, both exploded into unleashed fervor: a parting of lips, darting tongues that wet each other's mouths. They purred like kittens. Svetiia settled into Kovansk's lap, lips still locked, while his hands found the ties to her top, which dropped to the floor. He buried his head in her softness, and lashed at her breasts with hunger. She fumbled with his T-shirt, lifted it in an instant, and went for his shorts.

A trail of remaining clothing followed the duo into Svetiia's bedroom where he easily lifted her to a standing position on the bed. Unembarrassed, as Iliana would be, he thought, and in his full view, she watched him stare admiringly at her body, and caress it while she moaned and gyrated with delight. Both plummeted to the bed, lips locked, then searched, and found each other's warm places, as passions climbed. Svetiia writhed with pleasure. Oligoff knew just what she wanted as deep staccato breathing defined his target, and tenuous clutches at his back affirmed he found her magic.

Exchanging dominance, Svetiia savored his manhood until close to cliff's edge, and then paused when he whinnied for more. Repeatedly, she brought him near finality, and left him flaming with wilder desire. Both finally exchanged cries of satisfaction, in unison; warmed, and relieved by each other's white-hot lairs.

Several times thereafter over the next hour—neither counted—the same build up and conclusion to their sensual overture produced a symphony of ecstatic and exhaustive pleas to continue, until both relaxed supine in each other's arms, for a spell of recovery.

"My God, what have I been missing? No hateful commentary afterward, you showed no shame ... showed me your most beautiful body, no unpleasant aftermath, nor expressions of unfounded anger. Why did I not follow my instincts and choose you when we began to tease one another in our early days here?" *And, no deformed leg to reckon with,* he mused.

"We are doing it now; better late than never, my handsome Kovi." *Better late than never. If Iliana only had a clue what her fiancé was up to right now, she would kill again. I have half a mind to tell her, in exchange for the insults and accusations she cast my way yesterday. I was ridiculed for trying to help the spoiled little bitch.*

"Doctor Oligoff here." Kovansk answered his cell to Iliana's angry voice. She demanded to know where he was, why he left, and when he would return. Having fallen into the arms of another woman—Iliana's closest friend, no less—put him on the immediate defensive. "I ... I ... needed some ... er ... time to think about your predicament, ongoing hatred, and your continuing reluctance to be frank with me. I have to know full story for my own protection. Concord was not my idea, not in least, and I never meant harm to the man."

Screeching loudly, Iliana accused him of disclosure to the authorities, entrapment in some bizarre way, and, maliciously, not owning up to driving the getaway car, or participating otherwise in the travel planning. "You're in as deeply as I," she then reminded him. "You will not get off the hook that easily, not if I have anything to do about it." Where are you, Boris Oligoff?"

As usual when she used his given name, he raged, snarled, as his forehead rippled like a washboard, and then ended the call.

The phone rang again. "Do not ever do that to me again, Kovi. We have much to discuss. Come home now." She reconsidered, melted some, and added, "Please, Kovi."

Kovansk spoke from a wicker rocking chair on Svetiia's front porch, a bath towel around his waist. "I went to Svetiia's house after … ah, I …ah, stopped at the hospital to sign for a patient's discharge. I wanted to know what she knew. I do not understand why you cannot tell me of this Bostovitch, and how tightly he wound you into his triangle of terror. Because of your silence, he beat Svetiia, left her with bruises, and a leg laceration.

"She did nothing to deserve it, tried only to protect your identity, which, it seems, is now clear to those who investigate the incident. Your not being straight has hurt me and Svetiia, and it has to stop. Either you come clean with everything or we are through. I am going to see Bostovitch now."

"How dare you speak with Svetiia, Bostovitch, and try to subvert me. I will not allow that … might even go to the hospital, and tell your partners what you have done. You will be through, Kovi … down for the count." Iliana's dark eyes burned with fury; she tugged wildly at her short black hair with both hands and pulled small locks from their follicles.

Infuriated with her allusion, to inform his partners; again he disconnected. "I do not need her acting this way with me," he said to Svetiia whose arms enveloped him from behind, while her lips brushed his left ear.

She nuzzled his neck and replied, "Try to understand her, Kovi. You may not realize how she suffered … molestation for years at the hands of her father. She's so angry with men, she cannot distinguish you from the rest. "I know you were always good to her, nurtured, and tried to understand. Her leg and her past relationships, however, are symptoms of a troublesome fixation that requires treatment, in all probability. Such delusions are hard to erase, and typify psychosis, supported by many of her other behaviors— murder for one—if that is even close to being true. I did not spend more than four years in psychology studies for nothing, and know the woman like my hand's back."

"Svetiia, I had best go, but I want to see you again, and soon, I hope. Maybe I can help you out of your ties to Bostovitch. I will work on it today."

CHAPTER 27

MOJAVE

Desert oven heat mediated quickly. The diving sun lost its heating power, and gave in to stretching shadows from the local mountains to the southwest. Iliana, furious with Oligoff, and her sudden feelings of abandonment—however unaware she may have been at the time—turned an acceptable and understandable emotion into irretrievable rage. That only exacerbated her experience of uncertainty about his motives.

Pacing back and forth in Kovansk's kitchen, Iliana extended her dogged ambulation into the spacious adjoining den; and could have worn a pathway in the floor. She held a damp dishtowel tightly in her hands, wrung it into knots and whipped at the counter top, furniture, anything in the way; anything to quell her rising enmity. *What is he up to?* She asked herself like a broken record.

Why ... why does he now undermine me? What do I say if he finds out Chernya and I have been talking about more money for more of his services? Complicating things are Svetiia's unfortunate beating, and my inability to get any details of his death from Concord's old office, which makes me look worse and worse to Kovi.

"Damn him, damn! He could force me out; take my life away as Papa did with my virginity and delicate dignity when I was so young and helpless. I will not allow him to do it. Murder once, murder twice, what's the difference," she wailed aloud, and limped upstairs to the bedroom to retrieve Kovansk's Colt .45 semi-automatic pistol from beneath the mattress, on his side of the bed. The coal black piece felt heavy, ominous, deadly, and foreboding, yet an inexplicable glow draped over her as she handled it. Sweat from her fingers left clear fingerprints on the flat metal surfaces, a reminder that a forensic specialist could easily determine the shooter's identity if not used with gloved hands.

Casually, but with determination, she flipped the piece from palm to palm. Iliana removed and replaced the magazine, cocked it, and ejected the chambered cartridge. She picked it up from the floor, examined the copper-jacketed hollow-point slug, and replaced the bullet into the chamber. *That baby is designed to mushroom and rip a two-inch hole through a piece of flesh.* She aimed it at the window, mock fired and remembered detailed instructions Kovansk gave her the many times they took guns to a nearby canyon for target practice.

The sudden focus on possible victims drew upon her face, a glazed and impersonal expression, as she pictured them in the sights: her first fiancé, Dr. Ilya Gosnov, her father; Kovansk; and finally, though incongruously, her best friend, Svetiia. "Do I have to kill them all, to bring peace to my life? How would I ever do it? Who will help me? Bostovitch? No! He will do nothing of the kind unless he makes a fortune from it. How can I get the cash he requires to investigate Concord, and finally get rid of the man, if he still lives?

"Papa is gone, burning in hell, I hope. That will leave only Kovi... Svetiia, too, if she has deceived me. I have no idea where my first love went—the yellow little coward ... stood me up at the alter, as he did, but a week before our wedding. I ask very little, only that I might run into him someday." Gripping the .45 with both hands, she checked the safety, applied pressure to the trigger with her right index finger, and popped an imaginary round into his chest. Swept backward from the force of the shot, he dropped to the floor, quivered, and spewed blood from nose and mouth.

"I'm sorry," he wheezed through the frothing crimson fluid that seemed almost real to her—an apology—all Iliana wished from him, or any of her wrongdoers. Bewildered with the drive she felt, she saw a hideous face reflected in the entry hall mirror, and stared at it disapprovingly. Her self-hatred glowed. In lieu of replacing the pistol in the bedroom, once she viewed the image of her disturbed, distrusting countenance, she hid it under folded dishtowels in the lower kitchen drawer, closest to steps that lead to the garage. If he noticed the piece missing from the bed, she would say she thought she heard an intruder.

Iliana was surprised to find so much money in the wall safe buried in the rear of their walk-in closet, the combination to which Kovansk gave her after installation. *Either Kovi received some large cash dividends, he had more than he said he did when escrow closed, or he did not spend what he claimed, to purchase the partnership.*

Filled with disbelief at the neatly stacked, thick bundles of one hundred dollar bills—and bearing an irrepressibly gleeful grin—her discovery could be the ticket to hire Bostovitch for his final effort. Combined with what little she retained from her father's estate, the total was enough, and much more, to make Cheryna drool; she knew. Carefully counted, $275,000 lay stashed in the steel drawer she slid from the encasement.

Should I take it now from the lying snake or leave it until Bostovitch completes his task, and wants his pay? 'I am so strapped for money,' Kovi has whined repeatedly. Possibly he has a progress payment to make soon, or he is growing a money tree for himself. It could disappear. If I removed it now, however, and he discovered it before Cheryna demanded payment, he would throw me to the dogs. I would be wiser to let it be, tell Bostovitch I am ready to proceed, and give him a small advance from my own funds.

When he has done the work, I will pay the balance, if any. So long as Concord is dead, I am off the hook without disturbing this stash, to take it later if things deteriorate further between us. "Perhaps, in time, there will be more," she said aloud, while she gloated over her discovery. Carefully, she replaced the bundles as she found them, closed the safe, and reclined in bed to contemplate her next move.

What is Kovi doing with all that cash? She wondered. Who are those two investigators … homicide detectives … whatever they may be? Before she approached Bostovitch to finalize price negotiations and agree on what next he would do, she had to know. *I will ask Svetiia … make peace with her after my sudden rudeness, and the uncalled-for accusations I directed her way. If anyone is innocent it is she, poor thing, in such a bind with the* Bratva *and knowing only what I told her … no details … certainly not that Concord died at my hand. That could only have come from the two men who called on her.*

"Devushk, wait Devushk," Iliana, called loudly, when her old friend answered, "please, please do not hang up on me."

No surprise, a dial tone ensued. Iliana called again and pleaded for a chance to explain. "I am so sorry, so very sorry about my remarks when last we spoke. Completely wrong, I was out of order." This time Svetiia listened, though only peripherally, while she waved her hands to dry freshly applied nail polish. I want us to talk, get together, and I need your help, if it's possible."

Svetiia spoke, "I have enough problems with Bostovitch, his gang, and my apparent loose lips, for which he smacked me around again, as he did a few months ago, for holding back some of my income after a very tough week of abusive clients." She could not help but picture Kovansk's admiration as she stood on the bed before him. And she still quivered from the thrill, when he hovered above, looked so dreamily into her eyes, with want; his gentleness, and the offer to help extricate her from the impossible situation.

"I … I do not know what to say; you were so unforgiving … so many years of closeness … taking me on the way you did. Are you completely out of control? What about this murder charge they are trumping up? You are a wanted woman and I do not need these inquiries, or any association with violence allegations. Bostovitch covers my back with police, for my escort services but, murder? I do not think so."

Seething, feeling her pulse quicken as adrenalin rushed through, and bellicosity bubbled inside, Iliana, for once, held her tongue. Wisely, she allowed Svetiia to continue without interruption.

"What did you do that makes the inquirers so determined to find you … Kovi, too, poor. …?" Again, Svetiia felt Kovansk's romantic moves and soft whispers.

"Damned Kovi," Iliana snapped an interruption, "what did he tell you? What do you mean, 'poor' Kovi?" Why was he out to see you? Did he? Did he tell you anything, Svetiia?" Iliana felt herself losing it again, and breathed deeply to restore her borderline calm.

"Kovi … ah … stopped by, yes … because, er, he said he is in the dark about your ties to *Bratva* and how beholden to the mob you may be. He is a doctor with a reputation to preserve, is most worried of his connection with you, apparently wanted for murder, and how covert you have been with him."

"Covert? My God, you have no idea … naïve thing; he is involved as well.

"They just do not know he. …" Iliana said too much and fast retreated to the reason for her call; to repair torn ties with Svetiia and to ask for help. She had to know the investigators' identities and Svetiia might have the key, she reminded herself. "It has occurred to me that these men are passing out rumors and may work for Bostovitch in an attempt to … ah, extort money. They think I have the funds Papa left, but Kovi used the money to acquire the hospital partnership and I am not a source for more. Could you be of help?"

She touched a soft spot alluding that the mob chewed at her feet, with which Svetiia quickly identified as a victim of Bostovitch herself. "OK," she answered, "what do you need?"

"*Devushk,* I want you to come with me to Orange County, to make a call on the insurance claims office, tied to an investigation of things which occurred during my birth. Long story, I can tell you on the way. I am terribly curious; do the men who came to see you, possibly work there? Could there be a connection with Bostovitch, somehow?" Again, she played on Svetiia's hatred of the Russian mobster. "I simply want to know if you recognize either of them. We will just walk in, like we own the place, look around, and leave. Could you, please?"

Svetiia agreed. They made arrangements to make a fast stop at the offices of Concord, Stansbee and Fitch.

CHAPTER 28

LOS ANGELES

Boris Kovansk Oligoff parked directly in front of the *Minsk* bar. Mid-morning, the area was far different in the light of day, from the macabre appearance it presented when Stansbee and Concord stopped there. Traffic grew heavy, children from adjoining residential areas skateboarded on the sidewalks, women with infants pushed grocery carts and strollers in both directions, and several nearby Persian restaurants bustled with customers eating beneath multi-colored umbrellas that shaded outside tables.

He gave the inconspicuous lounge a momentary suspicious look. Kovansk walked toward the draped doorway. He stood out like a sore thumb: shiny black alligator cowboy boots, light gray linen slacks, and a blue scrub shirt beneath his charcoal topcoat.

Kovansk passed by the tough guy and waited for his eyes to accommodate, once inside the near-dark interior. Familiar music of his country played on cheap speakers. The interior smelled of pungent cigar smoke. He still wondered why he was there, when his eyes met the bartender's stare from the rear of the room. She gestured him to move forward. He spoke easily, in Muscovite Russian, and the greeting was returned, not by the redhead female behind the counter, but by a heavy voice behind him, of Russian origin, he surmised.

"Welcome to *Minsk*," the voice continued, "and do feel free … be seated." Bostovitch pointed to the bar where one man stood while he sipped an espresso with both hands, and then to the three vacant booths. "I have not seen you before. You new to area? Nurse, doctor, are you ... big new clinic on Pico Boulevard?"

Kovansk murmured an indistinct response, sat on a stool at the front curve of the bar, pointed to the male next to the register, then to his drink, and said to the bar maid, "One of those, please."

Almost overly solicitous to the few daytime customers who visited the seedy bar, Bostovitch introduced himself as, "C." He spread a wide smile. "I own the place. We have sandwiches, *pierogi*, cheap caviar, I must warn you—not our finest beluga from home—but is acceptable. Today our *pierogi* is stuffed with codfish or pork, topped with sautéed onions. The stumpy Russian host eyed Kovansk, his fit figure, and motioned impatiently for the bartender to hustle his coffee.

Appetite lost from an unseemly odor of the Polish dumplings in a steam cabinet behind the counter, Kovansk courteously asked, "Is there a Mr. Bostovitch here?"

The mobster grinned again. "I am your man, and you are ... Sir?" He extended a knurled hand to Kovansk and noticed his long, slender fingers. They shook before the doctor could respond with his name. "Are you the surgeon they call, Kovi?" Bostovitch sensed his identity right away.

"Doctor Oligoff, yes ... so nice to meet you. Kovansk withdrew his arm after a perfunctory shake, worried his hand—a delicate one, almost designed especially for neurosurgery—might be crushed. "I ... I am here to speak with you about my fiancé, Iliana Gosnov. I do not know or understand what you have done for her, what is expected of her in return, and how you think I fit in with her ... ah ... her ... current difficulties. What can you tell me about any police investigation currently underway?

"Can you help me?" Each query Kovansk put forth to Bostovitch brought an increasingly perplexed, unfocused stare. He inquired with almost desperate curiosity. It quickly became clear to the doctor that he crossed the line, and should never have let on that he knew of the stocky man's probable connections with their assault on Concord.

"Well, Doctor, you have me on the spot, do you not?" Bostovitch's expression paled, his smile and skin wrinkles disappeared. He grabbed Kovansk's arm too firmly for comfort. He meant business—serious business. "Iliana has spilled too much from her bilious, running little mouth, and should never have done so. I am a *brigadier,* just so you know."

Kovansk blanched from confirmation of his suspicions, set his cup down, and saw the man's eyes turn a steely gray.

"If my boss ever hears your talkative girlfriend has told you of our involvement, she and maybe you, too, my good doctor, could easily end up among the missing. I will warn you again; you are dealing with *Bratva*, just in case she has not mentioned it. Iliana borrowed money and owes us, big time." Bostovitch lied. He saw a look of surprise and frightened pallor sweep Kovansk's face.

Oligoff knew of the mob, remembered its domination of Moscow's underworld when he lived and studied there, and nearly passed out when told Iliana borrowed money, the worst-case scenario for a woman, he knew.

"I … I do not know what to say to such a threat. Iliana has told me little, the very reason I came here to ask for explanation. How deeply is she indebted; what else have you done for her besides extending a loan? Are you to conduct any further activity in her behalf?"

"Now, Doctor, that is quite enough. If you wish those little hands to continue operating, you would do well to ignore *Minsk*—L.A., me, and our … ah, private financial dealings, with … ah … clients." Bostovitch grimaced, released his clamp-like grasp on Kovansk's tensed biceps, pulled back his left coat lapel, and exposed his Glock-filled shoulder holster.

That was enough for Oligoff, whose broad training in Russia beset him with well-oiled *Sambo* combat and disarming techniques. Years of work and successful street encounters there, reinforced by frequent up-date seminars in New York while in medical school, unconsciously came to play. The most important technique he remembered, when faced with a weapon, especially to take the aggressor by surprise at the first sign of threat. Never think for a moment that negotiations might result in mediation, weapon withdrawal, or submission. "Get in first," were the bywords on the marquis that flashed in his mind.

Oligoff heard his instructor, an ex-KGB agent—with more hand-to-hand kills than a Moscow prison guard, and a master in the art—yell his most frequent caveat, "Take him, now! Never, never wait for opponent's next move." A fleeting instant passed. His time-forced preplan went to work. Subtly, he planted both feet on the floor; Kovansk inspired deeply, and stood up straight before Bostovitch could grab the pistol. He exhaled a gust of air with a bellow, drove freshly oxygenated blood to his sinuous musculature, lifted his right thigh in a flash, and with a snap, let loose a powerful lower leg kick to the back of Bostovitch's thigh. A stunning impact, it took the surprised man off balance, nearly fractured his femur, and threw him to the floor in a nanosecond.

The Glock tumbled from his hand and bounced out of reach beneath the bar. Before Bostovitch could react further, instinctive movement ensued while Kovansk surveyed the room for possible intervenors, a vital and instantaneous assessment of further hazards.

Bostovitch's leg crumpled with the searing pain of a well-placed and disabling jolt, which immediately rendered his left hamstring tendon useless. Kovansk leapt behind him, wrapped his right arm around the opponent's neck, positioned like a vice, so the inside of his elbow joint could crush the larynx with an extra tug of his left hand. A bit more pressure and vertebrae in the neck would fracture. Bostovitch, an accomplished combatant, but overweight and rusty, chocked a hacking apology while he struggled for breath, until Kovansk eased some and his color returned. Two men in dark polyester suits sprung from a booth; both brandished pistols, and moved stealthily toward the foray. The redhead barmaid grabbed a butcher knife from the sink and ran around the register.

Kovansk, outnumbered, and vulnerable, yelled authoritatively, "No one moves another muscle or this man is a dead, fucking *svenya*, a Russian pig. *Sambo* does it easily for me. Take another step and I crush this man's neck." Gasping to breathe, Bostovitch motioned them to comply, and at his prodding, stood up with Oligoff who shuffled backwards toward the front door. Bostovitch dropped to the doorstep. The doctor ran to his car, and tore away, northbound on Robertson Boulevard, before anyone inside could absorb what happened.

What the hell have I done? God forbid, I am soon to be in their sights. Now what? He mused fearfully as the downtrodden, urban landscape sped by in a blur. *They will come after both of us.* He pictured Svetiia's beating, how narrowly she escaped fatal injury. *She may be blamed for my being there. I must place her elsewhere and swear her to secrecy for now. First, I will pay her debt and, since the mob is in it for money, members may relax efforts to keep her in service. Then, she and Iliana should stay apart—no associations, so neither can be blamed for releasing sensitive information, until the investigators are identified.*

"Iliana, Kovi here." He spoke from his cell phone, while he entered the westbound I-10 Freeway.

"Where are you, damn it? Why did you just drive off like that and leave me hanging ... not knowing where, when...."

Kovansk interrupted. "Please, *popka* ... no time for that, not right now. Serious trouble is brewing. This man, Bostovitch, *Minsk*—L.A. bar. ..."

"She cut him off similarly. "Tell me you did not call him. You did not go to the bar. Kovi, you did not! He is a deadly bastard; he and his cutthroat cronies ... the worst in Los Angeles, maybe anywhere ... ruthless, and uncompromising. What the hell were you thinking? *Bratva*: that's who they are. Is that any surprise? Why did you not think I had good reason to keep him away from you? Now you have stepped in the trap's jaws. What, exactly, did you do?"

Kovansk rubbed his wrinkling forehead, tried to retain composure and avoid altercation after the tongue-lashing. "I drove to the *Minsk*, down on South Robertson, went in, and nearly got shot by asking a few innocent questions. I needed to know, since you concealed it, what is Bostovitch's connection?"

A gasp came forth on Iliana's end of the line. "Oh, Dear God, no!"

"I had to use two old *Sambo* moves to disable him, when I foresaw trouble, and got the devil away with my life, thank you to martial arts studies in old country. Now what? Can we pay your bill and quiet things down? I do not want us to be looking over our shoulders forever."

"Pay him? I owe nothing ... yet. I paid for everything he did, in full. He is lying if he says I owe him. Come home and ... I ... I promise to explain."

Kovansk did not argue though his feelings directed otherwise. *Why did she not tell me truth ... everything ... before*, he thought, *when I still trusted her? She has turned into Russian shrew, yes, a* Desmana moschata: *covert, underground, devious little insectivore ... works in the dark, cannot be relied upon, for anything. How will I get her out of house and away from hospital?*

"Who gave you the idea I owed him money?"

"He claimed you did, when I asked him how he was involved."

"Well, ask him to show you a note or something to verify his claim. It is simply not true. I paid him well, for everything, and we are only at negotiating stages, about more ... ah ... additional services." If you return to *Minsk* again, ask for paperwork to confirm his claims. There will be none."

"No chance I go back and get killed as I walk in the door. Never again, after way I took Bostovitch down."

My God, Kovi is dead meat, once Bostovitch decides how and when to retaliate. You do not hurt that man without a vengeful act in return, but of more serious consequence. I must call, try to persuade him to back down. I should be able to disable his anger by holding back payment for the next job over his head, until he promises to leave Kovi out of it. He started it by drawing his gun. He should respect Kovansk for the successful attempt to protect himself.

"I have had enough of this for now. Do what you must do and we will talk when you get home," she clipped.

Oligoff screeched to a halt in front of Svetiia's apartment, killed the engine, and ran to the wide-open front door without locking the car. The hardwood floor glistened in the afternoon sun that beamed boldly into the living room, lighting it brightly. An older Hispanic woman, dressed in a white blouse and starched slacks to match, on hands and knees, busy washing baseboards, ignored his knock. He stepped in, called to Svetiia, and stared about the partially vacated room in disbelief—astounded, at what he saw.

CHAPTER 29

LAGUNA BEACH

Aaron answered the cell call from Jim Gibson, his retired detective friend, who had news to report—though not completely what Concord hoped he would hear. A fax from the FBI arrived during the night, a report on the fingerprints Gibson lifted in Washington. "Aaron, I think we have a positive ID; at least I would bet on it with fairly high odds, from a couple good pulls off the map. That *Minsk*—L.A. match book cover, of all things; sure glad you stuffed your pocket with it."

Aaron remembered almost kicking it to the curb when he saw the matchbook on the road the morning of the shooting, however, the investigator's penchant for the coincidental and the telling, urged him to bend over one more time, and at least look at it. He preserved the evidence because it touted a Los Angeles business. What would the odds be for a local to have discarded it there, he wondered?

Startled with the news, Concord—who still maintained his disguise, as did Stansbee—seated himself on an uncomfortable vinyl couch in the living room of a furnished Laguna Beach apartment rental, for which he just paid a first and last month's rent deposit. Svetiia Kosnoff sat across from him, looked apprehensive, and wore a less provocative outfit than usual: natural linen slacks and a matching silk blouse, the tails of which she tied in a loose knot to expose just enough of her flat stomach to whet her appeal. A print silk scarf closed her neckline from view.

She could be a schoolteacher, Concord mused. Perched on a wooden kitchen barstool, Svetiia rested her feet on one of many cardboard cartons, still unpacked, and brought from her Santa Monica triplex, when Ken, Aaron, and two movers quietly piled her worldly belongings into a small rental truck that morning. She left no forwarding address with the Post Office and said nothing to neighbors or property owner about the relocation, per the investigators' strict instructions.

Svetiia willingly moved at their expense, to avoid another confrontation with the mob, when Concord and Stansbee suggested sequestration could be life saving for the time being. That intention evident, the frightened young woman took a different viewpoint toward them. She promised no contact with Kovansk or Iliana, and certainly, Bostovitch.

Compassionate, caring, and clearly understood, the men convinced her she was neither a suspect in the shooting, nor an assumed co-conspirator. During a telephone call from Aaron the night before, she became convinced that Iliana was definitely their target. She committed murder, they said. They needed her current locus, but Svetiia had not yet softened enough to disclose it. After the unforgettable tryst with Oligoff, she pledged to herself that he, too, would be protected for the time being.

Interest piqued, Svetiia listened to Concord's side of the phone conversation.

"Yes, Jim, I understand your thoughts and the doubt, too, but you've hit the nail on the head with her." Aaron trembled with anticipation and flashed excited glances at Svetiia. "If the matchbook prints trace to Iliana Ona Gosnov, that confirms our findings, as well. She is our girl! We can now put her in front of the house on the Hood Canal." For Svetiia's continued confusion, he went on: "We still need to explore motive, but we'll get that put together when we find her.

"My thought is that she left the matches on purpose, to wind Bostovitch into the foray as a possible blame shifting effort … set the cops sniffing up a different tree. Why else would they have appeared by the mailbox? Just about all we need to place her in cuffs, my friend. However, let's hang a little longer; just watch, and wait for more nefarious activity on her part. That we can't find this Kovi, or the weapon, to prove she was the shooter, may give the DA some concerns unless we can trip her on a further effort to snare a member of Concord's family." Once again, Aaron grinned at Svetiia, who listened intently, but remained far from the connection that Aaron Concord, the "dead man," sat right before her.

"Now, for the map. What did you get there?"

"Well, more than one person planted finger tracks on that piece of evidence. Iliana left a few partial ones, which is good, while most were from others.

"Concord's home locus was circled on the map, to tie another knot in her noose. Then we picked up two prints owned by an Alexander P. Grapple of Santa Monica. Did some checking and found he is the owner of a book store—Coastal Literary—in your area ... Santa Monica Boulevard; which carries a full line of out-of-state, local road maps, and atlases. I'm going to email a colored copy of the map cover and Gosnov's passport photo the FBI sent, to help you there. That'll be your job ... stop at the store, test their recall.

"Further, there are prints of one Boris K. Oligoff, a Moscow immigrant, all over the damned map. They show an address near Harvard University. Might have been a student there. Would he be the driver?" Gibson jumped ahead. "There are some on the map cover, traced from California DMV records, to a Bridget Doffler of Culver City, down by you, also. Think a surprise stop there could bear fruit?

Aaron looked up at Svetiia, watched her facial expressions, and body movements with care, then asked, while he momentarily pulled the phone away, "Who is Bridget Doffler?"

Svetiia turned palms up, raised eyebrows, most innocently shook her head, and whispered a convincing, "No idea ... never heard the name. Why?"

"Just wondered." *Doffler isn't in her circle,* he concluded to himself, satisfied with the obvious lack of name recognition.

"This Boris chap, a Russian, no doubt, like you said, yup? Gibson remarked.

Concord lighted and nodded approvingly. "Bet his middle name is Kovi. At least the initial K is more than a strong hint. Great news, Jim. See you ... er ... ah ... call back in a couple of days. Oh, and Jim—thanks, Buddy. Great job! I'll tell the lieutenant what a decent forensics man you are," Aaron said for Svetiia's benefit.

"Well young lady, you're in the middle of a great town, close to markets, shopping, and safely out of Bostovitch's clutches until this quiets down, we get him behind bars, or he appears satisfied with the payoff we'll make to him. Eleven thousand dollars, right?" Svetiia, flushed with embarrassment, nodded and expressed a genuine, "Thank you," with her bright blue eyes.

"You won't need wheels right away, but if you do, just whistle, and we'll figure out something. In the meantime, stay out of touch with anyone who might know Kovi, Bostovitch, or Iliana, and you will be safe from any more roughhousing." Aaron handed her five hundred in twenties for groceries and other immediate needs. *Just a question of time before this woman melts from kindness and hands us Kovi and Iliana on a silver platter. They can't be far away.* Aaron got up and walked toward the door, stooped forward, and winced from his awkward sitting position on the cheap couch.

"You know my current, er … profession, a highly paid escort, though I do have a psychology degree, and some post grad units in the field. Dreamed of being a nurse. I can begin to repay you and your partner, oh … today … tonight, if you like," she said sheepishly.

Aaron turned and quickly stepped to the outside landing. As beautiful and appealing as Svetiia appeared, Peggy awaited at home. He longed for his wife and the flying break they spoke about almost every night, after he left her in Washington.

Back at the office conference table, the two investigators brought one another up to date with recent findings. Stansbee began, "The girl, whose two fingerprints stood proud on the map, is out of the ring … a clerk at the book store where the likely culprits bought the Olympic Peninsula map. Our man, Gene Dempsy, who worked on another case in West L.A. this morning, stopped by the shop. Let's see here … yes, also saw one Bridget Doffler."

Stansbee read from hurriedly scribbled phone call notes, "She described Iliana Gosnov, exactly as I remembered her when she came to the office. Has to be the same woman. As for the male, Doffler remembered him as black-haired—cut neatly, curly, and fairly short—small goatee, tall, slender, and athletic, with a deep Russian sounding accent.

"He's your man in the van, A.C. Could well be Boris K. Oligoff. Svettia should see the photos. Watch her carefully when you flip them out; look for a lie. She'll try to cover for them; we know that already. We'll try that tough Ruskie, Bostovitch. Would he give Oligoff away? Maybe when we arrive bearing money—the eleven grand, tonight—to buy out Svetiia, we'll get a friendlier reception than before.

"The bookstore clerk plowed through sales records, found the couple paid cash … no credit card record, unfortunately … bought a couple books, too.

Very interestingly, she recalled Iliana wore a fancy black denim jacket, jeans, and black boots. DKNY?" He asked. "Still have your button?" Aaron nodded and opened the small manila envelope on the table, to confirm.

Stansbee waited in the truck, engine running, in a parking space at the south curb of Laguna's Coast Highway. Twenty five miles offshore, Santa Catalina Island stretched across the horizon—a dark violet sleeping giant surrounded by the blue Pacific—reminded it was months since he last fished its crystalline waters. Business boomed, and then Concord's problem erupted as a further diversion from his favorite pastime. *Sure need some rest and relaxation*, he thought.

Aaron emerged from the apartment building where they set up Svetiia Kronoff, bore a broad grin, and waved a folded sheet of white paper in each hand as if flags of surrender. He slammed the pickup's passenger door and belted in, before his animated rambling began.

Winded from the uphill trot, Aaron spoke, but reflexively panted the while. "I took in all her expressions … saw them beforehand … all … all, before I pulled out the FBI pictures. Showed her Iliana's first. Blushed, then, she did … bright red cheeks all of a sudden … breathed deeply, clasped both hands together to cover her shaking. Needed little more; a sure confirmation was evident, when I asked if the female in the photo was Iliana.

"Then, the *coup de grâce*, Kenny. I gave her a few minutes to regain composure … whipped out the small Oligoff passport photo, a poor one at that, but, no question; she knew the man. Oh, she reddened like a ripening apple again, more that time, breath held until she almost popped. Her feet began to tap as she feigned doubt, and scrutinized; to say nothing of obviously engorged jugular veins, and pounding carotid arteries. She is a very poor liar … too nice a girl … clearly recognized Oligoff. I asked if it were him, and, without thinking, she said, 'That's … no, not … Kovi.' Flushing suddenly, she turned a momentary gloss white … realized the cat was out of the bag.

"We have our murderous duo. Lets high tail it over to the *Minsk* ... see what Bostovitch says. FBI has Oligoff down as a doctor," Stansbee said. "Tried the university on a hunch and got some good feed from their personnel records clerk; I know her from handling cases there. His last address is in Beverly Hills. We'll hop by there, on the way back, with our phone company garb, and see what gives. Then I have to go home for a while, take the wife on a little break. She's losing patience to say the least.

"Meanwhile we have Svetiia on our side. Sooner or later, she'll spill the beans, as her comfort level with the safe location and with us, increases. I can feel it. That SOB, Bostovitch, and his underground clan abused and marginalized her far too much. We need only a current address and we'll be home free, ready for release to the cops ... this entire scenario.

CHAPTER 30

LOS ANGELES

This time, a bull of a man backed Stansbee and Concord—six foot five, two hundred sixty seven pounds, size thirteen shoes, and fists to match. Obie Pacette, legitimate piece-carrying, first generation Samoan, a security guard in uniform or street clothes—circumstances dictating which attire—accompanied operatives from the office when violence loomed. During potential tenuous interviews, his presence permitted frank conversation to pervade, in lieu of the physical challenges which could otherwise be expected.

When briefed beforehand, Aaron suggested that Little Obie—dubbed that by men in the office—keep his hand on the huge Remington long barrel .44 magnum revolver he holstered on a figured black leather police belt. Obie served a twenty-one year stint with the Santa Ana P.D. in Orange County, as tough an outfit as existed in Southern California; retired, and began his own company. A kindly man, clean-shaven, jet black but graying hair, and coal eyes, he retained his homicide detective demeanor: direct, loud—when he wanted to be—cocky, understanding, and downright intimidating. A more united front promised to present at *Minsk*—L.A., in contrast with the gunpoint submission which dampened their prior visit. Far from Kovansk's aggressive behavior, however, Ken and Aaron left their previous visit under trying but tolerable, businesslike circumstances.

Obie would lead the threesome past the goon in front; they planned at first glance. They would go directly to the booth where Bostovitch always perched, so his trained eyes could see the front and rear entrances. They were to seat themselves before Bostovitch could react. Obie said it would put the Russian on the defensive right away and, thus, set the confabulation's tenor on their terms; not his.

"On second thought, let's park in the back lot," Obie said with a crafty smile, "surprise the guy and bounce in from the rear. Always takes bar staff by surprise, if someone they don't know drops in from behind. Did that all the time when I'd call on a small lounge, looking for a perp. Now, Aaron, you've got the $11,155?"

Concord patted his inside jacket pocket. "All here, Boss."

"Kenny, you put that piece of yours in your belt, just behind the buckle so the Ruskie can see it; spread your coat lapels apart, and we'll take full charge from the beginning."

Hurriedly, the three men entered according to plan. They approached Bostovitch's table before his henchmen at the bar took notice, slid into the pleated vinyl semicircle, and crowded both sides of the surprised mobster.

"I thought I told you not to come back, gentlemen, and you waltz right in, bring this big kid with you. Supposed to worry me ... eh? I don't think so." Bostovitch looked clearly agitated with the sudden intrusion into his territory, just as Obie predicted.

The butt of Pacette's magnum stayed visible above the table. He kept his hand on it, as if he expected trouble.

"So what brings you cops or whatever you are ... telephone men ... eh ... here with this overgrown vice dick? Want some girlie action or. ..?"

"Enough small talk, little fellow. Just listen to the man here and you'll know." Obie gestured to Concord to fill the next void.

"Well, C," Aaron began, "we saw the remains of Svetiia after you slapped her around, and left her to her own on the bedroom floor."

Bostovitch's attention focused sharply. The dim light in the bar seemed to darken as his expression tightened; his hands grasped the table, and he turned his gaze across the room to the bar.

"Svetiia wasn't shy about the incident, said you just went into her something awful ... really left the girl bruised and cut, for God's sake. What kind of a squealing little rat, are you, to pound on a small, helpless woman like that?"

Stansbee and Concord met eyes. Both politely interrupted Pacette's tactics; well-practiced good cop—bad cop strategy at work again. "We have Miss Kronoff in protective custody, Pal, so forget pulling that one again. Furthermore, we are here to speak about her debt. Just how much does she owe?" Concord thought it possible Bostovitch might have had a lower figure in mind.

The mobster's withdrawl of a small notebook from his inside coat pocket, prompted both Stansbee and Obie to move their hands instinctively toward their weapons. "Jumpy, are you?" Bostovitch mocked, while he opened the dog-eared booklet to a page entitled, "S. Kronoff." Clumsily, he punched numbers into a small calculator. "That would be, ah … let's see, simple interest this month, plus, hmmmm … er, seems to be about $11,155." Obie and Concord glanced approvingly and nodded toward Aaron who withdrew the money and pushed the packet to the Russian.

"Count it," Obie directed Bostovitch who reached for the cash with shaking hands.

The mobster flipped the envelope from one hand to the other, eyed the others with suspicion, and wondered, *why would they pay for Svetiia?* Money was money, however, and it counted to exactly what he said Svetiia owed.

"Better assure us this will be the end of her indentured slavery. If not you'll spend time in the big house for tempting federal law, my friend," Obie stated with no evident doubt in his expression. "You're through with this Little Lady … all done. Is that understood? Now may we have the note … anything she signed for the advances?"

"You fellows might be interested in our not using notes or other … ah, such instruments. *Bratva* has no need for them when we can clip a finger off at any time. Our borrowers know that. You fellows like a beer, anything … dinner? What detail are you from? Work with Sullivan or Kaminsky, do you? Eh, eh?"

Stoic looks dropped over their faces. Stansbee broke the silence with his phony accent. "Now that we've agreed you will leave her alone, tell us about our doctor pal, Kovi? Where does he now live? We know you and he had a quick chat."

"Chat? He damned near killed me with some smooth *Sambo* moves, came in here like he owned the place, pulled me down. He is good and fast, all right. I'll knock off the fucking wimp surgeon … break all fingers if he meddles again. Wanted to know what my association with his girlfriend,

Iliana, was all about, and it is about nothing. I have nothing to do with girl. Nothing, I tell you, though I could use her in my escort service, eh, eh. ..." A supple grin surfaced for a moment.

"Where does she live ... Kovi and her together?" Aaron asked.

Bostovitch thought again, how he nearly suffered a fractured femur by Kovansk's lightning fast and unforeseeable kick, and opted out. "Don't know...somewhere in Beverly Hills ... all I know. Now, if there is nothing more, I do thank you for the payment ... will be sorry to lose my very best little helper; but a deal is a deal. We keep our word when the other side keeps theirs. We shall leave her alone. I do not want her singing about me or any of my ... ah, er ... activities anymore. Can you handle that with her?" He reached across the table and solidly shook each man's hand once.

"Handled," Obie affirmed, as he wriggled out from the booth, followed by the others, leaving Bostovitch alone at the table, seemingly pleased. He began to count his bounty once more, as they single-filed to the rear door.

"Not a bad business," the mobster uttered, "a good day it is!"

Chernya Bostovitch answered the phone from his table in the *Minsk* bar, noted familiarity with the caller's number, but he did not recognize it until the man spoke, in his best and most humble Russian.

"Mister Bostovitch, it is Doctor Oligoff, with an apology for my rudeness and ill manners, ah, the other day. I hope I did not hurt your leg." Bostovitch listened and waited for more, while he massaged his thigh behind the knee. He wondered how he would take the skinny doctor out, if their paths ever crossed again.

Oligoff could hardly think, bearing in mind his complete shock at Svetiia's apartment being vacant, and no sign of her or her belongings as he walked through the unit. The cleaning woman offered no help, nor did her employer, to whom Kovansk placed an immediate call before leaving. Svetiia cleared out, cleanly disappeared, and he could easily see why.

"Sudden fear of my life," the doctor said, provoked his offensive action. "I saw you reach beneath your coat, I thought for your gun. I was there, in your territory ... alone ... too vulnerable. My fight or flight response honed to fine edge, a reach for your gun ... no one to watch my back; I had to do something and fast. Reflexes finely taught in old country, required an instant decision: run and get shot on the way out of your bar, or take my chances with hand-to-hand combat. I practiced *Sambo* for many years. I am sorry, Sir, that we did not finish our business. Iliana's affairs are my affairs, and very sadly, the troubles she has brought upon herself have become my problems. I have to ask for your kindness, to help me understand what you two are cooking up in the *borchst* ... my favorite Ukraine meal, by the way."

No response came forth.

"I know you have *pierogi* much of the time at the bar, but is there ever a day for the beet borscht ... old country recipe? Mister Bostovitch, are you on the line?" Silence reigned while Bostovitch crafted his next move with Oligoff. His brain raced with ideas.

Finally the stocky Russian replied. "You have plenty nerve to call ... you would be doctor. If your fingers turned up in an envelope we mailed to your big-mouth lady friend, you might not be so good at *Sambo,* or your surgery either, eh?" Oligoff shivered with the prospect of more violence. He came close to a dive through the red light, and skidded to a stop; front wheels just over the limit line. He pictured selling pencils by the hospital door, dolling them out with clubbed hands, disguised to preclude recognition; having relinquished his Porsche, new home, and all he worked so hard to attain.

Iliana did this to me. Why did I keep things going with her, once I knew she was bad blood? Why? Stupid me ... should have known when she said she would kill her first fiancé if she ever saw him again. The light turned green and he accelerated south on Robertson Boulevard again, toward the *Minsk.* "I did not mean to offend you, Sir, and never meant harm," Oligoff continued.

What to do with this svenya. *Teach him lesson, today? Or, see what is on his mind?* Bostovitch had a flash of better judgment and asked why Kovansk called. "What do you wish of me, to make me punching bag again?" He could not help but respect the doctor for his guts, the strength, accuracy of his kick, and the deft with which the almost fatal strangle hold ensued, before he hit the floor. "That was some pretty cunning *Sambo* work Doctor, commendable, as a matter of fact. I was good at the art myself ... one time. No hard feelings," he lied. "None; now, what do you want?"

Oligoff recalled Svetiia's mention that it would take some $11,000 for the release from the mob's jaws. He took the chance, pulled cash from his Beverly Hills bank on the thought of buying her out, prepared to risk a lump of money that pleased Bostovitch more than gratification from threats he brandished.

"I am on my way, if you give me assurance I will not be harmed. I came to pay Svetiia's obligation ... eleven thousand, I believe she said."

"Why, yes," Bostovitch replied—arched eyelids barely contained. He turned a wide smile that graced his jowls—which he failed to override with the pan face practiced in advance. "It ... ah ... about that amount ... yes ... close enough ... a little more, but I will accept your offer as payment in full."

"Be there with the money in a few minutes and you assure me, do you; that I will be unhurt, and will leave, as I arrived, in one piece, with all my fingers?"

"One piece, of course; you are the man bearing gifts ... buying Svetiia's release."

Seated at his usual table with Kovansk, Bostovitch felt uneasy with the double payment he was about to receive; but the doctor called him, he chuckled to himself. *How could I refuse? If this brainless, elitist sucker wishes to part with his money, I am one step closer to buying car like his, and no tax to pay.*

The mobster flipped pages in his notebook as he did not long before, found Svetiia's record, murmured some calculations, and confirmed, "Eleven thousand would do it."

Unhesitatingly, Kovansk passed the bundle of cash across the soiled table, within Bostovitch's grasp. The bar owner grinned. Silver caps on his right front teeth flickered brightly as the neon sign went on and off in the window. He grabbed at the bundle, and carelessly stuffed the bills into his coat pocket, unable to quell the smile that showed all his teeth this time.

"Now that we have Svetiia settled, you will relax your grip on her? No more beatings? No more servitude, correct?"

"All true, my good man, and thank you. Now if that is all, I have work to do. He pointed to a stack of receipts and the journal on which he worked.

Probably keeps two sets of books, the greedy bastard, Kovansk mused. *Bet he takes home more than I do, and likely quit school in sixth year.* "By the way, we never finished speaking of Iliana and what work you are doing for her. Might you fill me in? I ask you, please; tell me what I can expect in coming weeks. I cannot take chances she will be found by the law, spill the beans, to put me in bull's eye." He looked for clues—what Bostovitch was thinking—but saw the mobster's best poker expression sweep away his grin, and learned nothing.

"Iliana and I may do some more business, or not … depends on pay I need, risks taken, and what exactly my, er … staff and I … ah … do for our pay. You do understand, how I respect her privacy?"

"Is there anything I can do for you … encourage your assistance, to fill me in, so I know whether to stand by her or not? It would be worth a good sum to me, and you, too. I am thinking, say, uh, five thousand dollars."

Bostovitch laughed aloud; his slightly protuberant belly shook, and he clapped open palms to the table. "That is good one. You take me for stupid man, eh?" He leaned forward with a stern stare, while crimson filled his cheeks and forehead. "You really think you are smarter than me? Tell you what; I give you thirty seconds to run like antelope on the steppes; no fingers chopped this time, OK?"

Oligoff looked around, panic-stricken, saw no heavies approaching, but left their table for the door, and the relative safety of the public sidewalk, with nary a look behind.

Filled with deep and eerie laughter, after Oligoff made his exit, Bostovitch still had some inclination to remove the surgeon's fingers for the lasting leg pain he suffered, when Kovansk dropped him so unexpectedly. *This young man may be good for more money, however, far more important than revenge, which usually pays nothing for one's risks and efforts.*

"His day will come. In mean time," he patted the wad of hundred dollar bills, and said to one of his assistants who came to sit with him, "this is not a bad business; not such a bad business, at all."

CHAPTER 31

Kovansk returned to Santa Monica for one further effort to locate Svetiia. Residents of single-family homes nearby were unaware of the woman's departure or any of her daily habits. That she had a small car, but frequently walked or rode taxis to the local business district was their only offering. Others alluded to a curious nocturnal lifestyle, and commented that her curtains, usually drawn closed during daytime hours, gave rise to assumptions that she slept days, and worked nights, even on weekends.

One next-door neighbor, Annie, a middle-aged floor nurse at the Medical Center, whom Kovi met years before, said Svetiia stumbled on hard times. "She only scratched out a living," the informant said, though she remembered Iliana, when she lived there, as a, "contemptuous bitch, who never had much to say—except non-stop raves about her job, and her volatile relationship with Doctor Oligoff."

Discouraged that Svetiia moved without notice, Kovansk tried, but could not withdraw his pressing desires to see her again, and began to wonder. *Did she seduce me just to get help ... to facilitate release from Bostovitch's grasp? Was I a fool to spring her from mob? Could she make a more trustworthy mate? What will Iliana do? She may discover I am interested in the woman.* Reluctantly, and with no further avenues to pursue at that time, Kovansk turned toward the desert, and resigned himself to make the best of Iliana for the night.

Concurrently stirred in Iliana's mind, however, were auras of suspicion and doubt, vociferous, anger-laden accusations of disloyalty, as she limped back and forth through the house, confused by his apparent lack of understanding. Uncontrolled shrieks of epithets periodically drew her toward Kovansk's intrusion into completion of the mission to eradicate Concord from her life. She panicked at the thought that she and Oligoff could be identified as the assailants, that all too soon, their whereabouts would become clear. She had to make a move, she concluded, as her Kovi raced toward their desert home.

Nearly 10:00 PM, Kovansk not yet at the house, Iliana festered with fury to the point of hysterics, in a continuing battle with herself to justify the shooting. Though she tried to shun its ever-present stealth, guilt chewed at her from every angle. "Concord deserved the shotgun blast. He obfuscated my birthright to economic recovery by removal of telling documents from the hospital chart. He did it with malice, to save insurance company dollars." She paced and stomped with her bad leg, alternatively on the hardwood and tile floors, from one room to another. As her petulance grew, she demanded answers: Concord's motivation for the ethical breach that threw such jeopardy into her life.

He damned well earned pellets in his face, his house shot to pieces, and a widowed wife. What should I have done, coddled him as Kovi would have it? What a little wimp he can be at times. And what does Kovi appreciate of the pain, the embarrassment, and anguish I have suffered at Concord's hand? No matter that Mother's senile anesthesiologist was the real culprit—my own family, Papa himself, a strong contributor.

Her frustrations and blame combined to a heated tempo when she heard the unmistakable roar of Kovi's Carrera as it plunged into the garage, and the one final engine wind-up he always managed, before coming to a stop in the center stall. The electric door rolled closed. He stepped into the kitchen to find Iliana waiting: hair disheveled, clumps of it pulled from her head, strewn about the white tile floor. Attired in a full-length, black nightgown, she ripped one strap during a rage, and left that side to hang off her shoulder. Sunburned face—marred with charcoal runs of mascara down almost violet cheeks—she looked worn and haggard from earlier tantrums. Unwashed dishes festooned the sink and counter top; but one light burned in the entire house.

Burdened with a deep urge to turn tail and leave, Kovansk nearly backed down the steps to the garage, once he took in the ghastly sight.

Spellbound for a minute or two, the silence broke with her words. Beforehand, however, Iliana silently coached herself—nothing gained to offend Oligoff and take the risk he might be pressed to leave again.

Must keep my composure. God knows, I lost it all day, while I cursed, blamed, and ranted over my fear of being identified, and found ... arrested and jailed—to suffer that, and my crippled leg, for the rest of my life. Can't overlook getting my hands on the money I discovered in the safe ... need it to finish my job.

"Hello, *popka.*" She sometimes used the same nickname he called her, however impertinent to a male. "I have had a ... a ... trying day ... missed you terribly ... lots of emotional and physical pain to wade through." She thought about the cash hoard she discovered, then grimaced while she lifted her gown to the waist. "Look at the bruises ... a fall down the stairs after my afternoon nap." Kovansk cringed at the fresh contusions and abrasions, curious if Iliana became unsteady from self-medicating earlier.

"I am so ashamed; squealed at you on the phone as I did. You simply tried to seek information I withheld from you. So sorry." She wept lightly, overdramatized terribly, and threw herself into his arms. The two stood in the unlighted rear entry, embraced, until she calmed herself.

What is that perfume I smell on his coat? I swear, it is something familiar, but not mine. Has my Kovi been with someone else? Could it possibly have been Svetiia? She has always had a crush on him and he remarked from time to time, how lovely she was. Could that be hers? It is such a familiar odor. I will call the little slut, fish for more information about the investigators ... put some pressure on her for the full story, if there is one.

Oligoff, uncomfortable with closeness so soon after he became the subject of her wrath, struggled hard to appear consoling and compassionate. He trembled with relief when she pulled away; unaware she discerned another woman's scent. *Is this girl bipolar? Am I failing her ... unsupportive when she needs it most? Is she completely unconscious when she succumbs to these rages? Her dishonesty; where does that stem from? Is it only this Concord or, as Svetiia suggested; her father's sexual liberties when she was a child? She is hopelessly out of control, in any event.* Kovansk felt Iliana's dissatisfaction with his coolness. His reaction was to pry, in hopes she would talk further and more openly.

"*Popka*, you are so troubled lately, not the same person you were before we went to Washington. Has remorse filled you with the hatred that manifests at such inopportune times? Are you still determined to keep venture alive and virulent? It has separated us so much. I am drawn into your sphere of sadness, regret, and pain, then pull back my feelings, and my willingness to help you through it.

"You have done a horrible thing: shot a man while he sat, innocently, in his own house ... his castle ... a safety net we would likewise consider. Why? You had your reasons, any therapist could not help but define as hopelessly complex, while sadistic, and unjustifiable from any perspective. It is no wonder you suffer."

Iliana bolted, unwilling to accept Kovansk's far too self-serving and exculpatory monologue. She flushed and then whitened; her heart leapt forward to a near fibrillating pace; she backed to a chair by the door, sat down, and dropped her head to fisted hands that shook uncontrolably.

A blind stare toward the floor; the young woman wept, genuinely this time, but fast recuperated to a feisty retaliatory state. "Goddamned Aaron Concord, and to hell with you, too. Concord ruined my life and deserved to be shot, in the face, if that is what occurred ... hardly punishment enough. I do not even know if the man is dead, or alive and on my trail. And you! You and your pomposity. You act as though you had nothing to do with it.

"May I remind you, Boris Oligoff, that you accompanied me on the exploratory trip ... in your Porsche; then you stole the van, drove it to the scene, waited while I fired—over and over, again—never asked me to stop at any stage of the effort.

"You have the nerve to cast stones my way? An accomplice, sure as hell you were, Baby! Never think I would not bring you in, should we be caught and I have the opportunity for a reduced sentence. Those two men sniff at our heels like Russian Wolfhounds, as we speak. I have strange, recurrent feelings each day when I arise from bed; there is a connection somehow with them and Concord; but not the police."

Iliana stood up, limped to the foyer, and looked at herself in the mirror. Badly fatigued, she felt unsightly, defamed, frighteningly exposed, and her countenance was a match ... a perfectly miserable fit, she thought.

Livid with her allusions that overstated his involvement, Oligoff looked at her hatefully. He harbored thoughts of crushing her chest with a fast elbow impact to the sternum; then, while on the way down, a vicious chop to the nape of her neck, to fracture a cervical vertebra and finish the job. *What has happened to us? I must keep my cool ... humor her until she comes out of this funk ... sits down to discuss what she has received or is expecting to get from the mob. I must decide what to do before we're exposed as the actors in this three-ring circus. Next attempts to locate us could be at our at home, or the hospital. That would be it. Things have become critical; it almost seems we are being taunted. Iliana is evidently more than willing to cross me and make me bad guy, if police do question us.*

Maybe I should accept the offer for Chairman of Trauma Surgery at North Moscow University's Movontov Trauma Center, and leave U.S. immediately. The waiting list of surgeons who wish to acquire equity positions at Joshua would make it easy to sever ties there and recoup the investment. The Russian medical center, world renowned for their advanced cancer therapeutics, added depth to the opportunity. *Their last offer included lucrative side benefits: full reimbursement for all taxes paid, a chance to buy a beautiful university-subsidized home in the suburbs, in a down market and; along with moving expenses; a new Land Rover™, such a high salary, too—offers still grow as we continue to communicate. Should I accept a part time teaching position at the university's medical school for a few years, the government would relax loan to Papa, for farm. We would all be better off from the change..*

Oligoff slowed the fast positive thinking to weigh the adversities, "Those brutal winters ... weather I could never forget. A quick decision maker, in itself," he said aloud, "if it weren't for murder charge I may face, with the law or someone friendly to the Concords, so close behind our every moves."

Since he bought into the desert hospital, Dr. Oligoff kept doors open for the position in Russia, with continued phone negotiations that he purposely dragged on with ostensible passivity, to keep the hospital's interest afire, yet give him more room to evaluate the direction his life would take. Meanwhile, two interesting offers from other finely equipped facilities in St. Petersburg, enlivened things. "I would have to do everything quickly and beyond Iliana's vengeful claws," he muttered almost too notably. He turned to see her atop the stairs, unaware his hurried musings became audible.

CHAPTER 32

"What a lovely flight it turned out to be ... that cold front loomed so ominously, when we left. I grew a little worried, we couldn't complete the itinerary we planned. Can we do that route down the coast again, when it clears next time?" Peggy spoke briefly and finished with a gasp when Aaron dropped the collective, to reduce power. The sudden altitude loss captured her breath for a moment, when the helicopter descended rapidly. Aaron brought the nose up to stop forward motion, increased power, leveled the aircraft and settled to the pad up the hill from their cabin. Peggy took their luggage to the house with the golf cart. A frantic cell call interrupted his post-flight check.

Jim Gibson, his flying buddy and retired police investigator reported the latest news. "Aaron, so glad I caught up with you. Where have you been ... off flying without me, I'd guess? Finally, took your missus for that long promised trip? I called to tell you we have a positive on our Kovansk Oligoff, the shooter's van driver; Doctor Boris Kovansk Oligoff, that is. Yup, nothing less than a brilliant surgeon ... U.S. trained, with our taxpayer dollars ... Harvard boy living the high life now, in Beverly Hills. I learned by some phone work that he has been in the states close to ten years ... very well respected and, interestingly, has been seen during recent stake-outs at that *Minsk*, ah, the Russian Mob-owned Los Angeles beer bar ... on Rober. ..."

"We've discovered him, all right," Aaron broke in, "we just haven't found where he hangs out or works. I think that will break, though, when

I go back south, day after tomorrow. My ex-partner and I can work a little more on the best informant we could ask for, Iliana's girlfriend, who has been jilted by Iliana and manhandled by the mobster bar owner one too many times. She's the best source for of both culprits' latest digs," Concord went on. "Correlated by all our informational sources overlaid, we've frigging got them ... no doubts this time.

"Jim, could you be of a bit more help and arrange surveillance, 'round the clock, perhaps with former or reserve officers, not serving in any official police department capacity, in case the limping girl reappears; simply 'a security project' we do not wish reported to the police. I'm still concerned she might snoop around to confirm she got me ... or not, in the first assault."

"Roger that; let's begin when and if you're fairly sure she intends to come back for a look-see. You give her a few more intimidating cell calls and it should provoke her to show. We should cover your mother's place, too, since she could ID Oligoff and Iliana by their descriptions, when they looked for you in the Seattle area—albeit with their guises—and by his Porsche. 'One dead, what's another,' they could easily reason?"

"It's true," Aaron replied, frozen in fear for a minute or two, that his aging mother lay so exposed, alone at her house in Redmond. "Think I should send my wife over there again, Jim. We just flew in; she could leave immediately, before things get too warm down south. That would eliminate her car from visibility in the driveway. I'll rent at the airport and leave my car there. The place would thus look like death indeed visited. I'd expect they would then go to Mom's. Better hire a few off duty cops for her safety if you would, when I call ... they're headed this way."

"Good as done, my friend, good as done."

"Thanks, Jim. We'll soon fly our brains out again."

Midnight brought a light rain or heavy fog to the Los Angeles area; often the two were indistinguishable close to the coast. Immune to the coolness of the night, coming from comparative warmth of the Mojave Desert, a fiery hot female navigated at top speed, southbound on Robertson Boulevard, en route to *Minsk*—L.A., hopeful Bostovitch made a hasty decision to help her.

Iliana Gosnov kept eyes to the rear, and drove with blind hope that she could thusly avoid a traffic stop. While she maintained a close watch, she muttered to stay awake, and to review recent developments. "I hope C will be satisfied with the $125,000 I took from the safe this morning. I'll tell him it's all I have; it's everything I could scrape together. Kovi cannot be angry at my action.

"After all, the entire contents of the steel drawer, $275K, should have been paid to me as reimbursement ... what I loaned him from Papa's estate, for the hospital share. It's really my money; it is due me. He owes me an explanation, as I would owe him for not disclosing this morning's withdrawal. Kovi can be damned for not telling me how it came about, however, and when he placed such a large sum there.

"The no good wimp doctor ... no backbone. 'I will take no more risks,' he said. Oh, he belongs in surgery, not in the real world, where he would support me until it's all over. I will do it myself. Maybe Bostovitch will help me with his personal expertise. He has some ideas, he warned me could be expensive, but at least he has some ideas. I need to remove myself from the Southland for a while, anyway, until the escapade completely blows away."

Iliana merged toward the curb and stopped in front of the bar on the opposite side of the street. Dark, cold and yet misty, the city's smells were so different from those of the desert, where the air, comparatively filtered, is smooth to intake, and does not cause that noxious cough Los Angelenos grow to tolerate. She loped across the busy street and came too close to being struck by a fast moving truck.

"Damned L.A. drivers," no mind paid to her mid-block crossing without crosswalk protection. An L.A.P.D. van—red, blue and yellow flashing lights galore—followed behind the offending pick-up, a stern reminder to the woman, that she could well be in the same spot as the truck operator, and all too soon. She shuddered and her hands tremored as she limped, inviolate, to the entrance, pushed aside the obstructive velvet curtains and ignored the bouncer who maintained his coarse look and asked for her ID.

Directly to Bostovitch she ambled, around disheveled chairs, and slid into the booth where he usually worked, at his silent behest; naught but a stern smile and a bored wave.

"Iliana ... a surprise indeed, and such a late hour ... must need something from old C, heh?" He hand signaled to the bartender for two vodkas and they arrived as she sat down. "Now, let us get to work." Half his glass disappeared in one gulp. "I received good training, as I told you before, to fly our Russian MI-8 helicopters in covert operations and open conflicts, for several exciting but perilous years.

"I flew the better part of 3000 hours in them, all over the Caucasus— high mountain missions and trainings for our troops and those of favored nation partners. In fact, they used Bostovitch, when I was young and adventurous, to establish safe flight ceiling when, with co-pilot and crew chief, we did numerous set downs at the summit of Mt. Elbrus, 18,510 feet above sea level, highest peak in the range. I remember, too, night missions in Middle Eastern deserts and in the hinterlands of Azerbaijan, Kazakhstan, along Russia's western borders and, yes, even in Moscow to transport State Police in hunts for intruders: drug traffickers, terrorists and. ..."

"Please, Mister Bostovitch; where will this be taking us? Iliana interrupted, "can't we get to the poin. ...?"

"Rude little thing; are you not? C has a plan for us both if you will show me some respect and patience, please ... you young spitfire, eh?"

Iliana fumed, turned from him to apply needed self-control and assumed, he saw in her face, the sudden ruby-red facial coloration of the beet borscht he sipped when she arrived. "So sorry; my uncle, Papa's brother from St. Petersburg, lost his life in an MI-8, a terrible collision with another, when both pilots vied for the same landing space on a ship, prototypically adapted for the Soviets' fledgling assault fleet. Until accepted into medical school, my father opted as a possible alternative, to attend army helicopter flight training. Your mention of the MI-8 triggered my recall."

While she elaborated on the memory, Iliana craftily mediated the vile attitude she was about to spring on the mobster, to speed things along. OK, C, I just wanted to throw a bit of gasoline on the fire. I apologize for my impatience." She glanced twice at her watch and hoped he took notice.

"Pay no mind; I can get carried away whenever talk moves in the direction of those flying days ... full of excitement, they were. Indeed they were. To continue with my background, I was also trained to fly a similar aircraft, America's workhorse of the day, their Bell 204-B or UH-1 ... the Huey, so well known for their massive use as transports and gunships in Vietnam. It was the better of the two helicopters and it so happens our organization has a couple of them, used for many duties, er, ah ... certain projects."

He failed to elaborate; they were kept by the mob to unload illicit drugs from ships at sea, inside the limits of the Air Defense Identification Zone. Deliveries then followed to a few drop zones at private pads and airstrips on the Olympic Peninsula. They get used, too, for frequent deposits of body bags—heavily weighted to sink the contents ... badly behaved *Bratva* agents or decedents contractually executed for others—into the depths of the Pacific.

"In fact, best of the two, N998 Delta Zebra; a cheap surplus purchase from Canadian Mounties; we fully rebuilt to every detail, has a proven flight record since organization acquired it. We operate it beneath a corporate veil, Northwest Aquatic Surveys, Inc. Yes, Bostovitch is one of few pilots with authority to fly it—on *Bratva* missions, of course. Very reasonable rate, I might add, since you are repeat customer. $1000 per flight hour, plus fuel and other out of pocket costs, is a bargain for such a fine old bird, the ideal platform for ... er, disposal of certain things ... ah, and its large sliding doors for ease of ... ah, er cargo handling. We would make good use of the bird for my plans in your behalf. You pay twice that hourly rate to a charter company for pilot, aircraft, and crew chief.

Iliana squirmed at the price and thought, *there he goes again; C is high binding me as far as he can push, with outrageous profits to his organization and as usual, a coffin or servitude as the payoff motivator.* Her temper revealed itself again, with a flush of deep violet ear color and this time, a contrasting look of pallor in her face, as blood rerouted to vital organs with the adrenalin rush. Bodily reaction to her sudden rage was so apparent that Bostovitch mediated before she could retort. "Now, Little One, do lower your voice, for there is more ... my plan to deal with the problem."

"It is getting late and I. ... Frustrated with his story telling, Iliana slumped.

"Formerly co-owner of investigative agency as obituary said, he may well be the one, with old cohort, who chases you ... for him but a game. He bats you around as cat plays with ball of yarn. If true, as I now suspect, he probably has you and Kovi in his sights by now, ready at any time to place what he has gathered, in front of County Sheriff. Arrest warrants would follow immediately for attempted murder and other serious charges. A decent term in prison will come next after very expensive trial."

"First the SOB messed with medical records, which denied me a decent life, and now he plays with me in some kind of sick game? If you are correct, I will take the risk; to end his life as he did mine. His termination seems the only route to settle my irrevocable compulsion, my wish for payback. So, what do you then propose?" she asked grimly.

Bostovitch removed a manila folder from his briefcase on the booth seat, slid the papers from inside and spread them out, fan-like, on the table. "We have found, while we waited for your expected response, that Concord is owner of a small helicopter—a lightweight compared to our 8500 pound Huey. My people there have seen it rolled outside the large building behind and uphill from the house which took your shots."

"Yes, yes, we saw the building ... his hangar, I guess, but thought it a large garage. A light was on inside, but I did not know ... an aircraft kept inside?"

"FAA Registration Office says it's an R-44™, tiny by comparison and quite vulnerable to a Huey's powerful rotor downwash. If I should drop in by steep descent from behind, pull up nose ... a quick flare or recovery, just above, and force it to become unstable from the ensuing turbulence, he could not likely recover, would roll and drop like shot goose.

"Using suitable subterfuge, my man, already on the job, was told by fuel pad attendant at Bremerton Airport, that Concord flew nearly every good weather day, and toward dusk, showed up for full tanks and usually, a few cups of coffee. 'Nice man,' informant said ... flew half the time alone and often flew with guests, one of whom he knew, a recently retired Sheriff's deputy.

"You making some connections from those we are beginning to make, are you? Yes, I think we have those 'telephone men,' the cause of your recent troubles ... at work for Concord, if he is not one of them. Tomorrow I should receive Concord's photo from Department of Consumer Affairs. I would have shown it to Svetiia, if only I gave her a little lighter hand last week. I had to remind her, is better a ... er ... ah ... to show more respect and nicer manners to *Bratva* in future. But she has gone, left her apartment in a great hurry after Doctor Kovi paid. ..."

"Kovi ... what about Kovi? What did he tell you in the bar, C? He did see you here, did he not?" Iliana jumped from her seat, stood up and leaned across the table, face to face with the mobster. Before she could recover her composure, she demanded answers again. "Spill it, now, Mister Bostovitch, or I'll come gunning for you, too, after I blast holes in that two timing Kovan...."

"Shut that flapping mouth and get hold of yourself," Bostovitch cut her off and growled, "I will not put up with any more of your senseless threats."

His menacing glare stopped her bluster mid-way; he sat back down, and tried to breathe deeply to attain an element of control.

All eyes in the bar focused on Bostovitch and Iliana until icy gawks from the mobster turned curious onlookers away. A quick and very angry scowl toward Iliana when she began another rant, and he brought down his thick, sinewy right hand to clash on her left clavicle with such a thunderous impact, that she crumpled to the seat and slipped from consciousness. As if in a drunken stupor, her eyes lost their luster, she shook her head repeatedly, slurred to immediate submission, and uttered a meek apology.

"I am so sorry for that demonstration. You surprised me with such staggering news, goings on, however, that I just recently began to suspect myself. My former girl friend and my fiancé appear too fond of one another and work to my exclusion in the shadows of my recent upsets. You, Mister Bostovitch, seem to know much more about them than you have thus far said.

"Don't forget, you are an added conspiracy suspect in this crime, beside Kovi and me. I planted a paper matchbook like this one, in the area where I fired a few rounds and left ejected casings. She picked up one of several that lay on the table; waved it back and forth as she explained. "I finally concluded it was this matchbook which led investigators to the *Minsk* and the many inquiries here in Los Angeles, the only source of further connections … none other than yourself, as hub of the wheel. You talked too much and led investigators to discover my identity. Yes, you and your talkative Ukraine whore, Svetiia."

Incensed that Iliana could be stupid enough to say such things and worse, to speak of her effort to frame him, he flamed inside, but contained what might have put an end to their conversation, and simmered his retort to a relatively cool one. "Well, you ignorant little bitch; do you or do you not wish my assistance? I will tell you something else you do not yet know."

Bostovitch quickly weighed the value of not saying more, though in the end, felt obliged to get even for the accusations she made. Worse and more worrisome were her suggestions that she would speak to his inclusion as a co-conspirator in a plea bargain effort for her own leniency. *That was wrong thing to imply to me, an active member and local* Bratva *boss. At right time, she is piece of Russian breakfast toast—to be cleaned from the plate and digested. I should deal with her as I would any offender.*

He watched Iliana fulminate, steamed to the boiling point by then, when he said most sharply, "Doctor Oligoff paid me eleven thousand to buy out your friend's full obligation, just to clear up things between us somewhat more."

He knew the risk he took: she could dismiss his plan and he'd lose the $150,000 previously quoted for Concord's disposal. *Where else might she go?*

Bostovitch is her only alternative, he silently reasoned. The expected rebuke did not shoot forth. Instead, copious tears of horror and self-pity poured down the young woman's cheeks, accompanied by the deepest, most forlorn sobbing to which the tough mob leader had ever borne witness.

The upheaval birthed a temporary release of the tenacious hold that tormented Iliana over decades of self-loathing, combined with the concomitant hatred she held so solidly for men. This would add one more male to her list, at the top of which now sat her Kovi, she quickly but sadly ruminated.

"Now, just for now, let's dispose of these bouts of anger, redirect them where best purpose is served and get along with plans to take out this Concord, we can now see is alive. I have arranged," Bostovitch said, "for N998 Delta Zebra to be available, on call and flight-ready while you and I do some more fact finding here and when we travel to Seattle. Do you think you can stand working with me?" he asked with a gentle snigger.

"I think Concord's demise will put an end to police curiosity. FAA accident investigators will cite pilot error as cause of accident and that should end it. Homicide would no longer be an issue. We will then put everything behind and go our separate ways."

Iliana calmed some, enough to think more clearly, see through her rage, and get back on point: to enlist the help suggested by Bostovitch, employ his ideas, and go forward to face the truth about Aaron Concord's life. *It is time,* she thought, *that I try to negotiate for a lower figure.* "The $150,000 you quoted, I do not have. I scraped together absolutely everything and could gather no more than $125,000. I brought it with me and I'll hand it to you now, with your promise that you will return any money not earned. I want his skin; so here is my payment in advance." She took a stuffed manila envelope from her sack purse and dropped it in his lap.

"That falls far short of my quotation," he said and hesitated almost to the point of Iliana's alarm, "however," he grinned to exhibit the silvered teeth and went on, "It will work for what I have planned, my young lady." Bostovitch nodded and had to struggle, not to show his excitement. He reached forward with his hand, lightly grasped hers where Iliana held it close to her body, and shook it a few times. Her tears cleared by then. A stiff but decipherable smile curled her lips upward and revealed her very white teeth, which teased Bostovitch's fancies, as Iliana's lovely features always did for him.

"I am pleased you will accept amended terms and want to get going, full scale, as you say." He looked a bit ashamed. "I must admit, since time is of essence, that I already began further work needed before we go north for, er, our ah ... final business. I have two one-way tickets to Seattle. We leave tomorrow night. You should relocate there or consider Canada, as I have. Look around area, when business is done; decide where you might live, for a time, at least.

"After disposition of ... ah, our target, you and Kovi should not associate for months; no calls, nothing, while fruitless investigations are under way. Leave your car at house, take only essentials for now, and if he asks, tell Kovi you stay with relatives in New Jersey. Leave cell phone and real ID at home, too. I have new papers for us both, passports, too. You must leave town. Maybe just minutes away, your pursuers could close in with blink of eye."

It was far too real and almost too quick for Iliana to digest. Simple nods, though, during Bostovitch's frank instructions indicated her stipulation to the program he planned. She decided with little deliberation. Kovi would be left to his own devices and, at all costs, Concord would pay for his taunting fakery, beside the original act for which she grew to despise him so fiercely.

"There is fresh news. Davidov, my best man, called me with most interesting advisory, shortly before your arrival tonight. I truly believe Concord did not die by your shotgun.

Iliana winced as if something painful were said, but she seemed lost for words.

"Happy and unhappy, eh?" He thought for a minute. "You do not have heavy sentence to face ... good news, hmm?" He is still around. Bad news, if he's your objective once more and you wish me to complete job. Good news for C, true?" Bostovitch's jowls shook as a throaty titter came forth.

"Davidov used police connections and informant inside phone company to learn more: no report to police ever occurred and more important, no Coroner's report was filed in Mason County, local jurisdictional authority.

"That type of injury would provoke automatic report to Medical Examiner. Phone at his home and cell were canceled day after shooting and, here it is, Little Thing: person carried his ID into company office, signed his name to close his numbers and call records next day.

"Yes, old ones switched to new and unlisted numbers the very next day, also. It had to be him. He must be at bottom of all questions and threats to you, Kovansk, Svetiia, and others in L.A.; his way to pull all of you out of hiding," Bostovitch said, as he stood up and helped her from the booth seat, "You look shocked ... enough excitement for one night eh?

"I am sorr. ..."

"Oh, do not mention." He rubbed her back a little too low and slow for her comfort, and quickly withdrew his hand when she limped ahead. "No matter now, Iliana; you have paid large fee and now it is up to *Bratva* to earn it and finish things. Using suitable subterfuge, his wife answered his mother's house telephone yesterday and said he was in Orange County for a few more days..

Iliana breathed easier, though with mixed emotion and massive confusion. Her face flushed almost grey.

"Charges are already ringing up, as new facts are unearthed and our activity intensifies. He will be back up north soon and we shall be ready when he takes to the air."

CHAPTER 33

Laguna BEACH

Late afternoon on the outside deck at *Las Brisas*, a busy cliff-side restaurant just north of Laguna's Main Beach; Aaron Concord, Ken Stansbee and Svetiia Kronoff met for Margaritas, and to discuss recent developments. The sun, close to its final fall beneath the ocean horizon, sparkled a bright orange reflection that shimmered straight to where they sat, and drew streams of compliments from most patrons who filled the glassed in, outside bar area.

Svetiia affirmed she had no contact with Bostovitch, Iliana or Oligoff. "I never felt so isolated, but I called no one on the outside, I promise. No calls received, either." Though indebted to the two men, she still kept the little secret to herself that her feelings for Kovansk never waned, and in fact, stole slowly, since last she saw him, to an almost irrepressible level of desire. She did not volunteer, either, that she found Oligoff that morning after many dead-end telephone efforts ... a senior member of Joshua Trauma Center's surgical staff. Further inquiries led to his home number which she planned to call that very night. *I cannot chance losing him to that thieving Iliana, who would probably turn police on him in as the instigator of the crime, to save her own hide. I will stick by him no matter what happens.* Loosened by the strong drink, she lost conscious connection to the conversation as her thoughts ran unchecked and to her horror, practically became audible.

She fought hard, to resist the urge that finally pushed her to attempt contact with her recent lover. Her mind once more filled with toe-curling imagery from which she was unable to dissociate: she, standing sans clothes on her bed in Santa Monica, Kovi standing on the floor, admiring and caressing her without relent, followed by the episodes of wild lovemaking.

Aaron nodded to Ken, who smiled subtly, relieved his cohort was about to tell Svetiia the truth ... who they were and what their plans were for Iliana. "Svetiia," Aaron said for the second time, and a third, "Svetiia, are you OK? You looked a million miles away just then."

"OK, yes, all right ... OK ... just lost it there, a moment. ..." Kovansk faded from her mind enough for lucidity to return and her glazed eyes to look alive again. "So sorry, what were you about to say?"

"Ken and I have to tell you some things you may find somewhat shocking, but here we go just the same. Are you ready ... sitting down?"

"Of course, given what's gone down already; little could surprise me." She pictured Iliana in cuffs at the local police headquarters; Kovi, a new spark in her life, affixed to the chair next to her.

An interruption to her racing thoughts, the clarion nearly blasted her from the table at which they sat. "My name is Aaron Concord, and I sit here, alive, well, and filled with apology that we had to deceive you. To my left is my former partner, Ken Stansbee, now president of Concord, Stansbee and Fitch, malpractice insurance investigations in Newport Bea. ..."

"Svetiia," Stansbee stopped him cold, as the woman gasped, her head dropped to her right shoulder and she slouched down in her chair, completely out. She fainted straight away from the sudden disclosure; shocked in all probability, that this was no longer a homicide problem, that Kovi would not face such fearful penalties. Aaron dabbed an ice water-soaked napkin to her face and she recovered with immediate cogency. Speechless, though, she made no comment, heartily sipped her second drink to the bottom of the goblet, and leaned forward, toward Aaron, as if to say, "Well, get along with it, then. What's this all about?"

"That brings you up to date with the whole story and the full truth that we hope will explain our reasons for being circumspect for so long. Most of our activity was successful because of information you provided us, with design or not; it made no difference." Stansbee stretched as he usually did when bored or fatigued. "So, we are about to release our files to the Mason County Sheriff but we will wait until we have addresses confirmed for Kovansk and Iliana. Any time that info will pop up, but the cops in Washington will likely request arrests via the Sheriff of the county in which they now live, I suppose somewhere in L.A. or Orange."

I have to warn Kovi, must tell him the news ... a good reason to call, even if he does stick it out with Iliana. He will be overjoyed that there was no death, and only a pinprick of an injury from the one pellet Mr. Concord said struck his shoulder.

Back into the conversation; Svetiia's faculties once again were disconnected from her musings. "I will walk to the apartment and work off the sudden surprise and that second drink."

At that, the men arose; Svetiia stood and gave each a heartfelt hug. "Thank you once again for the generosity you showed, the huge sum of money you paid Bostovitch to clear me from *Bratva's* grasp, the beatings I suffered ... and. ..."

"All because," Aaron cut in, "through you, we were able to identify and make contact with them. Do feel free to stay here in Laguna for the remaining month and a half for which we paid, but remain *incognito* for your best safety, until we can be sure mob actions will not come your way again. Don't forget, if you hear from either Dr. Oligoff or Iliana Gosnov; notify Ken or me immediately. That will not only help us get them arrested; it's for your own safety."

CHAPTER 34

"I will take next four days off work schedule, to complete much unfinished personal business. Nothing to worry about. I must finish paperwork for new accountants. Just write me out for usual work hours, please," Kovansk asked Liz Doudry, the day shift charge nurse in surgery, at Joshua Trauma Center. Oligoff had his eyes on her at one time, until told of her husband of twenty-one years; two of her three children still at home. A fiery redhead, with lovely features, she was a close match to black and white screen actress, Ingrid Bergman. Tough when she needed to be, Doudry ran a tight ship, while always willing to go over the line to help, "her brood of surgeons," as she playfully referred to staff members who operated there.

"Of course, Kovi, I'll do the necessary, but before you go, look in again, again at the lady who fell through her picture window ... Pearl Fleming. A floor nurse thought her thigh, the one with the terrible laceration, swelled more than it should, since you saw her in the morning. Maybe the drain needs adjusting. Otherwise, you're clear." She glanced at his backside and smiled when he walked from her office, sighed too loudly, and forced her gaze back to the following day's surgery schedule. "By the way will Gosnov ask for more time off, as well?"

He avoided a response. Almost crazy with fear, he trudged at a fast pace along the crowded corridor to see the female patient whose upper leg needed his attention. He found himself deeply morose, alone, and fearful beyond reason, so vulnerable to his impending discovery, that he needed more time to make many potentially life-changing decisions. How long could he stand being on the run? He could not help but wonder. *What about Iliana?* he worried, no idea where she stayed the last two nights. *Why has Svetiia not called? I must find her and try to talk about us for a while.*

"There it is, the silver Porsche Carrera registered in DMV files to his old residence. It has to be the 'little silver sports car,' Mother said the couple parked in front when they looked for me the first time in Redmond." Aaron practically yelled to Stansbee when they turned from Golden Poppy Road into the doctor's parking lot across from Joshua Trauma Center's emergency entrance. "I knew we were close when his talkative former neighbor in Beverly Hills prompted our expanded search and all but gave him away this morning. It was a long shot to drive this far," he continued, "but he's ours. He will be leaving soon; let's wait, tail him, and try for his home address while we're here.

Aaron said nothing. He feared they might be recognized and that a confrontation could ensue with the one who drove the shooter's van and permitted the effort to try for his life. Nearly face to face with Oligoff, his hands trembled when the tall, lanky, black haired surgeon, wearing green scrubs, exited the hospital building, turned away, and ambled slowly toward the Porsche.

"That's our man, A.C.," barked Ken, "we'll let him drive off the lot and down the street a half block, keep our distance, and take no risks of being seen on these lightly traveled streets."

Unnoticed by Stansbee, Aaron fumed out of control, felt an anger rush, clenched fists and grasped the door handle, prepared to go for the young physician.

"If he's driving far, we'll regret that we didn't bring another vehicle to switch back and forth, which reduces suspicion so well. We used to stay on the trail of the most evasive subjects that way," Stansbee recalled.

When Oligoff paused to exchange words with another doctor, Aaron opened the door. Were it not for his partner's instant snake-like strike for his belt, and the restraint with three fingers that held him in the cab, he would have incited an altercation. A phlegmatic redress from Stansbee, Aaron settled back in the truck, and regained his composure, though with notable difficulty.

"You damned well scared the hell out of me, old friend. Already on edge, a fight or Oligoff going for a gun were big worries, and then your sudden move.

"'Whoa little pony,' I said to myself; 'not on my watch.' I said.'

Oligoff darted across an undeveloped section. The white pick-up stood out far too much, which forced the men to fall father back. The Porsche then slowed abruptly and swerved into the wide approach to Desert Isle, a gated community of large, two story, Spanish style homes built around and within a dense cluster of Joshua trees. Kovansk waved at the guard as did Ken and Aaron when they arrived at the closing gate, not far behind. "Yes, we're with Kovi ... Doc Oligoff, and got a little lost ... thought we would just slip in after him. We're golfing together out at Pine Canyon Country Club this afternoon." Kovansk was well out of sight by the time the guard, too lazy to call the doctor, opened the gate and waved them onward.

"By the way, Ken slowed and asked the guard, "Doc, and his Porsche ... an impossible combination to follow. What's his address again?" He flashed one of his comely grins.

"22354 Avenida Matilija."

"That's it; thanks ... second thought, we'll do a one eighty and get some beer. To darned hot to be swinging clubs quite yet. Back at you in a few ... names are Clint and Gary."

Back to the guardhouse ten minutes later, the two investigators rolled forward as if beckoned toward the opened gate to avoid the phone-the-resident routine. They drove past the driveway where the Carrera was parked, without turning heads toward the house.

"Don't look now," Ken muttered, "but that black VW Passat in front, plate number, 'I M N RN,' is registered to Iliana Gosnov. Your shooter, A.C., doubles as the doctor's girlfriend. We learned through Svetiia's careless slip that confirmed the relationship, when we spoke with her a few days ago. The Terrible Two live together.

"Make it real easy for cops to pick up both in one scoop," Ken went on, "the block wall in back faces open desert, so the posting of one man just outside will prevent escape by that route. They can also go right through the doctor's entrance at the hospital and direct to the surgery wing to nail them, for that matter, but a nighttime arrest at the house would create less commotion."

"I would call today's activities just plain lucky, Aaron replied. I'm quite ready to go with Jim Gibson to the Sheriff's office in Shelton and pile on some poor detective's desk, all that we have accumulated. Physical evidence, Jim's findings and our reports to the file should be everything they'll need. Fingerprints, her tennis shoe prints I cast, the *Minsk* matches, my photos of the damage, the selfie of my shoulder wound, photos of the van, the Porsche, testimony we've elicited from so many witnesses; everything should pile up to provoke admissions, guilty pleas and efforts toward sentence reduction. Some jail time; minimum of five years, would be nice, eh? I won't worry about them regrouping after serving a decent amount of time. Should be a damned good lesson learned."

CHAPTER 35

"Oh God, Kovi, I have worried so much about you and how Iliana tries to make you as guilty as she knows she is. The woman has gone mad, I fear. I am afraid to effect contact, even to call her. When you answered the phone, I realized I left you no way to get in touch. To stay mum, however, was and still is for that matter, a strict admonition by Mister Concord, the kind man she thinks she killed, and his partner, Ken Stansbee, who now runs the investigation firm of Concord, Stansbee and Fitch.

Kovansk's eyes nearly popped from their sockets; he inspired deeply then gasped with the news of Concord's survival. His heart accelerated wildly, almost to the point of fibrillation. His tightened facial muscles met with a wash of numbness across his forehead. His mouth opened for a reply, but he could not speak.

"Their fine work, I regret only for your sake, led to your and Iliana's identification, Bostovitch also; that horrible ogre."

Kovansk's vision remained blurred; and his shock still buried an intended reply, when she continued. "Thank you so very much ... can't thank you enough, very importantly, for your unexpected gift, for the present time, at least, which enabled me to get clear of his filthy hands.

"I learned very recently that Mister Concord, most unwittingly paid a similar amount, unaware you, too, did the same, that very day. Bostovitch: horrible, greedy *svinya* that he is; the pig said nothing to Concord of your sweet gesture and helped himself to both payments.

"Freed, thereby; heaven only knows how many more months of servitude I had in store. I shall be eternally grateful to you both and as time allows, fully intend to repay you. So much else to say, Dear Kovi, but. ..." While she spoke, she longed for his body hovered over hers, the way his hips subtly oscillated to extend the wild ecstasy she felt when all her sensations culminated into the memorable emotional and physical explosion; and those non-stop compliments and kisses. So distracted she was, that she unintentionally obscured his reply until her dreamy memory faded.

Kovansk found himself completely bewildered on several counts. He, too, looked into his recent sexual experience with Svetiia as she rambled; and the strong appeal he felt, for years, when Iliana and she lived together and he often saw her there. While veritably stunned to find Concord averted death, with naught but the minor shoulder wound, he smiled broadly at the implications of reduced penal exposure. Oligoff felt inestimable relief. Where Iliana went, he could not answer, at Svetiia's light prodding.

"Iliana cleared much of her clothing and small, personal items," he explained with some embarrassment, and added that she left her car in the driveway. He hated to mention that she took $125,000 from their safe and that she emptied their low balance joint checking account that very morning. Their conversation thickened with increased affirmations of care and longing, until both became so stimulated that Kovi, in the midst of intensive planning for himself, opened the door to further and immediate contact.

His Carrera raced toward Laguna Beach. He felt protected by the anonymity of the freeways he would travel. The long trek, while foreshortened by continuous visions of Svetiia, nude on her bed, awaiting his caresses, allowed much time for thinking of and planning his next moves. His mind spun wildly, too, while he forged a pathway to change his destiny.

CHAPTER 36

BREMERTON, WASHINGTON

"Iliana, Davidov—Bostovitch's best man, known for his unforgiving cunning, viciousness, and tendency toward violence; Ivan Brorkiev, fellow *Bratva* boss from Seattle; and Bostovitch, the pilot—boarded the Huey helicopter in the early morning at Bremerton Airport. "A few flight minutes southwest to Aaron Concord's cabin on the waterfront, we will, among other things, survey possible routes there and back, and familiarize ourselves with charted wilderness areas or wildlife sanctuaries, over which flights under 2000' above ground level are restricted." He turned behind and spoke on the intercom, mainly to Iliana, while he flipped switches, checked caution lights and went through the lengthy pre-start check list.

Bostovitch flew about Mt. Olympus with some frequency and presumed Aaron enjoyed, as he did, also, recreational flights over permitted areas around Mt. Rainier, the most heavily glaciated peak in Washington, an old volcano that reached to 14,440 feet. His monotone voice again broke the intercom silence as he finished his check. "Stand by gen DC voltage-27.0, main gen-28.0 volts, temp-26.0." Engine rpms ran up and prompted the low rpm warning horn beep as they climbed to and passed through 6100. "N2, engine rpms ... at full power ... 6300, NR, rotor rpm-320, everything's ... all good to go."

Responding to the small collective pull, and concomitant forward pressure to the cyclic in his right hand, and little changes to pedals, the bird lifted just enough to be light on the skids. More power took the copter's nose into the wind, to a stationary hover a few feet above the pavement. Cleared to take off, it moved easily forward and nose down to 40 knots, and with more power, and forward cyclic, Bostovitch gained speed over the taxiway. He climbed to 1000 feet, turned straight and level to the southwest, and spoke to the passengers whose eyes remained glued to the windows and the passing terrain below.

"We will fly direct to Highway 101, just past Hood Canal, turn to the south and follow it to the Concord home. Keep eyes peeled for some open space, with dirt road, and possible line of sight to his hangar, up the slope from the cabin. We will circle and I will evaluate for a set down, where we may wait for him to take off when he flies next time. It will be his first experience with clear air turbulence. OK, Iliana Gosnov?"

He glanced at her and saw a frightening grin peel across her face. She fumbled with the intercom and returned a terse but pellucid reply, "It would not be too soon if we surprised him today."

An hour of circling over would-be spots for setting down, Bostovitch decided on a small field with a level area, free of trees and power lines, in front of what appeared to be an abandoned farm house. Surrounded by woodlots, the landing zone lay at the end of a grown over dirt drive way, at least a quarter mile long, that connected with a one lane paved road.

"Perfect ... a good spot Davidov, even if Federal Air Regulations say, 'No landing on private property without owner's written permission.' We can always say, ah ... er, 'Low oil pressure warning light flashed on and off, required me to land immediately. Turned out to be faulty sender.' How is that? TOT-turbine outlet temperature rose above upper limit. Had to land quickly to check, which forced us down."

"When sky opens and red helicopter rolls out, we light up turbine and get up and out to follow behind until he flies over wooded countryside. Then, heh, heh, we dive like Mongolian falcon and give him a most surprising LTE." That loss of tail rotor effect from the whirling vortex left behind and beneath a Huey's highly pitched rotor, in recovery from a steep and rapid descent and a nose-up flare to a near stop, is substantial. He knew from personal experience, formation flying in Russia and the steep valleys of Afghanistan, how such turbulence can negate the anti-torque action of the small tail rotor and send the affected aircraft into uncontrollable clockwise spinning, then rolling, out of control. "A Disney World ride could not be more fun, eh Davidov?"

His cohort murmured agreement and pointed to the field they chose as a temporary landing site.

A sudden flare slowed their approach speed to a brisk walk; Bostovitch selected a spot at the far end of the field and kept it in his sight until another flare stopped the descent to a five-foot hover. Davidov opened the large aft sliding door next to where Iliana sat and leaned out to survey the grassy spot.

Assured it was clear of fencing wire, posts or other obstructions, he turned and nodded at the pilot, who set the helicopter down as gently as stepping out a car door. Bostovitch was pleased; the view of Concord's place, a half mile away, was not ideal but possible from just up the grade, about fifty yards from their location.

More importantly, a report of their landing would not likely occur, he knew from prior experiences in that sparsely populated area. The olive drab exterior paint gave N998DZ an official appearance, usually mistaken for a military or law enforcement asset. While the others disembarked for a stretch, Bostovitch craftily worked out his next moves. He made sure via careful calculations that he had sufficient fuel and that weather at his next destination would hold steady.

He saw when aloft, Mt. Rainier was very clear, other than several separated layers of lenticular, lens-shaped, clouds that hovered around peaks, ridges and passes on the mountain, indicators of strong winds that poured toward the coast.

I will show them a good time, close-up views of some of the glaciers and will leave as fast as I came, to avoid complaints of breaching the 2000 foot above-ground level restriction once over National Park boundary. It's a weekday and few climbers would be on mountain with heavy snows above 6000 feet predicted to arrive tonight. Increasing clouds will help me, too.

CHAPTER 37

"All right, Jim, I will meet with you, and the Watch Commander at 4:00 PM tomorrow at the Mason County Building, and we'll lay it out for him, piece by piece." Aaron reclined on his Laguna Beach hotel bed and spoke to his friend, Gibson, retired Sheriff's Deputy.

"Subject to your thoughts, it appears we've an answer to every possible question, backed by evidence, or a solid lead that points to the name, address, and phone for all our witnesses, along with capsule summaries of how they will testify."

"Only one potential problem; there was no murder, so, the DA here in Shelton may feel uninspired to file, if she has the chance for some plea deals.

If that hothead, Iliana Gosnov, isn't shaken by the high bail that will be warranted and requested, some time in the tank could encourage her to boil down. Familiar as I am with the Mason County's District Attorney's office, they avoid a budget busting, long trial when they can, in deference to a plea and jail time. |

"This potential female defendant, a violent one, claimed so by every witness who has tangled with her, should be behind bars through arraignment and possible trial. What's to keep her from gunning for me again, if she is bailed, Jim?

"My wife, dog or someone else against whom she might harbor a grudge, will keep her quest alive for more assaults. As for the doctor, impending loss of his license to practice should keep him close by and peaceful.

"I will consider that strongly and the more I think about it, to avoid a rehash, we should include the DA in our meeting. Maybe we can get arrest warrants out in a few days," Gibson replied, "see you tomorrow. Bring everything."

"Alaska Airlines Reservations, may I assist in booking your flight to Sea-Tac in the morning, Mr. Concord?"

CHAPTER 38

"We have fuel enough and some time before dark, so we'll detour to get bird's eye views ... some of most beautiful sights in Pacific Northwest: the huge glaciers and rock faces of Mt. Rainier, eh?" Bostovitch turned to Iliana, smiled and winked at Davidov and Brorkiev who also sat in the cargo bay with her. "The sliding door we will open for better viewing of the terrain. Put your jackets on; temperature will drop below freezing as we climb to about 11,000 feet." Bostovitch nodded at the two men when Iliana leaned against the window for a better view as they overflew Gig Harbor and the Tacoma Narrows bridge.

"We must cheat a little and drop in at less than 2000 feet above ground, for better appreciation of the massive ice cliffs, seracs—huge ice columns, and deep blue crevasses, huge cracks in the larger glaciers. I fly above small clouds and drop in for a quick look, then move away from slopes to be legal again. Climbers report low fliers, eh, eh, want big mountain to themselves. We will steal it from them for a few minutes only. Look below ... open door Davidov, Puyallup River runs down to the west from Puyallup Glacier, starting just below us. It goes straight to its source, the massive wall called Sunset Amphitheater at about 11,500 feet."

As the mountain rose beneath them, their elevation above the amphitheater closed to no more than 100 feet. Buffeted by more than tolerable turbulence, the helicopter seemed small at the glacier's head. Gaping crevasses marred the icy white: seemingly bottomless swaths; azure blue, beautiful yet foreboding, hungry mouths.

Bostovitch nodded at Davidov. Below them and about ten yards down slope, an enormous crevasse beckoned. It was time.

Davidov surprised Iliana, unbuckled her harness and belt, and without a sound nor fanfare, sent her out the door, wildly clawing the air to stay upright. Iliana impacted gently on the fresh blanket of snow and, as the helicopter turned away from the headwall, the troubled young lady with an irrevocable hatred for men, slid over the upper precipice and torpedoed into the cavernous mouth ... down, down ... down. ...

Before he could regain airspeed, however, and, in an unwanted, uncontrolled descent; Bostovitch turned unwittingly into a dense cloud. He failed to relate to the instruments. Vertigo, the silent killer of many a good pilot, set in and his mind miscalculated that a right turn and forward cyclic were needed to correct what seemed an unusual nose high attitude. Instead, as his mind spun to achieve level flight, he swung the ship into the headwall and bounced to the ice, while rotor blades disintegrated—spun wildly into rock and snow. Over in seconds, the turbine ground to a higher and higher pitched whine, and exploded.

The helicopter bounced down the steep ice slope, across several small ones, until swallowed in a single gulp by an enormously gaping chasm. It bumped back and forth against the opposing vertical walls as it dropped into nothingness and finally stopped, nothing remaining but three badly mutilated and very dead men amidst a shattered, dismembered pile of aluminum and fiberglass.

A few gurgles from oil and hydraulic fluid that ran over engine hot spots and briefly ignited, ended the cacophony of blending metal and plastic, while soundlessly, small laminate shards and clumps of wet snow drifted slowly downward and danced back and forth around the wreckage like maple leaves falling on a windless winter night.

From the indigo darkness of another crevasse nearby, a female shook uncontrollably, tried in vain to extricate herself from the sub zero walls that held her, viselike, in their grasp. A long and plaintive whine, then she uttered in a faint and strained voice, "You did this to me, Kovi, Pappa, Aaron Concord, and you ... you SOB, Bostovi. ..." A barely palpable pulse pumped the last liter of blood through the massive laceration in her right thigh and left the voice muffled, then silent.

229

Flurries of the predicted snow fell over the mountain in dense curtains, quietly blanketed impact scars above two neighboring crevasses and swept from visibility, all traces of the airborne misfortunes that occurred not long before.

CHAPTER 39

"You have chosen Aeroflot Flight 107, LAX to Moscow. Baring unforeseen headwinds, our arrival should be as scheduled at 3:10 PM tomorrow. We are glad to have you as our guests and will do everything possible to make your flight a pleasant one," the smartly attired flight attendant said.

Seated in the Airbus A 330's first class seat 3-A, a man: tall, lanky, jet black hair, small goatee, whose long fingers—those of a surgeon—caressed the hand of a splendid, natural blond Ukraine female: sensuously dressed, pouty lips and large blue eyes; seated in 3-B, by the window.

"We will live the good life: challenging jobs, travel when we can, fall deeply in love, marry, raise a family with upper crust living standards, and take time for each other," Boris Kovansk Oligoff, M.D. spoke softly into the ear of Svetiia Dorita Kronoff. A dreamy grin, she squeezed his hand, placed open lips to his neck and flashed her tongue to add tickle to her long kiss. "I have always wanted you, Dear Kovi." Seats back, each closed eyes, dreamed of their endless loving the night before, and a long future together in upper crust Moscow.